LAWLESS

Book One of

The Merrick Chronicles

BRYCE SMITH

First published by Dog Ear Publishing
8888 Keystone Crossing
Suite 1300
Indianapolis, IN 46240
www.dogearpublishing.net

dog ear publishing

This book is printed on acid-free paper.
Printed in the United States of America

ISBN: 978-145756-843-5

DEDICATION

This book is dedicated to all the police officers who have been killed in the line of duty and all those who are still working to keep us all safe despite a growing number of people who do not appreciate their service. I pray the United States never sees the day when it is without them and finds itself without law and order.

ACKNOWLEDGMENTS

Countless people in my life have helped me write this book by continually supporting my family and me. No one has supported and inspired me more than my wife. I would like to thank the members of my editing team, who had their work cut out for them. I would also like to thank my publishing company, which walked me through the process of becoming an author.

Many of the people, events, and viewpoints in this book have been taken from people I have known as well as my own life experiences. However, I have changed and adapted the details to fit the story line, and they do not accurately reflect real life. This is a fictional book, and the viewpoints found in it are not necessarily in line with my own, but are meant to be thought-provoking and for entertainment purposes.

CHAPTER 1

It was midmorning on a clear October day, and Merrick Albright was going out for a short jog. It was his first day off and he was in no rush to start the day. For years Merrick was forced to run when he was in the Army and at first he hated it, but over time his body learned to tolerate it.

In recent years his dislike of a mind numbing run had changed with the discovery audiobooks. He now found himself running farther and more frequently, and even looking forward to his runs most of the time. Audiobooks were one of the rare advances in technology that he enjoyed.

Whenever he went out nowadays, it seemed like all he saw was a sea of mindless people moving around with their heads tilted down at their phones. He hated social media and had to limit himself from logging onto Facebook to less than once a quarter because if he didn't, he would become borderline homicidal. People were sharing way too much. They would post what they were buying at the grocery store, how bored they were in math class, or a million other trivial tasks that no one in their right mind would ever care to know about. He had no interest in Twitter or any other social network like it, and as far as he was concerned, those platforms were eroding the very soul of society and turning humans into empty-headed, antisocial lemmings.

As Merrick ran south on 32nd Avenue, he saw a mother pushing a stroller straight toward him. Even though he had never seen her before, he waved and gave a friendly nod. Merrick was six foot two and a little over two hundred pounds, with chiseled, muscular features and a commanding presence. Intimidating good people was an unfortunate side effect, but he found a wave and a smile often went a long way to set people at ease.

Most people took one look at Merrick, with his high and tight haircut and clean-shaven face, and guessed he was prior military. There were even days when he would wear his old military PT shirts to run in, and still the soccer moms he passed seemed to be wary of him. Merrick wondered if they would feel the same if they knew he was a cop. With anti-police culture growing, it wouldn't surprise him if they didn't.

As he turned onto 189th Street, his audiobook transitioned to the next chapter, and as it did he noticed a late-model Honda that looked like the paint job had been touched up with a can of spray paint and the wheels extended a couple of inches beyond the wheel wells. The car alone would have sparked Merrick's attention, but there were also three Hispanic males leaning up against the car and one more on the porch of the house the car was parked in front of. The three males ranged in age from about seventeen to twenty-five years old, all had short hair, and all were wearing more than the average amount of red clothing.

The area around Vancouver, Washington, where Merrick lived didn't have too many gang issues. White supremacist biker gangs were more common in the area than Hispanic-based gangs like the Nortenos or Surenos, but like most places in the United States, it was hard to go anywhere where these gangs didn't have some sort of presence. From their clothing style and the overabundance of red, it was a safe bet that these men were Nortenos members.

Merrick took a quick glance over his left shoulder to be sure there was no traffic, and then he jogged to the other side of the roadway and went up onto the sidewalk. It wasn't a matter of him being intimidated or scared. He was enjoying his run, and besides, why poke the bear if you didn't have to, especially on your day off?

As he continued in their direction, he was careful not to stare at them and provoke a conflict. In his peripheral vision, he could see them elbowing each other and nodding their heads in his direction. Then the youngest member of the group walked across the street and stood in his path, waiting for him.

The kid was small in comparison to Merrick. He was maybe one hundred fifty pounds and couldn't have been much older than eighteen. Physically this kid stood no chance against him. The kid stood there with his head slightly tilted upward in the classic Mexican gangster pose. His heels were together, with one foot facing Merrick and one foot facing out at ninety degrees. Merrick thought it was the stupidest fighting pose someone could have. To anyone who knew anything about fighting, to have your jaw completely exposed like that was like giving a Christmas gift to your opponent. That stance only gave way to poor balance and slow reaction time. The kid looked completely ridiculous, but there he stood thinking he looked like one bad mother. He was probably only issuing this challenge because he was counting on his friends having his back and thought that it would never be a one-on-one fight.

Merrick detested everything about gang culture. Gangs recruited troubled youth with shattered homes and brainwashed them into a false sense of belonging. They even referred to each other as family while threatening to stab each other thirteen times if they tried to get out. Merrick wanted nothing more than to go a round or two with all of them, but that would never happen.

Gangbangers' MO was to "jumping" people. They out number their opponent and are often armed with some kind of weapon. They all jump out of a car and attack the person from behind. Then they leave their victim beaten and bloody yet somehow still have the gall to brag about it like they had done something gutsy. That would be like Michael Jordan bragging about dunking on a fifth grader.

Merrick kept running straight toward the kid who was standing in his way. This time he wasn't concerned with trying not to make eye contact. It might have been a mistake crossing the road to try to avoid them. They probably viewed it as a sign of weakness and fear. Gangs love to be feared because in their warped little minds they see it as a form of respect and proof of how powerful they are. Merrick felt his day off slowly going down the toilet all because some gangbangers wanted to mess with him. When he was about twenty feet from the kid, he started talking to him.

"Mind if I borrow your phone, *ese*?" asked the young gangbanger.

Merrick had his earbuds in, so he just pretended like he didn't hear the kid and kept jogging. When he was about five feet away from the kids, he stepped down to the street, jogged right past him, and then got back up on the sidewalk and kept going. He knew there was no way the kid was going to run after him—not at any great speed anyway. One of the bright sides to gangbangers' hideous clothing style is that it is nearly impossible to run very fast with your baggy pants hanging low around your waist.

Merrick guessed that the kid would most likely return to his friends and get made fun of a little bit, and that would be the end of it, but there was also a slim chance of option number two.

He heard the rev of an engine behind him and the squeal of tires on the pavement. *I guess they picked option two,* he thought. This was not his lucky day. His pace remained steady as he retrieved his cell phone out of his pocket and used the emergency 9-1-1 dial feature.

"9-1-1, what's your emergency?"

"This is Deputy Albright. I am off duty and I am at about the 3400 block of NE 189th Street. I'm being chased by four armed gang members driving a late-model orange Honda Accord. I need Code 3 cover." He didn't wait for a response; he just dropped the phone into his pocket with the line still open.

Merrick was religious about carrying a concealed weapon every time he left home. The one exception was when he went running. It was too late for today, but he was calculating the practicality of running in the future with a concealed weapon. He wasn't totally convinced one way or the other, but made a mental note to at least carry a pocketknife next time.

The orange Honda pulled into a driveway in front of Merrick, and all four guys got out of the vehicle; none of them looked too happy. The driver was in his mid-twenties, about five foot nine and one hundred eighty-five pounds with just a hint of a gut. He was wearing an unbuttoned collared shirt over a white undershirt.

He slammed the car door shut behind him and walked right up to Merrick, who resisted the impulse to immediately drop him. Merrick took a step back and put up both of his open hands in the universal sign of "I don't want any trouble." It also allowed him to be ready to defend himself without looking aggressive.

"That was very rude, *ese*," the gang leader said, shaking his head.

Merrick had dealt with enough gang members to know rule number one: respect was everything. One sure way to get a gang member to fight, in his experience, was to disrespect him in front of his people. He still wanted to try to hold out long enough so the police would arrive, or to possibly find a peaceful way to resolve this. So he removed his earbuds and tried to be somewhat respectful. "Sorry, what can I do for you?"

The driver looked behind him toward his friends, who shook their heads in disapproval.

"I said you were rude to my friend, and I think you should apologize."

Merrick thought about apologizing, maybe even kissing their butts a little bit, but just the thought of it made him sick. Besides, showing even a small amount of weakness by trying to avoid them was what got him into this mess to begin with.

Even though he didn't want to admit it, the bigger reason was his pride. He was a man of principle, a man of honor, a warrior, and there was no way in hell he was going to let these little piss-ants intimidate him in broad daylight, not in his own neighborhood. He believed good people should not live in fear of leaving their homes because of the criminals who roamed the streets.

"Hey guys, I am just a guy trying to get some exercise. I'm not sure what I would apologize for."

"Doesn't matter. Just apologize anyway; it's the smart, healthy thing to do."

Merrick's blood started to boil, and he could hear the faint sound of sirens in the distance. The gang paid little attention to the sirens, and they had no idea the police were coming for them. He looked at the four of them and sized things up. He wondered if he could make this last just a little bit longer until the cavalry arrived.

The young kid who had first tried to stop him was on the driver's side of the car, leaning against the rear passenger door. The front passenger door was open, and a fatter, uglier version of the driver stood there, leaning on the car with his arms stretched out on top of the roof. The fourth male was another skinny young punk who was at the rear of the car, swinging around a bat.

They were right there openly threatening violence, but obviously not expecting any kind of resistance. They just assumed every normal person would fear them and back down from the four-to-one odds, but Merrick was far from normal. He guessed he could take out the first two guys before the other two could get into any kind of position to begin to attack him. So it really wasn't four against one. It was two fights of two against one.

"Well, what's it going to be, *ese?*" the gangbanger said, leaning in closer toward Merrick's face. "Or maybe you need a trip to the hospital to teach you a little lesson in manners."

Merrick lunged forward with explosive rage fueled by his survival instinct and years of training. As if working on muscle memory alone, he hooked the driver's right arm with his left arm. He held him close, and with his right arm he unleashed every ounce of his hatred of gangs into repeated palm-heel-strike uppercuts into the driver's jaw. Merrick could hear the devastating sound of the lower jaw breaking and the gangbanger's teeth grinding together as he delivered each blow. After a few hits, the driver's body went completely limp, and Merrick tossed him to the side.

The driver was definitely out of the fight and would be sucking food through a straw for a few weeks. Merrick's gaze lifted from the leader, and he saw the others looking on in disbelief.

Merrick moved toward the kid who had first tried to stop him, determined to take advantage of their hesitation. It wasn't until Merrick was right on top of him that he realized he was the next in line to suffer the consequence of messing with the wrong guy. He made an attempt to draw a spring-assisted pocketknife from his pants to try to better his odds.

Merrick saw the slow draw of the knife and was only a step away as the kid lifted the weapon in his direction. He stopped the knife's upward motion as he grabbed the wrist of the hand that held the knife. With his free arm, Merrick delivered a few quick but powerful elbows to the kid's face. His nose exploded and split open.

Merrick put his hand in the center of the kid's chest and pushed him backward toward the male with the bat, who was coming right at him. He shoved the small kid as hard as he could directly into the guy with the bat. The kid crashed into the oncoming gangbanger just as he was drawing the bat backward into a swing. They collided, and the kid with the broken nose bounced off the guy with the bat and rolled into the fetal position on the pavement. Two down, two to go.

The guy with the bat was caught off-balance for a split second, but that was all Merrick needed to close the distance. He ran right into the guy with the bat and drove him backward into the middle of the street. He wrapped up the male's right arm that held the bat, and he shoved his right thumb directly into the guy's left eye socket. The guy howled and shook his head in an attempt to free himself, but Merrick drove his thumb in hard while gripping the side of his face. Suddenly the pressure gave way and the eye burst. The bat dropped to the pavement along with the guy who had been holding it. One left.

Merrick quickly spun around searching for his final adversary. He had expected the guy to be right on top of him, but as he scanned back and forth, he couldn't see any sign of the fatter male.

He could hear multiple moans of agony and movement on the ground from the guys left in his wake. He then saw the Honda sway slightly back and forth like the vehicle's suspension was accommodating some kind of added weight. Then he could see it. The fatter male was in the vehicle and lying across the center console reaching into the back seat. Because of his girth, he was having a hard time. It took Merrick an instant to deduce what he was trying to retrieve: a gun.

He sprinted toward the vehicle. He could see the male had retrieved what he was looking for and was trying to get himself out of his awkward position. Merrick knew he would not reach the male in time to prevent him from aiming the gun. There was only one place he could make it to in enough time. He dove down hard on the opposite side of the beat-up Honda just as the male was swinging the pistol in his direction over the hood.

He saw a quick flash of light and a deafening explosion. Merrick started to hyperventilate, thinking he probably had seconds to live. His mind flashed to the one thing that mattered to him: his family. He pictured them at home right then, waiting for him to return from his run, and his heart ached to hold each of them one last time. He had never feared death, even as a child. He had lived a good life with more happiness than a person deserved. What he really feared was not being able to help those he cared about when they needed him.

He thought of his two boys: Reese, fifteen years old, and Indiana, twelve years old. He thought of how hard they might take his death. He thought about their future—how he wouldn't be there to support, encourage, and protect them. Last he thought of his wife, Lydia. She had always supported him through years of deployments and training. She had slowly changed him into a better man, a softer man, a man with a heart.

He forced himself back to the moment and fought to take a deep breath. As he did, he saw the open pocketknife on the ground, but as he reached for it, the fatter Hispanic male came around the corner of the car. He was holding the gun in one hand and glanced around at his friends before settling his focus on Merrick.

"*Muérete, saco de mierda!*" the man yelled as he walked closer. Merrick shifted his weight forward slightly as he prepared for one final futile attempt to take out the last gangbanger. He knew his chances were not good, but he would rather go down fighting then just sit there and wait for the end.

CHAPTER 2

Merrick stared into the face of the Hispanic gangbanger with the outstretched pistol. He had a teardrop tattoo under his right eye and scowled at Merrick with what looked like hatred or disgust.

Out of nowhere, a patrol car slammed into the Hispanic male and into the rear end of the parked Honda. The male was thrown twenty feet into the air and spun end over end multiple times before he landed face first on the street. Merrick pushed himself backward and was barely missed by the car. His head slammed backward against the cement. He lay there partly in a daze as he heard yelling and chaos around. The noise felt far away.

"Merrick! Merrick! Control, can I get an ambulance to my location, Code 3 for a down officer?" Deputy Chris Richardson knelt beside Merrick lying on the ground.

"No, I don't need an ambulance," Merrick said as he mentally recovered from having accepted his own death.

"Ha, thank God. You had me scared there for a moment," Chris said in relief.

"You were scared? I'm the one that almost got shot and then almost run over a second ago."

"You okay?" Chris asked, looking Merrick up and down.

"Yeah, I just need a minute." Merrick leaned forward and rested on one of his elbows, rubbing the lump on the back of his head with his other hand. He looked at the steaming mess of crumpled cars and bent metal just a few feet away from him. "Were you driving the patrol car?"

"Yep." Chris shrugged.

"Thanks. I owe you one."

"No problem; I was hoping to get a new patrol car anyway." Chris was smiling.

"Seriously, though, you saved my life. I am not going to forget that."

"Get me a maple doughnut and we'll call it even."

Merrick tilted his head at Chris and gave him a serious look.

"What?" Chris said. "I love those things."

"This might be worth two, even."

"Just make sure they're fresh; don't go cheap and get me the day-old ones."

"Shut up and help me get up, will ya?" Merrick asked as he extended his hand. Chris helped pull Merrick to his feet, and they both looked back and forth over the scene before them. Five patrol cars filled the road, lights on top flashing in the morning light and multiple sirens sounding. Deputies were cuffing up the Hispanic males and getting them ready for the imminent arrival of the ambulances.

"What a mess. I thought you weren't working today," Chris said with a smile. Chris and Merrick both used humor at times as a coping mechanism to lighten a situation that would normally be very sobering.

"I do hate it when work follows me home," Merrick joked. They both laughed. "So can I give you my statement so I can go home?"

"Sure. I would even offer you a ride home if I could," Chris said with another grin.

After Merrick gave his statement, other deputies offered to give him a ride home, but he decided to walk and take the time to clear his head. He replayed the events in his mind, thinking of what he could have done differently to tip the odds in his favor.

The more he thought about it, the more he was convinced that the only significant way to improve his odds was to arm himself. Merrick was a full supporter of the Second Amendment and of armed citizens. Even before he was a deputy sheriff, he had a concealed weapons permit.

His favorite belt buckle said, "God, Guns, and Guts Made America Free." Lydia hated it, of course, and each Sunday when she saw him wearing it, she shook her head in disapproval. To her credit, she never asked him to take it off.

Over the course of their marriage, Lydia had gone from not liking Merrick carrying a gun to having a gun of her own. She settled on the Glock 43 9mm single stack with Trijicon night sights. The weapon was amazingly accurate for its compact size, and it was a Glock, which in the gun world was synonymous with reliable. The only real downside was that the standard magazine carried only seven bullets. After shooting it a few times, Merrick ended up buying one too as a backup gun.

Merrick's phone vibrated softly. It was Lydia texting him, wondering when he would be home. He was not looking forward to explaining what had happened or how close he had been to not coming home at all. He decided he would tell her and the boys exactly what had happened and just leave out the little detail about the guy with the gun at the end.

CHAPTER 3

All Clark County deputies had a take-home car, which was a huge perk since they didn't have to load and unload all of their gear at the beginning and end of their shift. Everything was ready to use, and they knew exactly where everything was located. No one left coffee cups or forgot to take out their garbage. Arguably the best part of a take-home car was that deputies were able to drive to and from work without paying a dime in gas money.

Merrick's vehicle was a four-wheel drive Chevy Tahoe. He walked out to the vehicle, and placed his rifle in the mount and locked it. He stowed his snacks and water for the day, then backed out of his driveway. It took Merrick only fifteen minutes to get to the precinct, but he liked to be just a few minutes early to check his email. Briefing started at six o'clock and went to seven o'clock, but most of that time was spent BS-ing with the other deputies.

His sergeant was Steven Nash. He had been with the department for thirty years and wasn't afraid to stand up to the administration to defend deputies if they were in the right. Merrick liked leaders who took the fatherly role of not only teaching but also looking out for those underneath them. He had learned long ago in the military that not all those in leadership positions were good leaders. Having a leader you could trust was priceless. So for the last few years of his career, Merrick had chosen to work for Sergeant Nash and they had become friends.

Merrick checked his email at the briefing table as his fellow squad members came in one at a time and sat down. Deputy Baker walked into the room looking confused about where he should sit. Baker was a new police recruit who was less than impressive. The guy had no confidence in himself. He was so unsure of himself that he needed a pep talk to get the courage to do a simple traffic stop. Merrick had been training him for the last three weeks since his graduation from the police academy.

The police academy was five and a half months of dedicated police training. The instructors there could teach a lot of things, but they couldn't change a person's personality. Someone who was an introvert wasn't suddenly going to become an extrovert, and someone scared of his shadow wasn't going to suddenly become a confident cop.

From day one Merrick had a feeling this recruit wasn't going to make it, but a recruit got a fair shot to prove if he really had what it took.

Merrick hated failing recruits. First of all, it was a lot more paperwork to document someone who was continually failing to get better than it was to document someone who was steadily improving. It was going to be weeks of writing daily reports before the administration would eventually decide that Deputy Baker was not going to make it. No one wanted to be a cop in order to spend hours writing reports. Most wanted action.

Merrick hated writing reports, and if he had known how many he would have to write as a police officer, he might have chosen a different profession. Writing had always been a weakness of his even from a young age, but it never seemed to get in his way. In high school and college, he got As in just about every subject without ever having to study much at all. He was a visual and audio learner. He could recall virtually anything he saw or heard almost perfectly. So as long as the material was in the lecture, he would pass every test with flying colors.

The documentation wasn't the only reason it was difficult to fail someone. Spending twelve hours a day with someone for weeks made it impossible not to get to know them. Merrick had met Deputy Baker's wife and one-year-old daughter at their house one day when Baker had come to work with an empty gun holster. He didn't like the thought of Baker losing his job, but it was better than one day having to tell his wife that she was a widow because he got killed on the job.

Normal police work was like babysitting. Your job was to find those who were misbehaving and put them in time-out. Having to train a new recruit was like doing double duty. Always having to constantly reassure, correct, and guide someone while simultaneously making sure both of you weren't killed was exhausting.

The only reason that being a field training officer was worthwhile to Merrick was to get a chance to help mold the future generation of police he would be working with. In his opinion, the difference between good police officers and bad ones came down to how they used their discretion. Being a good shot, being able to run down a bad guy, and writing a good report were things a monkey could be taught how to do. On the other hand, being able to follow your gut and decide where the line was between justice and mercy was a rare quality.

Briefing started with Sergeant Nash handing out a few sex offender check sheets to the deputies who would be covering the beat the offender lived in. He also passed out a few flyers with photos of wanted people or people to be on the lookout for. These flyers changed from day to day and could be about anything. Sometimes they were about people who were threatening to kill cops, criminals someone was trying to identify, or a kid who was missing.

At least one of the flyers always seemed to be from out of town. Today there was a flyer from the Seattle PD, which was looking for a guy who had murdered his wife and was on the run. With new flyers almost daily, it was nearly impossible to remember any of them for more than a day or two.

"Graveyard had a stabbing call last night at about three o'clock, and detectives are still out there. It was at that burned-out yellow tweeker house on 50th Avenue," Sergeant Nash said as he poured himself another cup of coffee.

Heads around the table nodded because everyone had been there multiple times. Police called locations like this place "flophouses." Two years ago, the department almost got lucky when the place caught fire after a tweeker left a camping stove unattended. Every cop in the area was cursing at the firefighters when they came and saved the day by putting the fire out.

Firefighters were good guys, but they didn't face the same difficulties as cops. People didn't hate firefighters, they weren't sued, and they didn't have to worry about losing their jobs. Every day there were ten times more firefighters on duty than police, but they didn't do even close to half of the workload. While they were on duty, they slept, watched movies, went shopping, and barbecued.

Cops didn't hate firefighters because they had it good; they just felt underappreciated in comparison and were constantly getting screwed from a million directions while firefighters were getting new recliners at all their stations. They also didn't score many points with cops when they saved run-down drug houses from burning down.

Sargent Nash went on, "When they showed up, the suspect was on the front porch, naked and covered in blood. I guess he was yelling and smashing things on the porch as they arrived. The crazy guy decided to go back in the house and dove through the front window. Our guys followed him in and found him in the kitchen hovering over the female he had stabbed a couple dozen times." He paused and looked around the table to let everyone know he was building up to something.

"The guy was eating the victim's face off." He paused again and shook his head. "Just when you think you have seen it all, the world lets you know it can always get weirder. They ended up having to shoot this guy. All our guys are okay, but three of the graveyard guys are now on admin leave. So be prepared for more overtime coming up until they get cleared by the psychologist."

Everyone around the table exploded, wanting to know more details.

"Who was the guy that was shot?"

"What was he doped up on?"

"What happened to make them shoot the guy?"

"Look, the investigation is ongoing so I do not have all the final details, but I know the guy was doped up on bath salts," Sergeant Nash explained. "They tried to detain him but ended up fighting with the guy. Our guys shot him when he started trying to bite our guys."

After everyone settled down, the briefing transitioned smoothly into its second stage: the BS portion. During a regular shift, police officers didn't get a lot of time to bond with each other; they were too busy working. So part of briefing was time to just talk with each other.

"You know some family member of this guy is going to sue the department for killing their innocent zombie son," said Tom. Everyone shook their heads—not because they disagreed, but because they knew it was true.

"You know the world is going to hell when they won't even let you kill zombies anymore," Joe said, half laughing. Everyone joined in the laughter.

Joe was in his sixties and as sharp as ever. He loved his job, and being a police officer was as much a part of him as his right arm. When people asked him when he was planning on retiring, he told them "never." Being a cop was his life, and he was going to keep doing it until someone told him he couldn't do the job anymore.

"If we are having zombie problems, hasn't the world by definition already gone to hell?" Merrick added.

"Oh yeah, you're into that whole zombie apocalypse thing, right?" asked Klein.

"No, I am definitely not. I think that show is kind of dumb," Merrick said.

"Seriously? I love *The Walking Dead*. What is your problem with it?"

"I could only get through part of the first season, so that's all I have to go by, but I have plenty of problems with it. What cop in this day and age carries a long barrel .357 Magnum for a duty weapon and apparently has never had any kind of firearms training because he shoots it exclusively one-handed? Doesn't happen, but it looks cool for Hollywood. That and the whole zombie hype is dumb. It would be incredibly easy to take out an entire city of zombies."

"First of all, you think way too much when you're watching TV, man. It is a show, but you got me curious: How would you take out a *whole* city of zombies so easily?" asked Klein skeptically.

"I think it was in the first episode that it showed the main guy crawling in a tank, and it hit me: one armored vehicle with a full tank of gas is all it would take. Just drive down the streets with the radio bumpin' to bring them out into the street, and run them over. Five hours tops in one city, and all zombies would be dead. Well, okay, maybe not dead, but neutralized. Zombies are so dumb they can't open a locked door and are highly predictable. If I was on that *Walking Dead* show, I would be way more afraid of humans than any zombie."

Merrick could tell Klein was trying to find a flaw in his zombie killing plan, but after a few seconds he shook his head and said, "It's just a show. You're thinking way too much."

"Compared to most of the people we interact with, I will take that as a compliment," Merrick replied.

Seven o'clock came around, and the squad members slowly rolled out, all going their separate ways. As Merrick slid into the passenger seat, he reminded himself he had only one more week before he'd get to drive his own car again.

CHAPTER 4

"What's on the board?" Merrick said to his trainee.

"Looks like . . . four calls pending in Central, one abandon in 82, suspicious circumstances in 82, an alarm way out in 85, and a death investigation pending in 81."

Merrick sat quietly in the passenger seat, but he felt like he was dying a little bit. He was trying to let Deputy Baker make a decision about what call to take. Most trainees didn't make horrible decisions; they just procrastinated making one altogether and waited to be hand-fed the answer.

The car was idling as they sat in the precinct's parking lot. The only sound was Baker clicking on the computer, reading the details of each call he had told Merrick about. He waited until Baker had enough time to read each one four times.

"So what are we doing?" Merrick said, trying to get Baker moving.

"I guess we could go check the abandoned vehicle?" Baker said, making it sound more like a question.

Merrick wanted to lean over and punch Baker in the face. Abandoned vehicle calls were the lowest priority of literally any other police call, and the only reason Baker wanted to take it was because it was easy and required no real police work or thought on his part.

"What was the suspicious circumstances?" Merrick said as he refrained from assaulting his trainee.

"Guy walking, hitting himself, and yelling at vehicles," Baker said as he read the details.

Merrick didn't say anything, but looked at Baker with a stare that said, "Really, idiot, do I have to spell this out for you?"

Baker obviously got the message and dispatched himself to the suspicious circumstances. Last week Merrick had had a heart-to-heart with Baker and told him that he was struggling. He had said that Baker had no command presence and a problem being decisive. He had asked him to continue to push himself to overcome these issues, but to be open-minded that the job might not be for him.

In the last few years, the Washington State police academy had made a change that emphasized police were not "warriors" but rather "guardians" of the community. With all the hostility toward police and increases in police shootings the last few years, the academy was trying to rebrand police officers as kinder and gentler.

Most cops, Merrick included, thought it was one of those laughable political propaganda campaigns to call something by a different name and hope it might have an effect, but that wasn't the only change the cops had noticed. When new recruits started to flow into the department from the academy, they noticed a difference in their officer safety and that the recruits were failing to use force when necessary. On the road there was no noticeable change in public perception because of the new policy, but the academy had successfully trained recruits to second-guess themselves and to be wimps.

Every day when Merrick suited up for work, he remembered why he put each part of his equipment on.

Body armor—because someone might try to shoot him.
Radio—because his foe might be more than he could handle alone.
Handgun—because he might have to take someone's life to save another.
Extra magazines—because it might not take just one shot to stop his foe.
Rifle—because his enemy might be armed.

He wore over thirty pounds of gear during his twelve-hour shift.

Having been to war multiple times, Merrick knew what it felt like to gear up and roll out to battle. There was no doubt in his mind that every day he worked as a cop, he was going to war. Whoever said police officers were not warriors either had not ever been a warrior himself or had never been a cop; he guessed it was probably both.

In recent years all across the United States, police started being ambushed and targeted more than usual. Merrick wasn't exactly sure when the American people began turning on law enforcement, but he first noticed a big increase after the Michael Brown shooting in Ferguson, Missouri, in 2014.

All of a sudden, he was showing up on calls and everyone was recording him with their cell phones and yelling "F--- the police." It was no surprise that media outlets fueled the fire by saying that police were racist, using excessive force, and corrupt.

During his career, Merrick saw plenty of cops do things differently then he would have, but in all his time, he had never seen a racist or corrupt act. The average citizen thought that cops could shoot guns out of people's hands and that cops "shot to kill" because they were overly aggressive and must have wanted to kill the person.

Hollywood showed two basic versions of police officers in movies: good cops who were virtual supermen with unhuman skills, and corrupt cops who were in league with organized crime, planted evidence, and stole or did drugs themselves. Even though these two versions were almost nonexistent, they were the mental images that the majority of the public had of police officers.

The only silver lining to the masses turning against the police all across the country and some media outlets doing their best to make the problem worse was that regular good citizens were now going out of their way to say they were grateful for police and thought they were doing a great job.

Merrick looked out the window and thought about how much America had changed in the past few years. He was a patriot and loved the principles America had been founded on. Over the years, America had made plenty of mistakes, but overall he was proud to be an American.

Watching the last presidential election had changed all of that. Merrick had watched the top two candidates debate, but they said nothing about their plans for the country or what they would do to make it better. Instead it was an hour of each one trying to point out mistakes and flaws in the other candidate. Both came off seeming childish, petty, and corrupt. He couldn't believe that one of these people was going to be the person to lead the country.

He was embarrassed for his country, and while he knew better, he hoped the world was not watching and laughing at how far America had fallen. He was ashamed of how the generalization of Americans being fat, dumb, and lazy was slowly becoming all too true.

Deputy Baker and Merrick saw the male described in their call as they turned west onto NE 63rd Street from Andresen Road. A male in his midforties with shaggy hair and a short beard was making an interesting fashion statement. He looked like a homeless man dressed for a teenage beauty pageant. He had a feathered fuchsia boa wrapped around his neck, elbow-length cheetah print gloves, and black pinstriped pants that were either too short or were capris. To finish the ensemble, he was wearing three-inch white high heels.

"You can't make this crap up," said Merrick, looking at the guy.

"Control SAM 81 out with the male in the call. We are east on 63rd from Andresen," Baker broadcast over the radio.

"We are west," Merrick corrected matter-of-factly.

"What?" Baker said, confused.

"We are west, not east," Merrick clarified, showing only slight annoyance.

"Control correction—we are going to be west, not east, of Andresen."

Geography was a common problem among new recruits. The small mistake didn't bother Merrick; it was the least of Baker's issues. They looped around the Safeway parking lot, drove to the far north end, and parked about forty feet away from the male. Merrick got out and had to stop himself from walking straight toward the male and taking charge. Baker fiddled around in the car for a second and then walked toward the male, who began yelling at a car and telling it to slow down.

Merrick heard the tone in the male's voice and saw his tightly clenched fists. He looked back and forth between Baker and the male, wondering if Baker was seeing the same nonverbal tells he was. A veteran officer would have seen the prefight indicators and requested a second unit.

Baker walked all the way up to the male with no sign that he had picked up on the potential violent behavior. Merrick slowed a little bit, put his hand on his Taser, and smiled.

This might be an important learning experience, Merrick thought. When you were a field training officer, it was important to try to make sure your trainee experienced a wide range of calls and was put in stressful situations. Baker had already seen his first dead body, but he had not been in a fight yet. The most hands-on experience he had up to that point was when they arrested a female who had been in a fight with her boyfriend. She didn't fight Baker; she just pulled away from him and didn't want to be arrested. If Merrick was correctly reading this guy, Baker was going to have his hands full.

"Sir, can I talk to you for a moment?" Baker shouted at the male. The cross dressing male had been so focused on yelling at the cars in the street that he hadn't noticed Baker approach, and the sudden shout startled him. He twisted around and saw Baker.

"These cars are a danger to my welfare, health and safety. As a concerned citizen, I have an obligation to formally tell them they are in violation of code 3241.45 of the traffic law," the male said, sounding half-official and half-crazy.

"Sir, you just need to stop yelling at the cars."

The male suddenly rushed forward and, within a foot of Baker, pointed a finger in his face. Every muscle in his body appeared to be coiled with the intensity of his delusional convictions.

He yelled in Baker's face, "I have a duly verifiable obligation to be here, and I have broken no laws, and you can't stop me!"

Merrick had nonchalantly drawn his Taser when the male rushed forward but did not want to intervene too early. He had been waiting for this exact type of opportunity for his new recruit. Baker had been a bit too lax with his officer safety over the last few weeks, but so far it hadn't caught up to him. This was his baptism by fire—the perfect test to see if he had what it took to be a cop. Merrick wasn't about to cheat the moment.

Baker turned his head to look at Merrick, seeking the answer for what to do next. Merrick cursed under his breath, but not because his trainee was about to get his butt kicked. That was probably what he needed. He shook his head because of all the wasted effort that had gone into hiring this kid. All the testing, interviews, and five and a half months of police academy training had been a complete waste on this guy. Most untrained civilians had enough sense not to turn their back on a crazy nut-job who was up in their face, but Merrick wondered if Baker even had a lizard brain.

"I won't let you stop me!" yelled the crazy male as he punched Baker in the face. Lucky for him, Baker fell backward onto a patch of grass between the road and the parking lot.

Everyone was hit now and again, but Merrick wanted to see if Baker would get back up and engage the guy. He didn't. He just curled up on the ground with his arms up covering his head. The nutjob was kicking Baker with his white high-heeled shoes. A part of Merrick wanted to just let the guy keep kicking Baker; it was very entertaining, and Baker needed some sense beaten into him anyway.

Merrick holstered his Taser. He liked it as a tool well enough, but he still preferred using his hands most of the time. His hands never had a malfunction, and there was also added paperwork with using the Taser. In today's politically correct world, some moron had decided that punching someone was a lower use of force than Tasing them. Merrick thought that was absolute garbage, but he preferred his hands anyway.

"SAM 81, Code 3 cover at the Safeway on 63rd Street. We are fighting with this guy." Merrick ran up behind the male, and with his right hand, he grabbed a handful of the guy's hair and yanked him backward and down. He dragged the guy by his hair for a few feet until he was away from Baker, twisted his hand with the hair 180 degrees, and yelled, "Roll over!" He then pushed the guy with his free left hand, helping him turn onto his stomach.

Merrick knelt on the guy's back to pin him down with his body weight, still keeping pressure on his handful of hair. He swiped the small of the crazy guy's back with his free hand, then tapped his back and said, "Put your arms behind your back, bud."

The male did not respond and was babbling. Merrick twisted his handful of hair, heard a grunt of pain out of the male, and then repeated his instructions.

"Put your arms behind your back!" This time he got compliance and cuffed the male without further incident. In a way Merrick felt bad for the guy. Sure, he was crazy and dangerous, but it was really Baker's fault that he would be going to jail for assaulting a police officer.

"Control, we are Code 4, one in custody. If I can get just one unit to continue to my location." Merrick looked over to where Baker had fallen. He was sitting up on his butt and looking down at the ground.

"Are you okay?" Merrick asked. Baker didn't move or answer.

"Baker!" Merrick yelled with a little more emphasis. Finally Baker looked up and made eye contact.

"If you're okay," Merrick continued, "why don't you get over here and give me a hand?"

Baker rolled forward till he was on all fours and then slowly stood up. He was walking toward Merrick but going way too slow for Merrick's liking. Merrick stood the male suspect up and walked him to the patrol car. Baker followed with his eyes down on the ground.

Merrick turned to Baker to ask if he wanted to take over and frisk the guy, but the look he saw in Baker's eyes told him everything he needed to know. Baker was done, and not just for the day. Merrick guessed it was for good. Baker had finally discovered that he was not cut out to be a cop.

"Just get in the car," Merrick said as he shook his head and took out some latex gloves from his cargo pocket. He was in the middle of the frisk when the second unit arrived.

"What do you got?" Joe said as he walked up.

"Crazy guy popped my rookie pretty good," Merrick said with a smile.

Joe laughed and said, "And where might the rookie be now?"

"In the car licking his wounds." Merrick nodded toward his patrol vehicle.

"He okay?" Joe asked.

"Physically, yes, but I'll bet you ten bucks he is a no-show tomorrow."

CHAPTER 5

In his short active duty time in the military, Merrick had lived on two different stateside bases and had been deployed to Iraq. He loved to travel and see the world, but Vancouver, Washington, was more than just where he had ended up. It was home.

He had grown up there and gone to high school there, and while he didn't have family in the area anymore, Lydia did. She also had grown up in Vancouver, but on the fancier side of town. Her family had been there since the horse-and-buggy days. She had left to go to college, but had never really lived anywhere else and probably never would.

With only ten minutes left on duty, Merrick pulled up to his gated driveway. Lydia had been bothering him for a couple of years to get an electric motor installed so they didn't have to manually open and close the gate every time they left and came home. He knew he eventually was going to have to give in and get it, but for a multitude of reasons, it just hadn't happened yet.

He pushed the gate open, drove twenty feet forward, and pushed the gate shut. It got really annoying on rainy days, which were probably around 50 percent of the time in Vancouver. Today he was lucky—no rain.

Merrick opened YouTube on his computer and played "Wind of Change" by the Scorpions. He just sat in his warm car, closed his eyes, and tried to relax. He did a mental dump of the day's stress, of having to be constantly aware of everything going on around him. He always tried to make sure he took just a couple of minutes to transition between Merrick the police officer and Merrick the husband and dad.

The song ended and he checked the time—1744 hours. *Close enough.* He logged out of all his computer systems, collected his things, and headed inside. As he unlocked his front door, he could hear Indiana ask, "Is Dad here?" He was about to close the door behind him when Indiana ran up behind him, ambushing him in the entryway.

"So Dad, here's the deal: Joel's birthday is going to be at a paintball place in Salem and they need an extra driver. Could you do it? It would be so awesome. You could come in and play with us. Please, please, please?"

Merrick, holding all his gear, paused in the entryway and exhaled in frustration at Indiana.

"I should probably ask you later?" Indiana quickly said after he saw the look on Merrick's face.

"You should probably ask me later," Merrick repeated, nodding in agreement.

"Hey honey, I told him to wait!" said Lydia from the kitchen.

"Thanks for trying. I will be down in just a few," Merrick called out as he started up the stairs.

"Okay! Love you!"

"Love you too."

Coming home and putting all his gear away was just as much a process as putting it on. Merrick put his shoes in the garage, hung up his vest and belt in the closet, and stowed his firearms in the safe. Workout pants and a sweatshirt was his go-to outfit after a long workday. He washed his hands and face and then headed downstairs.

Merrick could smell Lydia's homemade Jo Jos cooking in the oven. She made them once every couple of weeks, and it was rare to have any leftovers.

"Smells good. What are we having?" Merrick said as he came back down the stairs.

"Jo Jos. Reese is outside cooking up the hamburgers right now," Lydia said as she gestured to the sliding glass door.

"Sounds amazing. What can I do?" Merrick said, feeling hungry suddenly.

"Can you slice up the cheese and take it out to Reese?" asked Lydia.

"Sure. Where did Indiana run off to?" Merrick glanced around.

"Grabbing more pickles out of the basement. How was your day?"

"Well, for Baker, my recruit, probably not a good day." Lydia stopped what she was doing and turned to face Merrick. "He got sucker punched in the face by a cross-dresser." Merrick couldn't help but laugh at the sound of it.

"He what?" Lydia said, not believing what she heard.

"He got punched in the face by a cross-dresser." That line was not getting old anytime soon. In the moment when his trainee got punched, Merrick didn't even think of how embarrassing it would be for Baker when the whole department heard the story. Only when he arrived at the jail and the booking staff almost crapped themselves laughing at the story did it dawn on him. On his way home, half of the department had sent him messages with some funny comment about what had happened.

"Seriously?" Lydia asked raising both eyebrows.

"Yes, 100 percent," he laughed.

"I want to hear more, but you can wait to give the details because I know the boys will want to hear this one too."

Merrick walked the sliced cheese outside to Reese, who had the grill's hood open and was moving some of the burgers around. Every barbecue had its hot spots, and to cook things evenly, you had to shuffle things around so they would finish at the same time.

Seeing Reese efficiently move the patties around on the grill made Merrick smile with pride. Merrick had learned how to barbecue from his father, who had barbecued at least once a week no matter the weather, and now every time he barbecued, it reminded him of time with his father. Merrick looked at Reese, who at fifteen was almost as big as he was. He wondered if he, too, would think of him when he grew up and was grilling with his kids. He couldn't help but notice how much of a man Reese looked like already.

"How you doing out here, bud?" Merrick asked, putting a hand on Reese's shoulder.

"Good—another five minutes," Reese responded, keeping his eyes on the burgers he was flipping.

Merrick set the cheese down next to the grill. "Anything new at school?"

"Not really. Just thought high school would be a bit more fun."

"What do you mean?" Merrick knew it was not like Reese to be negative.

"There are a few upperclassmen that are being a bunch of douchebags to us freshmen."

"What are they doing?"

"You know, just the normal stupid stuff." Reese paused for a second and then asked, "Do you remember my friend Matthew?"

"Remind me."

"Tall, skinny, has a stutter."

"Yeah." Merrick remembered the kid.

"They heard him stutter today, and then they just wouldn't let up on him. They were mocking him and imitating him. I wanted to punch them in the face so bad."

"I don't blame you. I wanted to just hearing about it. Did you tell anyone about it?"

"Like that would make it better for him," Reese said, glancing at Merrick.

"True. I guess we don't have to worry about a douchebag shortage in the rising generation." Merrick didn't like the term *douchebag* but used it in an effort to cheer up Reese. It was unfortunate that high school was such a harsh, unfair environment.

"Yeah, that's for sure," Reese said with a smile.

"Need a clean plate for the burgers?" Merrick asked.

"Please."

"Back in a sec." Merrick grabbed the plate that had held the raw hamburger patties and brought it inside. Lydia was taking the Jo Jos out of the oven.

"How much longer on the burgers?" she asked.

"He is putting on the cheese now."

"Okay, good; I am starving. The first batch of Jo Jos is done and the second one is in," said Lydia.

Merrick brought a clean plate out to Reese just as the burgers finished. "Thanks for helping your mother with cooking tonight."

"Not a big deal." Reese bent down to turn off the propane, then looked up at Merrick. "You have cooked for me a time or two," he said with a smile.

They walked into the kitchen, and Reese placed the plate on the island. Merrick then crossed his arms to prepare to say a prayer over the meal. The rest of the family crossed their arms as well.

Merrick had grown up in a strong Christian family. At a young age, he found himself in Sunday school asking deep, probing questions to his teachers. When they didn't know the answers, most gave responses like "We are not meant to know everything in this life" or "If we knew everything in this life, we would have no need for faith."

In his youth, Merrick had been merely disappointed and unsatisfied with these answers, but later in life he had come to truly despise them. In retrospect he found what those teachers had been saying with those statements to be disturbing. They essentially had been saying that there was no point in trying to understand difficult concepts and not to bother searching for truth because that was what faith was for.

If his religious education had continued in such a manner, Merrick probably would have forever been discouraged. But when he was fourteen, a new assistant youth minister, Corey Delong, had moved into the area. He was in his late forties, wore glasses, and was skinny to the point of almost looking sickly. Merrick at fourteen years old was six feet tall, one hundred seventy-five pounds, and the captain of his middle school wrestling team.

He wrote Corey off almost immediately when they were introduced. Everyone he had ever admired at that point in his life had a commanding presence that he could read instantly. They didn't have to be large, but they had a confidence and a boldness that was visible to anyone. Corey was less than commanding—he was invisible. It wasn't until Merrick heard him teach that his eyes were opened.

The first time they met was around Christmas, and Corey was teaching the story of Christ's birth. Merrick knew the story well; he had heard it, seen the movie, and read it himself. Corey started with how Zechariah, the father of John the Baptist, was a high priest working in the temple and how at that time the right to be a priest was passed down from father to son.

Merrick found himself listening intently to the details that he had missed when reading the Bible and that no one had ever bothered to share with him. Corey talked about how the famous Three Wise Men were not for sure "three" men at all. It could have been two or one hundred wise men, but hundreds of years ago someone made an assumption and guessed that there were three because there were three gifts given.

Corey also talked about how the Three Wise Men really shouldn't be in the manger scene since they were not present at the birth. Everyone in the room murmured with objections from what they had been taught their entire lives. Corey simply dove deeper.

He talked about how the wise men came from the east and were not Jewish. They were incredibly devout, educated, and faithful men who were not God's "chosen people" but came from a society that was so devoted that they had watched the heavens eagerly waiting for the sign of Christ's birth.

This was interesting not because the Jews were not eagerly awaiting the Messiah, but because nowhere in the entire Bible was there any prophecy about the Messiah being born when a new star appears. The Jews were clueless to the new star and what it meant. The shepherds in the story who came to Christ's birth were directed there by an angel.

The wise men started their journey when the star appeared in the sky, meaning they didn't even start packing until Jesus was born. They came from far in the east, not the town next door. There were no planes or trains to make the trip fast. The best-case scenario was it took weeks, if not years, for them to arrive, and when they did arrive, they didn't even go to Bethlehem. They went to Jerusalem and asked Herod where the Jews prophesied that the Messiah should be born.

These wise men must have come from a civilization that received prophecies about the birth of the Messiah that the Jews themselves did not. Who were these people? Did they have other scripture, and where did they go?

Merrick felt his mind shoot in a million different directions with thousands of new questions and possibilities, but he had to fight to push the questions out of his head for the moment because he did not want to miss a word of Corey's lesson.

For an hour Merrick was enlightened with historical knowledge and Jewish customs that altered his entire perception of the birth of Christ. When the talk was over, Corey asked if there were any questions, and a few kids raised their hands. Corey answered some; he simply admitted that he didn't know the answer to a few others but that they were good questions. There was something refreshing about the way he admitted so easily that he did not know the answer even though he was clearly very knowledgeable.

There was a complete lack of pride in Corey's voice, of having to be right. Merrick felt like a fool and a little guilty for judging him so quickly and so wrongly. Merrick didn't ask any questions because even then he was too overwhelmed by trying to soak it all in.

The lesson finished, and someone gave a closing prayer. People began to mingle and move toward refreshments, but Merrick didn't move. He was lost in thought, not over any of the specifics he had heard that night, but over the thought of what other Bible stories had so much more to offer. How many of the Bible stories did he just accept as fact because he had been told them a hundred times?

The more Merrick thought about it, the more frustrated he became. He felt like he had been lied to, or at least left in the dark. Why would his ministers and teachers teach half truths or even things that were not historically accurate? Why would they leave out critical details and parts of the stories that explained so much?

"You look like you have a lot on your mind," said Corey. Merrick was so lost in thought that he hadn't noticed Corey approach him. He scanned the room; everyone was on the east side of the chapel where the refreshments were. He knew he probably stood out in the pews all alone.

"I was just thinking about your lesson. It was amazing," Merrick said, still unable to grasp all the ramifications from what he learned.

"Thank you. I am Corey, by the way." Corey stretched out his hand.

"Merrick Albright," he said as he stood and shook Corey's hand.

"What are you thinking about?" Corey asked, sitting down next to Merrick.

"A million things." Corey didn't respond and just sat waiting for Merrick to say more. "For one thing, why am I hearing all those details you shared for the first time?"

"Probably the same reason why you are the only kid over here thinking about them."

"What do you mean?" Merrick was confused.

"Not everyone has a hunger to know the truth. Would it surprise you that there are a lot of adults that go to church here that have never read the New Testament?"

"No, I believe it." Merrick nodded, knowing it was true.

"Most parents and teachers just reteach what they have been taught and remember. They don't teach you the details and insights because they don't know them themselves. It's hard to teach what you don't know," Corey said.

"I guess that makes sense, but as ministers I thought they should be more knowledgeable; they should know all those details. I just want to know the truth—not passed-down assumptions and not a version of it. I just want the truth."

"I can understand that, but it is a little unfair to put all the blame on the ministers, don't you think? If you want the truth or you want to find Christ, you can't just sit here waiting for someone to spoon-feed it to you. You have to be willing to work to find it."

"Where did you start? How did you learn all that stuff you talked about tonight?"

"Reading and research are a big part of it, but I think it is more important to be open-minded. If you are not looking for it, the truth will pass right under your nose and you won't even see it. One of the best things you can do is to get together with others who share your hunger for truth and feed off of each other. There is synergy in trading insights and things that you have learned with others. Tonight you probably heard something that sparked a question or two in you. Everyone's brain works differently. You could ask a question that I never even thought to ask, but I should warn you about something."

"What?" Merrick asked.

"Your hunger to understand and to know things will not be filled when you find answers. It will only make you hunger for more, and every answer will lead you to ten more questions that are even deeper than the ones before."

Merrick looked down, then turned back to Corey. "I want to know; I want to understand."

"I believe you, and that is more rare than you know. Most don't question what they are told and don't ask for more than they are given."

"Not me; I always want to know more. It drives most of my teachers nuts."

Corey found true hunger in Merrick's eyes. They sat and talked for more than an hour after everyone else had already left. Finally Corey had to tell Merrick that he had to go home, but promised that it would not be their last discussion. True to his promise, over the next few years they had hundreds of discussions. Corey soon found that Merrick's mind was not only hungry but also had the ability to see things and draw conclusions that others could not. Their discussions became less student-teacher and more open discussions between two equal seekers of the truth.

CHAPTER 6

The clock in the briefing room read six in the morning, and Deputy Baker was indeed a no-show. Merrick had already checked his emails and saw nothing from Baker, so he decided to give him a call. The phone rang, but there was no answer. He left a message: "Deputy Baker, this is Deputy Albright. It is 0600 and you're not here at briefing. Give me a call and let me know if you're okay."

About five minutes later he got a reply via text: "Deputy Albright, I am sorry I did not call ahead of time. After yesterday I am not sure if this job is for me. I very much appreciate your help over the last few weeks, but I will not be coming in and will send a formal letter of resignation shortly."

"Well, Baker will not be coming in today," Merrick announced. Each squad member had some kind of a response.

"Better he figure it out now than later."

"Kids nowadays can't take a punch."

"He couldn't show up and say that in person."

Merrick didn't say anything. He just texted Baker back: "I understand. If you want my advice, take a day or two to think it over, and then make a decision. Keep me and the training sergeant updated with whatever you decide."

Baker texted back, "Thank you. I will do that and let you know."

The excitement of having the driver seat again was nice, but it was slightly tainted by Baker quitting. He was not the first and definitely wouldn't be the last. Clark County had about a 20 percent dropout rate for new recruits. Some, like Baker, washed out after realizing the job was not for them, but most were asked to leave. There were people who had honesty issues or attitude problems and couldn't take correction. Merrick didn't like thinking about people losing their jobs, even though it was for the best. So he needed something to keep his mind occupied during the downtime. There definitely was no shortage of criminals in the world and therefore police work from day to day stayed pretty busy, but every shift had its busy times and its slow times.

Merrick was currently studying famous military battles and their tactics. He was in the middle of reading some interesting side history about Custer and the Battle of the Little Bighorn when his phone rang.

"Danger Zone" from *Top Gun* filled his patrol car. He often found himself waiting an extra second to answer just to hear a few more seconds of the song.

"Hello?"

"Merrick, this is Nate Holden." Nate had been hired at the Clark County Sheriff's Office about the same time Merrick was. They had worked together a couple of times on the same squad. Two years ago Nate applied to be a student resource officer at Prairie High School. Nate had five kids, and the schedule allowed him to spend more time with his family. Merrick was happy that Nate was at the school his sons went to.

"Hey Nate. What can I do for ya?" asked Merrick.

"I am calling about your son Reese."

"What about him? Is he okay?" Merrick's mind raced with the possibilities of what might have happened.

"He got into a fight today," Nate said hesitantly.

"He what?" Merrick's patrol car was in drive, and he was accelerating toward the high school before Nate could say another word.

"He's fine—no injuries," Nate said quickly. "I guess a couple of kids were picking on a friend of his, and he threw two of them into a giant mud puddle."

"Okay. Where is he now?" Merrick asked.

"He is in the principal's office, and he's definitely your son. The principal tried to question him about what happened, and he told him that he wasn't going to say anything until he talked to his dad."

"That's my boy." Merrick laughed. He loved quizzing his kids on road trips about the law and their rights. He had taught them that just because they were in the right in a situation didn't mean they couldn't get into trouble. He knew too well that the difference between being in trouble and not was often just how someone worded things.

"The thing is the principal isn't too happy. Reese refused to answer any questions until you or your wife arrived. I tried to talk to him about it and tell him Reese was a good kid, but once he found out you were a cop, he didn't want to talk to me anymore. I am sure he thought I was just taking your side."

"I appreciate you trying," Merrick said.

"See you here in a bit. FYI, I think he is planning on suspending Reese—you know, the whole 'no fighting at school' thing." Merrick knew exactly what Nate was talking about. School policy across the country had changed, and kids were not allowed to defend themselves in school anymore. It didn't matter who had started the fight or the circumstances around the fight. The standard policy was to suspend anyone involved.

"Okay. I'm about five out."

Merrick pulled right up to the school's front doors, parked his vehicle in the fire lane, and walked into the main office. Nate was waiting for him at a little half door that divided the public from the school staff. Nate opened the door and walked Merrick to the back offices.

"Just so you know, the kids that got thrown into the puddle have their parents on the way. The principal said they are pretty upset," said Nate.

Merrick didn't answer because as they rounded the corner, he could see an enclosed office with windows all around it. Sitting comfortably in two chairs outside the office were two boys wet and covered in mud. Each had a towel on his lap. Inside the office Reese turned and looked at him. Then a bald man with a goatee yelled something at his son, came out of the office, and closed the door behind him.

"You must be Mr. Albright," the man said formally.

"Bingo," Merrick responded in a playful tone. The bald man's eyes instantly narrowed and his brow wrinkled.

"I am Principal Mikles, and your son is refusing to answer any questions about what happened." The principal made sure to emphasize "your son."

"That's my fault, but if you let me talk to him for a moment, I am sure he will be ready to make his statement."

"You mean you want to talk to him in private and coach him on what to put in his statement?"

"Yes, that would be great. Do you mind if we use your office?" Merrick said with a smile. He knew this would probably piss off the principal a little bit, but unlike most parents, Merrick knew the principal had no power to stop a parent from accessing his or her child.

"I do mind. You're not going to talk to your son and tell him how to keep himself out of trouble. Just because you're a police officer doesn't mean you are above the law."

Merrick looked around and could see the two muddy kids and office staff members glued to their conversation, but they were doing their best to appear like they were minding their own business.

"Maybe we should talk in private for a moment." As bad as Merrick wanted to chew out this guy in public, he knew it wasn't a good idea, and it was a *really* bad idea while he was still in uniform.

"Sure, this way." Principal Mikles stretched out his arm toward another office. Merrick walked inside and waited for the door to be shut before he said anything.

"Principal Mikles, I am not looking for any special treatment. I just want to see my son and talk to him for a few minutes, and then I am sure he will be ready to give you a full statement." Merrick tried to sound reasonable and calm.

"As a police officer," the principal responded, "I am sure you can understand that it isn't fair that your son gets coached on what to say when the other boys have already given their statements. He is perfectly capable of giving a statement without you holding his hand."

Merrick couldn't stand how pompous and power hungry this guy was being. He couldn't believe this guy was in charge of overseeing the development of hundreds of teenagers.

"Every teenager has the right not to say anything when questioned; it's called the Fifth Amendment. It is not Reese's fault that those other boys did not understand or choose to exercise their rights. Trust me, I know a thing or two on this subject. If you want a statement, then I am going to talk to my son first. If you don't want to respect that, then I will just take him home right now and you won't get a statement at all."

"You can't do that!" The principal shook his head and even raised his hand in the universal "stop" gesture.

"I can't do what, exactly?" Merrick said as he leaned toward the principal, unable to fathom how ignorant the guy was being.

"You can't just take your kid home." Principal Mikles shook his head again.

"Well, I find it a little hilarious that you want to argue the law with me, but I will humor you. Please tell me what authority you have to hold a child against his will and against the wishes of his parents? What authority do you have to refuse a parent access to their child?" Merrick turned his head and cupped his hand to his ear, begging him to come up with a half-reasonable argument.

"I meant that if you take him home without him first making a statement, then I will be forced to expel him," the principal said, backpedaling slightly.

"I am a pretty cool-headed man most of the time, but you're going to start pissing me off here pretty quick if you don't get your head on straight and stop trying to hold the little authority you have over my son's head. Just to clarify, you are threatening to expel my son if he exercises his constitutional rights or if I, as a parent, exercise my right to take him home. Is that really the legal position you are putting the school in? Because I will have no problem suing the school district." Merrick paused, and finally the principal seemed not to have an argument.

"I am going to walk in there now and talk to my son," Merrick continued. "If you walk in that office before I invite you in, then we are walking out of here, and you will be in a legal battle with your career on the line."

Merrick didn't pause or give Principal Mikles a chance to respond. He stormed right into the office where his son was. Reese got up and gave Merrick a hug. Reese was not a crier, but Merrick could see he was a little teary-eyed after they hugged.

"You okay?" Merrick said, holding Reese at arm's length and looking him up and down for any signs of injuries.

"Yeah, fine," Reese said dismissively.

"Tell me what happened." Merrick leaned back against the principal's desk.

"Remember me telling you about those seniors who were picking on my friend Matthew?"

"Yeah, I remember."

"Well, today before school started, some of us were hanging out in front of the school and Matthew was walking up to us. Those two senior douches came up behind him and they pantsed him, underwear and all. It was awful, Dad. He pulled up his pants and turned around to face them. Then one moved behind him and did it again. I don't know how many times they did it, but I ran over to them and I shoved one in the big puddle out by the gym entrance. The other one came at me and I told him to just back off, but he swung at me. I am not sure if he had ever thrown a punch in his life, but it was pathetic. Anyway, I closed the distance and pushed him back toward the puddle. He ended up falling into the puddle on top of the other guy. I thought they would come after me, but they didn't. Maybe because they were soaking wet. Then one of the office people came out with the principal and told us all to come to the office."

"You did good, and I am proud of you. You did exactly what you should have." Merrick leaned forward and patted Reese on the leg.

"Sounds like I will be suspended anyway," Reese said, hanging his head and not excited about his fate.

"We'll see about that, but no matter what, you did the right thing. Right and wrong don't always coincide with legal and illegal. The problem is we are not dealing with laws here. It's just stupid school policy, so don't worry about it either way. I am going to get the principal. Just tell him what you told me and you will be fine." Merrick got up and paused at the doorway. "Probably best not to call the kids douchebags when talking to the principal," he said, giving Reese a wink. Reese smiled and wiped his eyes.

Merrick opened the door to the office and saw the principal standing with his arms crossed and a very displeased look on his face.

"Principle Mikles, we are ready for you," Merrick said, trying to sound respectful, mostly for the office staff present.

The principal walked in, sat on the edge of his desk, and crossed his arms again. Reese recounted the whole story him.

"The story pretty much matches what the others said and what the witnesses reported. See, Reese, there was no reason not to just be honest and tell us what happened," Principal Mikles said.

Merrick interrupted, "So what happens now?"

"In accordance with school policy, Reese will be suspended for three days."

"What about those boys outside? What happens to them?"

"They are going to be suspended as well," Principal Mikles said.

"Reese, why don't you step outside for a second. I will be right out. I just want another quick word with the principal." Merrick waited for Reese to shut the door, then turned to Principal Mikles.

"You don't have an easy job, but you made this a whole hell of a lot harder than it had to be. I am not sure if you are just completely ignorant to juveniles' rights or if you intentionally violate their constitutional rights on a regular basis, but either way, this is completely unacceptable. You threatened to expel my son if he didn't talk to you, and all the while you knew he was the good guy in this whole thing." Merrick paused. "The cherry on the top is my son, the one you wanted to *expel,* is the hero that stopped two of your seniors who sexually assaulted a disabled freshman. Here is my one-time offer: Unless you want this whole story to be all over the news with a big headline of 'Seniors Sexually Assault Disabled Freshman at Prairie High School,' there will be no suspension for Reese. He will return to his normal classes today. Part of me wants you to personally apologize to my son, but I am not going to make you do that. I will, however, let you apologize to me."

"Mr. Albright." There was a long pause. "I don't know if I can ignore school policy . . ."

"No, no, no. You didn't hesitate for a second to violate school policy when you threatened to expel my son for simply wanting to exercise his rights. You have about ten seconds to make good on this, or we are walking out of here and you can sit here and wait for the news trucks to show up before school gets out." Merrick folded his arms and looked Principal Mikles right in the eye to signal that he was not bluffing.

Principal Mikles walked over to his office door and put one hand on the handle, and while looking at the ground, he said, "I apologize." He opened the door and called out, "Mr. Albright, can you come in here for a moment?"

Reese walked back into the office looking very confused. "Mr. Albright, I believe it is almost second period," Principle Mikles said. "You will not be suspended, so you are free to go back to class."

Reese looked back and forth between Merrick and the principal. Merrick walked over to Reese, gave him a hug, and told him, "I'll see you at home." Reese slowly walked off to class, glancing backward and trying to understand what had just happened.

Merrick turned back and stared at Principal Mikles, who looked away and wouldn't make direct eye contact. He stood there for a moment, then turned around and walked out of the office over to Nate. He asked, "You mind walking me out?"

"Sure." When they were out of earshot of the office, Nate said, "From the look on the principal's face, he had to eat a good helping of humble pie."

"I tried to keep my cool in the beginning, but he had to make this into a big deal. I think he is used to being God around this place, being surrounded by a bunch of kids and people that work for him. I took him down a notch, but the fact he was able to swallow his pride in the end and do the right thing makes me think maybe he's not all bad. Can you do me a favor?"

"Yeah, of course. Name it," Nate said.

"I need you to talk to those boys and their parents when they show up. Make it clear that they and their friends don't mess with Reese. You can always threaten to charge them with sexual assault and explain that they will be sex offenders for the rest of their lives," Merrick suggested.

"I already told that to the muddy duo over there, but I'll make sure that the parents understand. I wouldn't worry too much about Reese. I'll keep an extra eye on him, but honestly that boy is built like a tank and can handle himself. Any of these pretty boys mess with him, and my money is on your son."

"Thanks, but I'm not worried about him getting beaten up. I don't want the fight to happen at all. He's a kid and shouldn't have to be constantly watching his back at school. Today I had some leverage with the principal and was able to talk him out of suspending Reese. I'm not sure if I can do that next time," Merrick said.

"I get it, but look on the bright side: Reese is a freshman, and he just beat up two seniors. Every girl in the school is going to be all over him." Nate fist-bumped Merrick in the arm.

Merrick had to laugh. "We'll see how it all pans out. See you later, and be safe."

"You too."

CHAPTER 7

Reese was out of the house and running to Merrick's patrol car before he could even put it into park.

"Dad, what did you say to my principal to get me out of being suspended?" Reese asked with a big smile.

"Not much. I just talked him through his options, and then he decided it was the best option he had."

"No, no, you're going to have to tell me way more than that." Reese was still unable to wipe the grin off his face.

"Well, how about you let me change and then I'll tell you more of the story?"

"Deal, but I want all the details."

Merrick handed his patrol rifle to Reese. "Here, make yourself useful." Merrick never left his rifle in his patrol car. He lived on a little more than ten acres in a rural part of Clark County, so the odds of someone breaking into his patrol car were pretty slim. No matter the odds, though, he didn't want to take the chance of arming a criminal directly outside his house.

He watched Reese take the rifle and start moving toward the house. His walk was casual, and he held the weapon in the low ready position like he had done it a million times. One of Merrick's favorite pictures was of him holding Reese as a baby with earmuffs on him at the shooting range.

He had successfully passed on his love for firearms to both of his boys. Reese and Indiana both shot competitively in youth shooting programs, and while the firearms were officially registered in Merrick's name, both boys had multiple firearms. Last year Reese had won a regional competition and gained a couple of sponsors. Merrick couldn't believe that shooting might pay for his college education. As a father, he couldn't be more proud of both of them.

Dinner was full of laughs and jokes. Between Reese recounting his story of throwing the two seniors into the mud puddle and Merrick putting the principal back in his place, everyone was fully entertained.

"Indiana, don't you go getting any ideas," said Lydia as she pointed her finger at him. "You should never go looking for a fight, right?"

"I know, Mom." Indiana rolled his eyes. He was the baby of the family but hated it when Lydia was overprotective.

"However, if a fight finds you, then you finish the fight, right?" Merrick said as he looked at Indiana and shook a finger jokingly at him.

"Hell, yeah!" said Indiana, smiling in excitement.

"Hey! Language, mister!" Lydia rebuked Indiana, then turned her finger toward Merrick. "And you should not encourage them."

Merrick nodded in agreement, then added, "As long as you boys are always on the right side of a fight like today, I will always have your back." Lydia definitely did not look pleased with Merrick. "But you boys know with how backward things are right now that just because you're in the right doesn't mean you can't get into trouble. So choose your battles." Merrick looked up at Lydia to see if his added words had bought him a little forgiveness. She gave an approving nod as she returned to clearing the table.

"All right, boys, let's help clean up," Merrick announced.

Everyone had their normal duties. They had never been formally assigned, but over time everyone got comfortable doing a certain task and the routine stuck. Merrick had always done the dishes in the house, even before the kids were born. He had a process and found it somewhat therapeutic. Reese wiped the counters, Indiana swept the floor, and Lydia loaded the dishwasher and dried. Like a well-oiled machine, the kitchen was clean in no time.

"Reese, Indiana, I just need a few minutes with you tonight to go over the plan for the group activity this weekend," Merrick said as he dried his hands after finishing the dishes.

"We still doing the apple cider press and shooting?" asked Reese.

"Yep, that's the plan."

"What kind of shooting?" asked Indiana.

"A really simple bounding overwatch drill. Most of the adults are not as up to speed as you guys, so I'm going to need your help, both with being a safety and helping to train anyone that needs a little extra instruction."

"You want to go over this right now?" asked Reese.

"Yes, if that works."

"I need to use the bathroom for a few first," said Reese.

"No rush; just meet us in the basement when you're done."

Merrick and Indiana went to the basement. The house had been built in the 1950s, and before Merrick and Lydia bought the place, it had been on the market for a year. It didn't sell quickly because it was so dated inside. The house had been full of the oldest and ugliest wallpaper and carpet. It wouldn't have been so bad if there were one bad wallpaper and one bad carpet throughout, but every room had a different one, and the kitchen cabinets were old and falling apart. The house photos online were probably hurting more than helping. In fact, Merrick and Lydia probably wouldn't have even thought about it if Merrick didn't drive right by the place while on duty one day.

It was the location that really sold them on it. The property was toward the end of a dead-end road on the northeast end of the county. Merrick had loved the feel of the neighborhood as he drove in. All the houses were on at least five-acre lots and they all looked like nice, well-maintained homes. The property was completely fenced, including the driveway.

The home looked amazing from the outside. It had an industrial metal roof and an old-school stone chimney. On the northern boundary of the property, there was a large creek about thirty feet wide. During an appointment to check out the house, Merrick fell in love with it. Lydia wasn't too sure, but after Merrick drew up a few remodeling plans, they both became very excited.

The house was huge. It was four thousand square feet including a basement, two double garage doors, and a large shop. Merrick couldn't believe he and Lydia could afford it, and he couldn't believe how well it turned out after a full year of remodeling.

He had done most of the remodeling himself with a little help from friends in the construction trade. YouTube had been a huge help as well. He was definitely a visual learner, and after watching a few videos on how to do a project, he normally didn't have too many problems.

One of Merrick's friends growing up had a secret room hidden behind a bookcase, and Merrick thought that it was the coolest thing ever. Though he was fully grown now, he couldn't help himself from putting in a few hidden hidey-holes when he remodeled. Most of the hidden rooms were nothing special and just used for extra storage space. They definitely needed as much storage space as possible because before they were married, Lydia had been a shopaholic. Making the transition to married life wasn't easy for Merrick or Lydia. Both were independent people and used to spending their extra funds on whatever they saw fit. Having to justify the use of funds to someone else took a while to get used to.

Lydia was able to partly get over her addiction to shopping by becoming a couponer. Within a year Lydia moved beyond picking up an extra item or two at a discounted price and graduated into being an extreme couponer. Now it was normal for her to come home with a carload of things from the store that she paid only dollars for.

Part of Merrick's deal to get Lydia onboard with their new house was the promise of a storage room that was five times bigger and solely dedicated to her couponing stuff. So they had to change their office into a wall-to-wall storage room. The giant stockpiles continued to grow and grow, and Lydia was able to get her shopping fix each week. It had done the trick.

"Hey bud, grab an ammo can of the practice .223 rounds and a bunch of the AR mags, and bring them into the family room." Merrick grabbed the whiteboard and the dry-erase pens.

"Can we start loading a few while we wait for Reese? I'll race you!" Indiana said.

"Okay, son, let's see what you got. Count out twenty-eight rounds, then say go when you're ready." Indiana and Merrick counted out their rounds and then held their magazines at the ready.

"Go!" Indiana yelled, and both rushed to load their magazines. As they got toward the last few rounds, Merrick saw that he was just a second ahead of his son.

"Come on, don't let me win," Merrick egged Indiana on.

Merrick finished just as Indiana was loading his second to last round. He grabbed his son in a headlock and rubbed his head.

"Soon, son, soon—just not today." Merrick loved the spirit of competition but was careful not to give his boys false confidence by letting them win when they didn't earn it. Already both boys had outshot him, outrun him, or beaten him plenty of times at a million different trivial things. Beating their old man was far sweeter when they knew they deserved it.

"Who won?" Reese asked as he ran down the stairs.

"Dad, barely," Indiana said in disappointment.

"I'll take a piece of that. You ready to get beat, Dad?" Reese challenged.

"I'll tell you what. You and your brother go first, and I will take on the winner, but then we have to talk about this weekend." Brotherly competition was a beautiful yet scary thing. Merrick knew the boys loved each other, but by the way they competed, you'd think that they were ready to kill each other.

"I'll call go," announced Indiana.

"No way! Dad will call it. You're just trying to cheat already," Reese said in a demeaning tone.

"Just count out your rounds and let me know when you're ready," Merrick said, trying to stop an argument before it began. Both boys counted off their rounds and indicated they were ready. Merrick looked at the boys; they had pure determination on their faces. He thought that Roman gladiators probably hadn't looked this determined to win.

"Go!" shouted Merrick.

Both boys began loading with lightning speed. Merrick had thought that Indiana had given his all when he went against him, but he could see that going up against his brother had truly lit a fire under him. Indiana finished with Reese still having one round to go.

"Done! Done! And done!" Indiana proceeded to jump around in a victory dance full of a few inappropriate gestures. The overdramatic performance would have been overboard for the final touchdown of the Super Bowl.

"All right, settle down. Take a seat, you two." Merrick wanted to get to business.

"Dad, you still owe me a rematch, and I'm feeling on fire," Indiana objected.

"After that sad display, I think you need to prove you can win with a little grace before I give you a rematch."

The boys, with displeased faces, took a knee.

"This weekend we're going to have a bunch of people here that don't know how to shoot remotely close to the level you two are at," Merrick continued. "I need you guys to be teachers and not worried about showing off or outdoing each other." He paused and looked at both of them. "Can you handle that?"

"Yes," they both said in a not-too-thrilled tone.

"Yes what?" Merrick said with a grin.

"Yes, sir," they both said while giving the worst salutes ever.

"Okay. All weapons will be unloaded on the big gray folding table back by the cherry tree. The black folding table will be the ammo table here. All weapons, when not on the range, will be stored empty with their actions open. We'll split everyone into two groups. Reese, I want you here, and Indiana, I want you here at this closer station. Reese, have your person in starting position by taking a knee behind this barricade. When everyone is ready and in place, have your person call out, 'Cover me!' Indiana, if your person can't hear Reese's person call out 'cover me,' then just have them sit tight till they are loud enough to be heard. People have to learn to use their big boy voices.

"Reese, once Indiana's person starts to provide cover fire, have your person move quickly, but safely, to position two here behind this barricade.

Have them take a knee and fire two to three shots, then go prone and fire two to three more shots. Indiana, when you hear Reese's person begin to shoot, your person can stop firing, but have them stay at the ready and watch. We'll switch stations and run everyone through both sides. Questions?"

"You want everyone with topped-off mags?" Reese asked.

"Yes, I think it's good for people to get used to the weight of a full mag, and I have a feeling people will blow through all their ammo long before their partner reaches their barricade and have to do a mag change when they should be providing cover. That, or they'll be shooting so slow that they won't be providing decent cover fire. It takes just a little practice to get all the pieces of providing good cover, which is why we're doing this drill.

"We'll do a quick demo for everyone prior, but no crazy hotshot crap. Remember, you are the example, so no sprinting or crazy sliding in behind the barricade. Show them the safe speed you want them to operate at during the drill."

"How many targets do you want set up?" Indiana asked.

"I was thinking three for the person providing cover so they can practice transitioning between targets and just one for the person running. We can review the targets after each set and tape up the shots so we know how each shooter did. Any other questions?"

Both boys shook their heads.

"Okay, remember that right after breakfast that morning, I need you guys to help me set up everything and get the ammo and guns prepped. Then we need to pick apples for a couple of hours. Show-up time for everyone is at one o'clock."

"Are we using all our apples?" Indiana asked with concern.

"Everyone is bringing a few bushels, but we need to pick them anyway so we can make apple chips and applesauce."

Reese jumped in and said, "I vote for apple chips."

"That reminds me." Merrick quickly lunged forward and grappled Reese. He wrestled him to the ground and started tickling him.

"What? What did I do?" Reese howled with laughter as he was being tickled. Merrick pinned down Reese's arms against his chest and paused for a second.

"You ate all my apple chips, and if you eat all of them again before June, you're getting a royal butt kickin', boy."

Reese smiled. "But they are so good and . . . totally worth it." The tickling continued with new vigor for a few more minutes.

CHAPTER 8

On Saturday morning, the Albright family woke up one by one to the smell of crepes and bacon. A few years before Reese was born, Merrick and Lydia had gone on vacation to France, Germany, Switzerland, and Italy. In Paris Merrick and Lydia tried a crepe from a street vendor, and they were hooked. Merrick couldn't walk past a vendor without getting one for the rest of the trip. Once they got home, he looked up a crepe recipe by Julia Child, and from then on, crepes were one of their weekly meals. The boys typically ate four crepes each, so Merrick had to make a double batch of batter.

"I'll clean up. You two go and get ready," Merrick told Reese and Indiana.

It took only about an hour to set up the shooting range and get all the apple cider press supplies ready. Then they started picking apples. It was a beautiful October day, and the Albrights had ten apple trees full of fruit.

Merrick drove his pickup truck directly underneath each tree. The two boys picked what they could reach standing in the bed of the truck. Merrick climbed an A-frame ladder to get the ones that were a little higher. After three hours of nonstop apple picking, all of them were ready for lunch and a break.

Lydia had grilled cheese sandwiches and tomato soup waiting inside. Merrick loved good movies and would play one in the background while he was working out, doing projects in the garage, cleaning guns, eating, or doing anything really. He watched movies like most people might play music. Indiana said a quick prayer to bless the food, then Merrick put in the movie *Commando*. They ate quietly and enjoyed the Arnold Schwarzenegger movie, rich with one-liners.

"How much is everyone bringing to pay you for the ammo?" Lydia asked Merrick.

"Twenty dollars each. We're not doing too much shooting. It's mostly the mechanics and the moving that we're practicing."

"Moving? Are you making us run?" Lydia tilted her head to the side.

"It's more of a jog than a run, seventy-five feet max. If anyone can't handle it, then I'm not sure if I want them in the group."

"Just remember not all of us are trained hard-core killers," Lydia said before she took another bite of her sandwich.

Merrick considered arguing about being a hard-core killer but knew it was pointless. He was one, after all. He didn't blame the military for turning him into one, because it didn't. Being in the military merely helped him hone his skills.

His warrior spirit and killer instinct were present long before he joined the service. Earlier in his military career, he read a book called *On Combat*, which resonated with him and explained a lot about his personality. There had been times in his life that he thought something was wrong with him for enjoying conflict.

Merrick knew firsthand that not all soldiers and not all cops were true warriors. For some people, military or police work just happened to be the career they fell into. A true warrior, to him, was someone who came alive in the middle of a fight and who felt like his or her true personality could be finally unleashed.

Merrick looked at his wife and said, "I know. I will go easy on everyone, and we'll be training at the Lydia hard-core mama speed."

At the beginning of their marriage, Lydia refused to do any kind of training with Merrick. It wasn't until some people from church asked Merrick for some advice with home defense that things started to change. Over the next few years, Merrick taught the women at church self-defense. Family and friends asked him to teach classes on a variety of subjects.

Lydia showed up and participated in almost all of them. For whatever reason, when Lydia saw the interest that other people showed, she became interested too. When she got involved and participated, she seemed to really enjoy it.

Years later, Merrick put together a group of couples who he and Lydia enjoyed being around and who were interested in getting together regularly to train to be more prepared. The group helped motivate Lydia to train more often, but that was only part of his motivation to form the group.

Deep in his soul, Merrick had an unshakable feeling that *something* was coming. He had experienced a similar feeling when he was in combat right before something bad happened, but this feeling was different. It was more ominous, like it was not in the present but possibly sometime in the future. He had had this looming feeling about as long as he had his recurring dreams. Since both started at the same time and had been with him most of his life, he couldn't help but feel like they were somehow connected.

Merrick had learned over the years to trust his gut. When he first got to Iraq, he remembered getting that feeling one day while on patrol. His unit came under fire as they neared a market. Kyle Reese, a squad mate he had gone to basic with, was standing about twenty feet from him when he was shot multiple times and then fell to the ground. Merrick returned fire while running to get to his friend. He grabbed the back of Kyle's vest and dragged him to cover. The rest of the squad reacted and suppressed the enemy while advancing toward them. Merrick stayed with Kyle and started doing what he could to patch up the holes. Kyle said that Merrick had saved his life, but that was not how Merrick felt at the time.

A couple of days after Kyle was shot, Merrick couldn't stop feeling guilty because he had had a bad feeling that something was going to happen, but he hadn't said or done anything before the first shots were fired. The chaplain held a nondenominational service each week, and Merrick was one of the few who attended. He had a pretty good relationship with the chaplain even though he was Catholic and they differed on quite a few religious views. After the service, Merrick asked if he could talk to the chaplain for a second, and the chaplain happily agreed. Merrick laid out the details of what had happened and his feelings of guilt afterward.

The chaplain said that one possible reason people got the feeling that something was wrong, even though they couldn't explain why, was that the brain was hot-wired to jump to conclusions based on information that sometimes people didn't know they were observing. He said 80 percent of human communication was through nonverbal methods like body language, and while it was hard to describe a frustrated person's face or body language, once people saw it, they could recognize it almost instantly.

He said it was the same with a million other things, but when it came to survival, the brain kicked into overdrive. How quiet was too quiet? It is difficult to describe or put a decibel amount on it, but when you were there in the moment, your brain figured it out pretty quickly.

The chaplain also said the brain was an advanced computer designed to pull in data and make conclusions. He said there were a million different things that Merrick could have seen or heard while on patrol that could have triggered his brain to get the feeling that something bad was going to happen. Listening to those gut instincts had helped keep humans out of bad situations for thousands of years.

The chaplain then changed directions slightly and asked Merrick what he thought would have gone differently if he had told his commander that he felt something bad was going to happen during the mission. Merrick thought about it and realized that without being able to tell his leaders something specific, he would have just been told to keep his eyes open and his head on a swivel, which he always did anyway.

Merrick knew then that no matter who he had told about his gut feeling, the outcome would have been the same. He felt a little better, no longer weighed with guilt that he could have done something. Merrick thanked the chaplain for his time and left.

He stayed in contact with Kyle Reese even though Kyle's career in the military was over after that moment in Iraq. Kyle had lasting health problems, but no one would know it by talking to him. Merrick was impressed with Kyle's positive outlook on life and ended up naming his first son after his friend.

CHAPTER 9

Ryan Kerr and his wife, Amy, were the first to arrive at the Albright house. Ryan was Merrick's second cousin on his mother's side. They had grown up seeing each other at family events, but that had been really the only time they interacted. Ryan had recently moved to Vancouver, though, and they became more than just cousins; they became friends.

"Ryan, good to see you." Merrick walked up to Ryan and gave him a hug.

"Good to see you too. Has work been busy lately?"

"Always—plenty of idiots in the world."

Ryan always asked about Merrick's job and wanted to hear the latest stories. Merrick had made the mistake about asking about Ryan's job on a couple of occasions. Ryan was a mechanical engineer and messed around with software that tested the structural integrity of small metal pieces. It was a good job, but not the most exciting to hear about.

Amy got out of the pickup with two wrapped boxes. Merrick shook his head and said, "It isn't their birthday or Christmas. You can't keep spoiling them."

"Any kid with you as a father deserves a little extra love," Amy said in defiance.

"Presents are not love," Merrick pointed out.

"Aunt Amy!" Indiana yelled as he broke into a run. Reese must have heard the yell, because he came running over as well. Both boys embraced Amy with big hugs and big smiles. Amy was overjoyed by the attention and gave Merrick a "you were saying?" look.

She held both of the presents tight to her chest and asked, "Who is your favorite aunt?" Both boys enthusiastically chanted, "Aunt Amy, Aunt Amy!" as they jumped up and down. She extended her arms and gave the boys their presents.

Amy and Ryan were unable to have children of their own. Amy had brought presents for both boys when she first visited Merrick and his family. The boys had been excited and jumped all over her thanking her for the presents, just like they did today. She had brought them presents each time they visited since.

"Why don't you put those presents away before the Hale kids show up and get jealous?" Merrick suggested. The boys went inside with Amy, who was going to visit Lydia.

Ryan led Merrick to the back of his pickup and revealed two rifle gun cases.

"Good, you brought your rifles," Merrick said.

"Yeah. They are not as nice as yours, but I think we will be able to hit our targets with them."

"I'm sure they'll be great," said Merrick.

"Yeah, but I blame you for the latest addition." Ryan handed one of the cases to Merrick and nodded for him to take a look. He unzipped the gun case and peered in. He saw an AR-15 rifle with a new EOTech red dot optic on it.

"You got an EOTech! Nice."

"Your fault. Amy shot one of your rifles last time we were shooting, and she basically told me that she didn't want to shoot without a red dot." Ryan looked pretty happy about the development.

"Did you get one on your rifle too?" Merrick asked.

"Yeah. I couldn't have her outshooting me and making me look bad."

"I think you couldn't handle her rifle looking prettier than yours," laughed Merrick.

"Whatever." Ryan blushed slightly.

"Seriously, it is great. I think it'll help both of you getting your rounds on target faster. Have you sighted them in yet?"

"No, we haven't had the chance." Ryan looked apologetic.

"Grab Reese and tell him to help you get them sighted in real quick."

"Thanks. I don't want to hold everyone up."

"Reese will have them done in no time, but get going or you're going to miss all the fun chitchat."

Ryan and Reese jumped on two four-wheelers and headed down to the lower part of the property. Minutes later the Hale family pulled in with their charcoal Honda Odyssey. Merrick openly gave most men crap for driving minivans, but secretly there was much he liked about them—mostly the dual sliding doors.

While deployed in Iraq, Merrick knew a guy who lost a few fingers because of heavy swinging armored doors. He had argued that the military should go to automatic sliding doors on their armored vehicles, but like most good ideas in the Army, it fell on deaf ears.

"Bruce, that minivan makes you look like a stud. Lori, I hope you don't let him drive it around town without you; he might have to beat the ladies back with a stick," Merrick joked.

"You can laugh about it for a little bit longer, but you know you're getting one eventually. I've talked to Lydia about it," Bruce joked back.

Merrick walked over to Bruce and whispered, "You're probably right."

Merrick opened the back door to help let the kids out, and his heart melted when he saw the Hales' youngest daughter, Chloe. She was six years old and the cutest thing ever. She was wearing a yellow dress with flowers on it and had long blonde hair worn half up and half down. Merrick wasn't afraid of much, but the thought of having a daughter of his own was a very sobering thought.

Bruce worked as a local family doctor. He and Lori had four kids: Braydon twelve, Sessile ten, River eight , and of course Chloe. Anyone would think they were a picture-perfect family. Merrick had met them at church, and it didn't take long for him to like them. Once he learned that Bruce was a doctor, Merrick was all too excited to extend an invitation for them to join the group. For years he thought it would be extremely valuable to have someone in the group with the skills of a nurse or a paramedic. Having a doctor in the group was a huge plus.

Funny enough, when Merrick invited the Hale family to join the group, Bruce was hesitant, but Lori was all about it. Originally Bruce didn't think he would be a good fit because he wasn't a gun guy and wasn't even sure if he wanted a firearm in his home. Merrick didn't have a ton of doctor friends, but he knew that it wasn't easy to be one and that those who were in the profession took it seriously. The Hippocratic Oath that all doctors took was all about helping others and not hurting people. It was understandable for Bruce to have concerns about having to take a life. Merrick was glad that eventually he came around to realizing sometimes a person must take a life to save a life.

It took Bruce only a year of monthly participation in the group before he was ready to buy his first firearm. In the end it was the rising violence in the world that pushed him over the edge—well, that and Lori putting her foot down and telling him he had to. Both Lori and Bruce ended up being great shots and levelheaded shooters. Merrick was glad that Bruce had finally come around because he couldn't trust someone with his family if they weren't willing to defend them if they were in danger.

A few years before, Merrick almost punched a self-proclaimed pacifist at church who was arguing that Jesus was a pacifist and that everyone should try to emulate him. Merrick had heard this argument before from other Christians. They always quoted the whole "turning the other cheek" teaching and Jesus willingly letting himself be crucified.

Too many Christians picked and chose the scriptures they wanted to remember and forgot the ones that didn't fit with their agenda. Merrick argued that there was a time to fight and a time to show love—just like there was a time when Jesus turned the other cheek and a time when he started kicking over tables and whipping people to get them off the temple grounds. Merrick told the pacifist that while Jesus said to feed his sheep, he never told anyone to *be* a sheep. That was why Merrick chose not to be a sheep or the wolf that preyed on sheep. He was a sheepdog—one who would defend the sheep and stand up to the wolf. The only problem with sheep was that they were too dumb to know the difference between a wolf and a sheepdog, and they often ended up fearing them both.

At work Merrick came face-to-face with violent, evil people and knew the only thing that would result from turning the other cheek to these people would be to allow evil to spread and more good people to get hurt. Pacifists were idealists in Merrick's mind. In a perfect world where everyone was nice to each other and violence had no place, anyone doing any kind of violence would be a monster. That was why most pacifists had never been victims of violence, because the prayer of every victim in that moment was for someone to come to their aid and bring down violence on their attacker. This particular guy at church actually said that if someone broke into his home and hurt his family, he would do nothing and just trust that his family would be welcomed home by God. That statement nauseated Merrick.

The last family to arrive was the Dyer family. Mark and Miranda and their three boys: Will seventeen, Jake fifteen, and Travis thirteen. Merrick never quite understood what Mark did for work. He said he was on a board that helped manage a string of hospitals. What that entailed work-wise Merrick didn't know, but Mark seemed to have a lot of time off and a nice paycheck. Miranda worked part-time at a local music company she had started for children. The company was an outlet for Miranda to get out of a male-dominated house.

"Mark, great to see you guys, and you brought doughnuts," Merrick said as he opened the front door.

"Thanks for hosting. Me and the boys have been practicing, and I think you'll be impressed with our improvement," Mark said confidently.

"I am looking forward to seeing you guys kick some butt out there."

After ten minutes of everyone mingling and eating doughnuts, Reese and Ryan walked inside. Merrick waited for Reese and Ryan to grab their doughnuts and get settled before he started the meeting.

"Okay, everyone, let's begin. First, Lydia, do you want to go over the schedule?" asked Merrick.

Lydia pulled out her phone and opened her calendar. "The next meeting is scheduled for November 12 at the Hale home. Bruce will be teaching us first aid. Is everyone still available?" Everyone indicated that they were. "Then our Christmas party is on December 20 at the Dyers' home. We are doing a white elephant game with a survival-themed item. The item should be under $10. Miranda, are you sure you don't need people to bring something?"

"I'm sure. It's no problem. Just come hungry," replied Miranda with a smile, excited to host.

"Okay," Merrick said. "Thanks, Lydia. Before we go down and start shooting, I just want to go over a few safety things. We're training today, which means we're focusing on developing good habits, not speed. Only the people who are up to shoot will be handling their firearms. When you're moving, just remember to go as slow as needed to be safe. Once the range is hot, everyone not shooting has to stay behind the firing line at all times. Okay, everyone. Grab all your gear and load up in the trucks."

Everyone but Reese and Indiana piled in the back of Merrick's and Ryan's pickups. Reese grabbed the medic bag, and then he and Indiana jumped on the four-wheelers and headed down to the lower property.

CHAPTER 10

For a bunch of average Joes, moms, and kids, their shooting wasn't bad. Merrick scheduled about an hour's worth of tactical training once every quarter. It wasn't enough to make anyone proficient, but it was better than nothing. Merrick thought of the group kind of like the Army National Guard. They got together once a month, and practiced and prepared with the idea that one day their skills might be needed. Merrick was a realist and knew that their small band of shooters wasn't a battle-hardened squad, but he hoped they could keep each other alive if necessary.

He knew from personal experience just how little tactical training most National Guard and Army Reserve units got during the year. Between change of command ceremonies, sensitivity training, inventories, PT tests, drug testing, and a dozen other mandatory check-the-box training points, there simply wasn't enough time left for units to train on basic war-fighting skills. Overall Merrick's people got more trigger time and more one-on-one tactical training than most military members. Merrick bet that Reese and Indiana would give any Special Forces guys a good run for their money in a shooting competition.

Every adult in the group was encouraged to have an AR-15 with at least five magazines and some kind of tactical vest. Having the same weapon system meant that everyone could share mags and ammo. It also made maintenance and extra parts easy. When they wrote the group's bylaws, they included a provision that allowed only armed personnel to have full voting rights in group decisions. Anyone who was not armed or chose not to contribute to the group's defense was considered a refugee. The intended effect was to maximize their defensive force and minimize the chance for someone being a conscientious objector. It also drew a line between when a kid transitioned to being an adult in the eyes of the group. Once they were old enough to be counted on to defend the group, they got a vote in how thing should be done.

Over the years, people who met Reese and Indiana made jokes about them following in their father's footsteps. The truth was that Merrick didn't want either of his boys to join the military or be a cop like him. He wanted both boys to be able to defend themselves and maybe one day their own families. It was sad, but Merrick was starting to lose faith in the

American people and their leaders. He felt like America was just like the *Titanic*. It boasted about being the most powerful country in the world, and it had become so confident in its own superiority that it had lost sight of what had once made it great.

He felt that with how broken, corrupt, and ineffective the government was, America was slowly taking on water. Merrick wasn't sure if it was fixable, but it was time to at least start looking for a lifeboat. This group was Merrick's lifeboat for his family. So he took the training seriously because one day someone he cared about might depend on it. He hoped it would never come to that, but if it did, he wanted to make sure his family was safe.

Once the group finished the shooting drill, they drove back up to the house to make apple cider. Everyone took turns cranking the grinder wheel and throwing apples into the hopper. The young kids decorated caramel apples and watched *It's the Great Pumpkin, Charlie Brown*. In no time at all, everyone drank their fill, and each family left with five gallons of apple cider.

CHAPTER II

It was early Friday morning, and Merrick had just cleared from a standard two-car collision. He was enjoying the feel of being behind the wheel again. Deputy Baker had officially resigned, and Merrick was soaking up how peaceful and quiet it was in his car. He pulled into the parking lot of a church off 119th Street to finish the collision report.

Most churches had nothing going on during the day Monday through Friday, so their parking lots were the perfect spot for writing reports. Merrick had been in the lot for less than ten minutes when he heard the tones on the radio.

BEEP, BEEP, BEEP. "All units: active shooter at Prairie High School, 11311 NE 119th Street. Multiple reports are coming in of a shooter and students being shot," said the 9-1-1 dispatcher over the radio.

Merrick put the car into drive, floored it, and flipped on his lights. He fishtailed around the turn to the school. "Control David 81. I am thirty seconds out," Merrick managed to broadcast over the radio. He pushed harder and faster, keeping his focus on getting to the school as he mentally struggled not to be consumed by the overwhelming emotions of responding to Reese's school.

"Control copies, Code 33 on Channel 2."

The twenty seconds it took Merrick to drive to the school felt like an eternity. As he pulled up, kids were screaming and running in all directions as they poured out of the front entrance. He had to slow down because even though his lights and siren were going, the kids didn't seem to notice him until they were practically touching his front bumper.

"Move, move, get out of the way!" Merrick yelled and waved his arms even though there was no way they could hear him.

He pushed the release button for his rifle as he slammed on the brakes and came to a stop thirty feet from the main entrance of the school. He jumped out of the vehicle, rifle in hand, and grabbed his 5.11 go-bag that had extra supplies for exactly this kind of incident. Multiple shots rang out from inside. He didn't even think twice about his ballistic helmet and ran toward the front entrance.

"Control David 81. I can hear multiple shots coming from inside the main building. I'm going in."

"Control copies, David 81 going in, multiple shots coming from the main building," Dispatch echoed.

Merrick ran toward the front doors but couldn't see through the glass. Kids were still pouring out intermittently. "Where is the shooter?" he yelled at the kids, but it was like they didn't even register that he was there. Merrick wanted to stop each kid leaving and ask if they had seen Reese, but he knew that the best chance to save Reese, no matter his status, was to put down the shooter.

He paused for only a half second to scan inside through the front doors. There was no shooter visible, but he could see kids on the ground. Some were shot, crying in agony, while others lay motionless on the ground. Others he could see hiding in corners and under tables.

Merrick opened the door and moved into the school. As he did, the horror of the carnage before him was overwhelming. His stomach knotted, and he felt a sudden panicked desire to search for Reese among the wounded. He forced his emotions and focus onto his training.

Without any conscience thought, Merrick was moving again. He sank into search-and-destroy mode, thinking of nothing else but taking out the gunman. He started to move faster, knowing every second he didn't put the shooter down would cost more lives. He reached the main cafeteria and decided to go south, not because he heard more shots but because the trail of bodies led in that direction.

BANG, BANG. Merrick could see the muzzle flash through the south doors about 150 feet south of him. He broke into a run down the hall. The only thing that broke his focus was seeing Nate Holden, the student resource officer of the school, on the ground shot in the head. He felt rage build inside him as he kept running, and the thought of Reese was temporarily moved to the back of his mind as he pushed forward.

Merrick got to the south doors and could see the shooter walking outside another door to the right. He was a young man in his twenties with dark hair, holding two semiauto handguns with large extended magazines sticking out the bottoms. He was moving with his guns extended toward a girl who was wounded and lying on the ground.

Merrick crashed through the door to the outside. He didn't say "stop" or "drop the gun." He didn't say a word. His only response as he continued to walk toward the shooter was five quick and careful squeezes of his finger. The rounds found their mark, and the last shot went through the shooter's head to ensure no more would die at his hands. Merrick took a breath, relieved that the shooter was down.

BANG, BANG, BANG.

Merrick was thrown forward as unimaginable pain shot through the right side of his lower back. He hit the ground and spun toward where the shots were coming from, and then fired wildly while trying to stop the rain of bullets that were coming his way. A second shooter ducked behind the corner of the brick building. Merrick fought through the pain as he forced himself up. He moved quickly in a large sweeping arc as the shooter popped out from around the corner.

The second shooter peppered the ground with his shots exactly where Merrick had been only moments ago. He tried to adjust his aim to Merrick's new location, but Merrick's weapon was already on target. The second shooter looked like he was having a seizure as Merrick's weapon opened up with every round left in the magazine in less than three seconds. He had made a mistake thinking the first shooter was a lone wolf, and he wasn't going to do that a second time. He quickly dropped his empty mag and put in a fresh one, locking the bolt forward. He quickly scanned the area, looking and listening for any indicators of yet another threat.

Ten injured kids were on the ground in his immediate area. He could hear sirens very close and looked in their direction, and then he saw multiple Clark County Sherriff's Office cars pull into the parking lot at the school's front entrance.

He instantly felt like a weight was lifted off his shoulders. Merrick didn't realize it earlier, but being these kids' only hope was a heavy burden to carry alone. Now that the responsibility was shared with other officers, it didn't feel quite so heavy. He allowed himself a deep breath before he keyed up his radio.

"Control David 81, two shooters are down on the south side of the school, more than fifty injured, no indications of any other shooters at this time." Every breath made his back scream with pain.

"Control copies" came the response. Merrick looked back at the injured kids around him and noticed one of them was a football player with only a small flesh wound on his arm. He knelt down beside him.

"Hey bud, what is your name?" Merrick asked.

"Dalton," the boy responded, sounding dazed.

"Dalton, your friends need you right now. I know your arm hurts, but you can push through. Can you do that?"

"Yeah, I think so," Dalton said, looking up at Merrick.

"All right. Come with me. I need to keep my eyes open to keep us safe, so I need you to help me do some first aid. Come on, let's go."

Merrick walked over to a teenage girl who had been shot in the chest and was lying on her back. When he looked up, Dalton hadn't moved. He was just staring at the girl Merrick was now leaning over. She was coughing and had a panicked look on her face.

"Dalton, she needs you. Let's go," Merrick said, waving Dalton forward.

Merrick heard a door to one of the classrooms open and raised his rifle toward the possible threat. When he saw who was there, he almost dropped his rifle. "*REESE!*" Merrick yelled.

Reese peeked around the classroom door holding a fire extinguisher. He dropped it and ran toward Merrick. Merrick felt his eyes flood with tears as they embraced. For a few seconds, he completely forgot about the pain in his back.

Reese pulled away and said, "Dad, are you okay?"

"Yeah, I'm fine," Merrick said, caring only that his son was safe. But he was drawn back to reality when he saw a new group of a dozen police cars from multiple agencies speeding into the parking lot.

"What do I do?" Dalton asked as he knelt above the girl with the gunshot wound. Reese instantly dropped to his knees by the girl.

"We are going to help you; just hang on," Reese said to the girl. He grabbed her blood-soaked shirt with both hands and ripped it open. Dalton stared at Reese in disbelief. A tiny hole in her chest was bubbling bright pink.

"Use part of her shirt to wipe around the wound," Merrick said as he dug through his go-bag. He found a chest seal and handed it to Reese, who applied it over the wound.

"Help me turn her over and look to see if the bullet went all the way through," Reese instructed. Dalton glanced at him with an unsure look and then turned to Merrick.

"David 81, David 83?" barked Merrick's radio.

"Listen to him, he knows what he is doing," Merrick said to Dalton, and then he keyed up his radio. "Go ahead for 81."

"We are sending a few officers to your location, and the rest of us are going to sweep the school and make sure there is no one else. The next few units coming in should secure the main building so we can get medical in here to help these kids."

"81 I copy," Merrick said.

"I don't see any wound on her back," Dalton said.

"Dad, what should we do now?" Reese said, looking up at Merrick.

"If she can sit up, lean her against the wall, and we will see who else we can help," Merrick said as he continued to scan.

Reese and Dalton worked to gently move the girl up against one of the brick walls of the school. Then they ran together to a skinny, shaggy-haired boy who had been shot in the back and was lying facedown. They flipped him over, and Reese leaned down to see if he was breathing. After a few seconds, Reese started doing CPR.

"Reese, we don't have time for that. I am sorry, but we have to move on and focus on people we can save," Merrick said, knowing how difficult it would be for kids to undergo triage. He moved toward the next injured person but saw the boys hesitating to leave their classmate. "Guys, more could die if we don't try to save them. Come on." He put more authority in his voice.

"Seth!" Dalton yelled as they ran up to the next boy who was hurt. Seth had been shot in his upper thigh. He was grabbing at the wound with both hands and rolling back and forth in pain. Merrick reached into his cargo pocket and pulled out a pair of medical shears. He handed them to Reese, who started to cut away the boy's jeans.

Merrick tensed as a door opened. Three deputies came out with weapons up and made their way to Merrick.

"One shooter down over there and the other is over there by the corner," Merrick said to the deputies as they approached.

"Are you good?" asked one of the deputies.

"Yeah, I am good. If one of you could cover us while we try to do some first aid and then the other two can cuff up the shooters," Merrick suggested.

"On it," the deputy said while staring at the wound Reese had just exposed. There was a small bullet hole in the back of Seth's thigh, but the front was missing a chunk of meat and skin the size of a golf ball. Blood seemed to be flowing steadily from the wound.

Merrick slung his rifle on his back and knelt down by Jacob. "Reese, I will finish up here. Take the shears and go prep the next one," he said as he started to apply a tourniquet high on the boy's leg. "Dalton, once I get this secured, I want you to help this guy over to the wall. Then come find us again, understand?"

"Yes. Is he going to be all right?" Dalton asked with concern.

"This tourniquet should do the trick; he'll be fine." Merrick patted Dalton on the shoulder as he got up and moved over to where Reese was. They continued to work together in this way, moving from student to student and treating those they could save. It wasn't long before the school was swarming with cops, fire personnel, and ambulances. The SWAT team arrived and started doing a detailed room-by-room search of the school, while scores of firefighters and paramedics treated and loaded patients.

Merrick's adrenaline from the event faded, and he felt like he had just run a marathon only to have had a red-hot fire poker jabbed into his back. He found a bench near his patrol car and sat down. He sent Reese to fetch a few water bottles out of the car while he removed his vest. As he eased it off, he was relieved at the reprieve from the weight.

"Dad, your back! You've been shot!" Reese exclaimed as he ran back with two water bottles in each hand. Merrick strained to look down at his back, but could see his shirt was saturated in blood and sweat.

"Yeah, they managed to miss my plate back there, but luckily the vest stopped most of the impact. Let me down one of those waters, then we will take a look at it." He ended up downing both of his waters before Reese looked at his wound.

"How does it look?" Merrick asked.

"It looks like someone shot you point-blank with a frozen paintball round," Reese said.

"So I will live, doc?" Merrick asked, smiling through the pain.

"I am afraid so," Reese said as he gently taped the wound.

They sat together on the bench and ate all the power bars and snacks Merrick kept in his patrol car.

"Shouldn't we call Mom and let her know we are okay?" Reese asked.

"Crap, crap, crap," Merrick said with his mouth full. He got his phone out and called Lydia. "She is going to kill me if she hears about this from the news," he said as the phone rang.

"Hey babe. First of all, I want you to know that Reese and I are fine. Don't freak out, but there was a shooting today at Reese's school. Yeah, I helped to shoot the bad guys. I will tell you all the details later, but you should probably come and pick up Reese. They will be contacting all the parents shortly, and this place will turn into a zoo. I would bring him home myself, but there is going to be lots of paperwork stuff I will have to do before I go home. I will keep you updated and be home when I can. Love you."

As Merrick hung up, he noticed he had a few alerts on his phone. He had signed up a couple of years ago for a police app that texted him about any major events that occurred across the country. He was curious if they had already put out the alert for the school, so he opened the first one he saw. It said there had been a school shooting in Florida, but nothing about this one yet. He was not surprised. The parking lot was filled with flashing lights from dozens of police cars, fire trucks, and ambulances, but there was no sign of any news crews yet, thank goodness.

"Mom should be on her way to give you a ride home," Merrick told Reese.

"Can't I just stay with you?"

"I wish, but no. Sorry, bud," Merrick replied.

Merrick's supervisor, Sergeant Nash, walked out of the main entrance of the school, saw Merrick sitting on the bench, and walked over.

"How you holding up?" Sergeant Nash asked. "Oh wow, you did get hit." He stared at Merrick's back.

"I'm fine. It hit my vest," Merrick said dismissively.

"So you go Rambo and take out two terrorist shooters on your own and get shot in the process? You're going to be famous: TV shows, radio, book deals," Sergeant Nash said with a smile.

"Shut up. There's no way they are getting me on TV."

"National hero protecting our nation's youth from terrorists? We'll see." Sergeant Nash raised an eyebrow.

"Wait a second—how do we know these guys are terrorists?" Merrick asked, confused.

"They're Arab, Middle Eastern, or whatever people are calling them these days. They're in their early twenties like most terrorists, and oh yeah, they just shot up a school, so it's just an educated guess," the sergeant said sarcastically.

"I guess I didn't notice their race," Merrick said, trying to remember.

"You were a little busy getting shot, so I won't hold it against you. You know what happens now?" asked Sergeant Nash.

"They will get a brief statement from me today, collect my gun and clothes, and then I'll give my full statement in a day or two."

"Takes one man and a couple minutes to save the day, but it takes weeks and dozens of detectives to figure it out. Make sure that you have a guild rep there when you give your statement."

"Got it. Did you see Nate?"

"Yeah, I saw." Sergeant Nash looked at the ground and shook his head. "One of the commanders is heading over there right now to break the news to his family."

Merrick felt bile rising up in the back of his throat as he thought about Nate, his family, and the dozens of other families that lost kids. He turned away from Sergeant Nash and vomited all the power bars he had just eaten. After his stomach was empty, he dry-heaved half a dozen times more.

Sergeant Nash sat down next to Merrick once he recovered. "Feel better?"

"No, I feel like crap actually," Merrick said, wiping his mouth.

Sergeant Nash nodded thoughtfully. "I could see that. You have done a pretty piss-poor job today saving all those kids and killing the bad guys and all. I was thinking about kicking your lazy butt off my squad."

Merrick gave Sergeant Nash a look.

"Exactly," Sergeant Nash continued. "You know that is a bunch of bull. We do our best and save those we can. Save yourself some time and drop the guilt you don't deserve. People lost their lives today and it is tragic, but you, you saved lives."

"Thanks, Sarge."

"Yeah. I'll catch up with you later at your interview. Give me a call if you need anything before then." Sergeant Nash patted Merrick on the knee a few times.

Merrick took another deep breath, knowing that the process wouldn't be fast. The only thing that gave him a bit of satisfaction was knowing that it would be detectives writing the report and not him. As he sat on the bench, about ten cops walked past and asked him if he was okay after seeing his bloody shirt. Some who knew him told him he did a good job.

"You must be the famous Deputy Albright." Merrick looked up and saw a Vancouver police detective in dress clothes walking up to him.

"Well, that depends. Are you the one that's going to get this process started so I can go home?"

"I am one of them. I'm Detective Beck." He extended his hand. "Things are still pretty crazy here and it's a big scene, so it's going to take a while. Try to relax; be patient with us, and we will get to you as soon as possible. We have to get all the contact info for all the teachers and students before we can let them go home, and they're the priority at the moment."

"I get it." Merrick knew the drill all too well.

"Hey, good job out there. You saved lives."

Merrick nodded at the detective as he walked away, then turned to Reese. "I'm going to hop in my patrol car and see if I can get a little rest. You want to come?"

"Would you mind if I go inside? I think they're bringing everyone together in the gym, and I wanted to go check on my friends," Reese said.

Part of Merrick didn't want to let Reese out of his sight, but he knew an event like this was life-changing, and he wasn't going to deny Reese from checking on his friends. "Sure, bud. You got your cell on you, right?"

"Yeah."

"Just know that Mom will be here to pick you up soon. If she or I call, make sure you answer, all right?" Merrick said, still not wanting Reese to go.

"Sure thing, Dad." Reese hugged Merrick, who groaned slightly at the squeeze. "Oh, sorry, I forgot."

"I will get you back later. See you soon. Love you."

"Love you too," Reese said as he ran into the school.

Merrick gathered his things, slowly eased himself into the driver seat, and reclined the seat as far as it would go. He put his patrol baseball cap over his head to block out the light and breathed. He couldn't believe how tired he was. He heard his phone buzz a few times, but he ignored it, wanting just a few minutes to rest. It buzzed again and again.

After five more buzzes, he was ready to turn the thing off, but he decided to look at it just in case Lydia was trying to reach him. He took out his phone and saw that he hadn't received any new texts but had thirty-five special alert notifications. Merrick sat up; he was now wide awake. He didn't know what was going on, but his gut told him it was not good.

CHAPTER 12

At first Merrick didn't want to believe it, but after ten minutes of research, it was undeniable. That morning there had been a nationwide coordinated terrorist attack on the United States. The combined death toll was in the thousands, but he knew this event had much bigger implications than just the people who were already dead.

He remembered that planes were grounded for days after 9/11, the Patriot Act was passed, and the United States got involved in wars in multiple countries. Merrick was surprised that a message had not been broadcast over the radio letting all law enforcement know that there had been a nationwide terrorist attack. He picked up his phone and called dispatch.

"9-1-1 Dispatch."

"Hi, this is David 81. Do you guys know about the other shootings all over the US?"

There was a significate pause on the phone. "Yes, we have been made aware."

"Okay, and why aren't you putting that information out yet?"

Another pause. "We have been told to hold off on putting the information out because there's going to be an official message broadcast shortly." The dispatcher sounded apologetic.

"Last question: Who's telling you to do all this?"

"The FBI."

"Thanks," Merrick said, and hung up the phone. He got out of his car and walked inside the school. A few cops were hanging out in the lobby; none of them worked with Clark County.

"Where are they doing interviews?" he asked the group.

Some of them gave him a funny look for not having his vest on. "Main gym. You okay?" one answered, seeing the blood on his shirt.

"Yeah, thanks." Merrick gave them a nod and walked off.

When he walked into the gym, he could see the bleachers were packed with teachers and students waiting to be interviewed. There were also a couple of counselors holding hands or hugging kids who were distraught. Merrick saw the detective who had talked to him earlier across the gym and walked toward him.

As he moved across the gym, Merrick heard someone start to clap. He turned and saw Dalton, the boy who had helped him and Reese do first aid. He was standing in the bleachers clapping and looking right at him. One by one, everyone stood up and started clapping. Merrick instantly regretted coming into the gym. He felt like he had to do something to make them stop.

So he held up his hand and nodded in acknowledgment. Slowly the clapping died down, and the crowd began to take their seats. Merrick continued walking toward the detective, who now was very aware that he was in the room.

"You sure know how to make an entrance," Detective Beck said sarcastically.

"Wasn't my intention. Do you have a sec?" Merrick gestured for a private word.

"Yeah, I guess." They walked about fifteen feet away from the table and chairs that had been set up for interviews.

"What's up?" Detective Beck asked, sounding a bit confused.

"Do you know that there have been more than thirty similar attacks all over the US this morning?"

"What?" Detective Beck said loudly. There was no mistaking the surprise in his voice.

Merrick looked around and gestured for him to keep it down. "This is not just another school shooting. It's part of a coordinated nationwide terrorist attack. The FBI already has notified Dispatch, and they are going to be making a statement shortly. My guess is that someone from the FBI will be showing up here to take lead on this."

"You're serious?" Detective Beck put his hand on chin.

"Dead serious. Just wanted to give you a heads-up," Merrick said, then he turned to leave.

"Thanks. How bad is it?" Detective Beck asked as he tried to catch up with Merrick.

Merrick turned back so the detective could see the seriousness on his face. "My guess is it's going to be worse than 9/11."

"Okay. Thanks again." Detective Beck went back to the interview tables.

Merrick scanned the bleachers for Reese. When he found him, he motioned him to come over.

"Is Mom here already?" Reese asked.

"No. I just found out that there has been dozens of school shootings and other terrorist attacks this morning all over the US. This just turned into a much bigger deal than just one school shooting."

"Does that change anything?" Reese asked.

"It changes everything. Go finish saying goodbye to your friends and then meet me outside. I am going to call Mom and let her know." As Reese started to turn away, Merrick added, "Reese, let's not start a panic and keep this to ourselves for now, okay?" Reese nodded and walked back to his place in the bleachers.

When he was back outside in his vehicle, Merrick dialed Lydia, who picked up on the first ring.

"Merrick, is everything all right?"

"Yes, but I'm calling because I just found out that there's more going on. There were dozens of similar terrorist attacks all over the US this morning. More than thirty attacks, and they all happened at about the same time. The government is going to come down hard. I'm not sure exactly what they'll do, but my guess is they might even cancel school across the country for a couple days. When people start hearing about this, they're going to freak out big-time, and then it's going to get crazy, fast."

"Okay, what are we going to do? Are you coming home?" asked Lydia.

"I will as soon as I can, but I still need to finish up with this mess. I'm not trying to scare you, babe, but maybe you should pick up Indiana too."

"I am right by the middle school. I will just stop and pick him up right now. Honey, you are kind of freaking me out," Lydia said nervously.

"I know, but I am not trying to. I am sure things are fine right now. In fact, why don't you guys stop and fill up the car with gas and get a bunch of fresh groceries?" Merrick said, trying to downplay things a bit to make Lydia feel better.

"Okay, be there in a few. Should I just pull into the school?"

"No, you'll never get in. This place is packed. Go to the big white church on the corner of 119th. Text me when you are there, and I will send Reese over."

"Why don't you just come with us to the store and then home? They're not going to have you do anything else today, right?"

"Babe, I can't. I know it is stupid, but I have to sit here until they interview me." Merrick's heart ached.

"Okay. I love you."

"Love you too."

It was a harder conversation than he thought it would be. Lydia was scared because of a thousand conversations, books, and movies they had watched about societies falling apart. They had talked about how the beginning of a social collapse could be one of the most dangerous times.

Merrick felt a strong urge to go home and be with his family—screw waiting to be interviewed. He had to remind himself that the world wasn't falling apart yet. This whole thing could be a big deal like 9/11, but it didn't necessarily mean it would push the nation into chaos. He had, after all, just been in a shooting. Maybe he was being a little paranoid.

He decided to call the rest of the group members and let them know what was going on, but maybe he would try to downplay it a bit more. He dialed Bruce's number.

"Hello," Bruce answered.

"Hey Bruce, it's Merrick. Have you by chance seen the news?"

"No. What's up?"

"Well, I hope you're sitting down. There has been a nationwide terrorist attack on the US. There was even a school shooting here in Vancouver at Prairie High School." There was no response from Bruce, just silence. "I wanted to let you know because things might get interesting. I'm not saying we're activating the group and having everyone come over, but it's not a bad idea to fill up the cars, have the kids pack a bag, and start to pre-stage a few things. Hopefully, things calm down quick and go back to normal, but better to be prepared than not, right?"

Merrick waited, but there was no response. "Bruce, you there?"

"I'm here." Another pause. "You're serious. This isn't like a training joke or something, right? Why isn't it this all over the news?"

"It's coming; it just hasn't hit yet. When it does, it'll be easier to judge how bad it will be."

"Would you mind if I stop by and pick up my rifle after work today?"

"That's fine. I might not be home myself, but I'll give Lydia a heads-up that you might stop by. Stay safe."

"You too," said Bruce.

The other calls went pretty much the same. Merrick was finishing his phone calls when two black SUVs with tinted windows pulled into the parking lot and he knew exactly who they were: the FBI.

Over the course of his career, Merrick had worked with the FBI on multiple occasions. It normally involved a bank robbery or federal fugitive, and in his experience they were not fun to work with. They always seemed to have a one-way information problem. They wanted all the information from everyone involved, but didn't want to share their information with everyone else.

They depended on local cops and detectives to do all the hands-on work, but they never developed the gut instincts and insights of someone who worked the road. Merrick didn't care that they showed up, but he knew that with the FBI now "helping" things, it would be even longer before he got to go home.

CHAPTER 13

More than three hours ticked away as Merrick sat around at Prairie High School waiting to be interviewed. After Lydia picked up Reese, Merrick tried to keep himself occupied by researching what was happening across the country. He couldn't believe it was only a little after noon. He felt like it was five o'clock at least. It didn't help that he was tired, hungry, sore, and antsy from sitting for so long.

Researching the attacks all over the country was not enjoyable. He found out that not all of them were school shootings. There was a train with a suicide bomber, two or three incidents of vehicles running over large groups of people, a couple of mall shootings, one plane crash, and a few incidents at hospitals and a daycare center, but schools were the most common.

In Merrick's opinion, the worst of the attacks was the daycare center. Seeing teenagers dead was horrible enough, but the very thought of toddlers and preschoolers shot and killed by the dozens made him sick. He felt both a little shameful and a selfish kind of gratitude that his kids had survived when so many did not.

BEEP, BEEP, BEEP. "All units, all nets be advised due to the multiple terrorist attacks across the nation, the president has declared the entire United States in a state of emergency. He thanks all first responders for their heroic acts and hard work today. In order to protect US citizens from further acts of violence and to help law enforcement apprehend anyone involved in these horrific acts, the president is enacting the following: All US borders into and out of the country will be closed for forty-eight hours. All schools have been canceled for this coming week. There will be a nationwide curfew starting at 10 p.m. to 7 a.m. for all nonessential travel for the next seventy-two hours. All gun sales will be suspended for one week. The president asks leaders at all levels to help their citizens feel safe and remember that there is nothing that America cannot get through. There will be a broadcast tonight at 8 p.m. Eastern Standard Time when the president will address the nation. Please address any questions about how this will be implemented to your individual agencies."

CHAPTER 14

"This is Special Agent Matthews with the FBI, and it is October 18, 2019, at 1430 hours. We are here to conduct an interview in connection with the Vancouver, Washington, incident that occurred at Prairie High School. Deputy, can you please state your name for the record and your agency?"

"Merrick Albright with the Clark County Sheriff's Office."

"Deputy, do we have your permission to record this conversation?"

"Yes." At this point Merrick was ready to let the FBI pepper-spray him if it meant he could go home.

"Also present for the interview is Detective King with the Vancouver Police Department and Deputy Yates acting as Deputy Albright's guild representative from the Clark County Sheriff's Office. Deputy Albright, we recognize that you have had a long day, so we will try to keep this as short as possible. Can you start by telling us how long you have worked in law enforcement and any special qualifications you have?"

"I have worked for the sheriff's office for ten years. Military before that. I am a first aid instructor, armor, FTO, defensive tactics instructor, baton instructor, and on the riot team."

"Wow, that's quite a few additional duties. Okay, can you tell me what you did in the military?"

"I did a few different things while in, but I am currently in the Army Reserves as a Civil Affairs Officer." Merrick knew from experience that 90 percent of those in the Army had no idea what Civil Affairs was, so he was just waiting for this FBI agent to ask the question.

"What does a Civil Affairs Officer do?" asked Agent Matthews.

"I act as a liaison between the civilian population and our military. Before deploying, Civil Affairs does in-depth reports on every aspect of a country's culture, economy, leaders, etc. Once in the country, Civil Affairs helps minimize civilian interference with the mission and maximize their cooperation. Think of it like the Army's own internal State Department and diplomats."

"Well, I learned something new today. Let's move on to this morning. Can you tell us what you were doing just prior to being dispatched to the Prairie High School shooting?" Agent Matthews sounded like he didn't really care about the extra information about Civil Affairs.

"I was just west of the school in the Baptist church parking lot, trying to finish a collision report."

"Can you describe the route you took to get to the school and approximately how long it took you to arrive?"

"I took 119th Street to 114th Avenue by WinCo and drove south into the back entrance of the school grounds. I drove directly up to the front doors of the school. My guess is it took less than a minute to arrive."

"Why did you go to the front doors of the school? Did you receive any information were the shooters were?"

"No, there was no information yet of where the shooters were. I didn't even know there were multiple shooters at the time. I just saw kids running from the front doors as I drove up. I honestly don't know if I thought it at the time, but most of the large congregation areas of the school are right off the main entrance, so it would be the area a shooter could do the most damage," Merrick explained, really thinking about it for the first time.

"What did you do once you arrived?"

"I took a second to grab my rifle and my go-bag, then I moved toward the front doors. I heard a couple shots while I was grabbing my gear."

"Maybe this is a silly question, but what is a go-bag?" Agent Matthews asked.

"You can call it whatever you want, but it's a bag that I keep extra mags, water, food, and some first aid items in. You have it for when the 'big one' hits, like today."

"Oh, okay. Is that an issued bag?"

"No, I bought it myself, but there are a good number of deputies that have a bag like it."

"How many mags did you have for your rifle, and how many rounds do you put in each?" Merrick was only slightly annoyed by this question. It was asked at every shooting that involved police, and 99 percent of the time, it seemed unnecessary.

"I load all my rifle mags with twenty-eight rounds, and I had one magazine on my rifle, with one on my vest. Then four more in my go-bag."

"For a total of six magazines. Wow, seems like quite a few. Are you on the SWAT team or anything?"

"Have you ever been in a firefight before?" Merrick asked the agent, feeling his patience starting to run thin.

"No, I haven't," the agent answered slowly.

"Well, you would be amazed how fast you can go through ammo. In this job, you never know what might happen. Today is kind of proof of that, right? If you asked most of our deputies, I would bet they have at least four rifle mags in their car at any given time."

The FBI agent took a few seconds to make some notes. "Okay, let's continue. What did you see when you arrived? Was anyone injured or any sign of shooters?"

"I just saw panicked kids running out of the school, no shooters."

"Okay, please continue with what happened next." The agent gestured at Merrick to keep going.

"I went into the school and saw dozens of kids on the ground. I heard shots to the southeast and saw the muzzle flash from one of the shooters. I ran toward them, opened the door, and shot the first shooter." Merrick was trying to speed things up now that the agent seemed okay with moving on.

"What did you notice about the shooter once you saw him?"

"It's hard to say what I noticed when I saw him the first time and what I noticed once the event was all over, but I am positive he had a handgun in both hands and he looked like an adult, not a student."

"Did you give him any orders to stop or drop the gun?"

"No. He was in the act of shooting kids. I wasn't going to give him another second to possibly shoot another kid."

The FBI agent scribbled a few more notes down and creased his forehead as he wrote. "How many times did you shoot him and where?"

"About five times total, I think. Most of the shots I aimed center mass, but the last shot was a head shot."

"Why did you shoot him in the head?"

"To ensure the threat was neutralized. I didn't know if he was wearing a vest, and I didn't want him to still be able to shoot."

"Have you ever shot someone before?"

Merrick hated this question. Adults and kids always asked it once they learned he was either a cop or in the military. What people never seemed to grasp was that shootings were not happy memories and most people who experienced them didn't want to relive them every time someone asked about it.

"Yes, I have," Merrick said hesitantly.

"When and how many?" the agent asked matter-of-factly without even looking up from his notes.

"I would rather not get into the details. They happened while I was in the military, and they are not relevant."

"Why not? Is it classified?" the agent probed.

"No, it's not classified," Merrick said.

"Then why are you not willing to share the information?"

"I am tired. It has been a long, not-so-great day for me, and I don't feel like talking about other days in my life right now where I lost friends and had to watch people die. Hopefully you can understand that, but if you have to know, you can look up my military history and read about it." Merrick hoped he was blunt enough for the agent to take the hint and drop the subject.

"Okay, I guess that will do for now." The FBI agent wrote down a few more notes, this time looking less pleased with Merrick than he had at the beginning.

It took another hour to finish the interview. The FBI photographed Merrick and had him take off his uniform. They took his duty rifle and handgun. Merrick thought it was odd that they took his handgun since he didn't even touch the thing during the whole event, but he didn't argue. They took his magazines and counted all the rounds in each and photographed them. They also wanted Merrick's bloody shirt and pants. Luckily he kept an extra pair of clothes in his patrol car.

Merrick felt a little naked handing over his weapon, but luckily Sergeant Nash arrived and issued Merrick his new AR-15 rifle and a Glock 17 fresh from the sheriff's office armory. Merrick loaded his handgun and hesitated for a second while deciding whether to take the time to load his rifle mags as well since he was just going to be driving straight home. Then he started loading 233 rounds into his magazines.

CHAPTER 15

Merrick drove his patrol car home. He wasn't nodding off, but he felt exhausted. He pulled into his driveway at about 4 p.m. and parked. Reese was out the door of the house with a rifle in hand before Merrick was able to turn off the ignition. He smiled at his gun-toting son, grabbed the rifle out of his patrol car, and rolled out of the driver's seat. Reese wrapped him in a hug that almost knocked him over.

"Dad, I am glad you are home." At first Merrick thought Reese was glad he was home safe and sound, but then it hit him: Reese was glad he was home not because he was concerned about him, but because he was worried about what was going on in the world.

"I'm glad to be home too, bud. Thanks for holding down the fort for me. It makes me feel better knowing you're here to watch over your mom and brother." Merrick tousled Reese's hair.

"Well, do me a favor and don't need me very often. It was freaking me out knowing it was on me to keep them safe," Reese said seriously.

"No promises, but I will see what I can do. Good news is I will be off for a while with the shooting, so you should be off the hook for at least a little while."

"Did you hear anything more about what's going on?" Reese asked.

"Let's go inside and I'll tell you guys everything I know, but just know I am pretty done with people asking me questions right now, okay?"

"Okay, sorry." Reese and Merrick walked into the house and instantly smelled food cooking. Lydia was getting Merrick's dinner ready and Indiana was watching the news.

"Hey babe, smells amazing and I'm starving, but I really want to take a quick shower," Merrick said as he moved toward the stairs.

"Sure thing—right after you explain why I am finding out from our son that you got shot and not from you?" Lydia glared at Merrick.

"I should have told you that a round hit my vest, but can you give me a little bit of a break? After all, I have been shot today," Merrick said, pleading for a little bit of mercy.

"All right, but I am going to want to take a look at it and want to hear the whole story later," Lydia answered with her eyebrow raised.

"Mom, I think Dad is pretty done answering people's questions today. Maybe it can wait till tomorrow," Reese said as Merrick walked up the stairs. He appreciated the gesture but knew Reese was going to be in hot water with Lydia.

"*What* did you say? You do not need to involve yourself in my conversations with your father . . ."

Merrick didn't bother to listen to the rest of the butt chewing and jumped into the shower. At first the water hitting his back stung like it was on fire. In a minute, the excruciating pain settled into a dull ache. After a few more minutes of soaking in the shower, he was downstairs wearing a T-shirt and workout pants.

Merrick went straight to the medicine cabinet and took four Extra Strength Tylenol tablets. Lydia had made her homemade chili. He could tell she had put jalapeños in it; she didn't care for them but knew Merrick loved them. Reese and Indiana were sitting down at the bar; Lydia turned off the TV and walked around the island in the kitchen. She folded her arms and gave Merrick a look that said, "It's that time."

Merrick snuck one more big bite of chili before he started to explain. "When I heard there was a shooting at Prairie High School, I floored it but I couldn't get there fast enough. I got there first and took out the two bad guys." He took another big bite. Lydia drummed her fingers on the table, waiting for him to continue.

"I didn't expect there to be two shooters. I dropped the one and the second guy started shooting at me. One of his rounds hit my vest," Merrick explained while not making direct eye contact with Lydia.

"Cool," Indiana said as he tried to lift up Merrick's shirt to look at the wound.

Lydia smacked Indiana's hand and said, "Not cool."

"Honey, I know you're upset, but please remember these guys were shooting at kids, and Reese was there. I would have run in there in nothing but my underwear to stop them if I had to," Merrick said, trying to lighten the mood. "Plus there is a silver lining to this whole thing."

"I am going to give you a pass tonight, but we're going to talk about this later. I understand and appreciate what you did, but I am *not* okay with you being shot at and not telling me about it. And what could possibly be the silver lining?"

"With all this craziness going on, I am going to be on admin leave for at least a few days while they're investigating the shooting."

"Thank God for that," Reese said with a huge sigh of relief.

They all looked at Reese and laughed.

"How did those guys get the drop on you, Dad?" Indiana said in a puzzled tone. Indiana had played enough paintball and airsoft with Merrick to know that his dad always seemed to be one step ahead and could smell an ambush coming. He seemed surprised that some run-of-the-mill bad guy would even stand a chance against his dad.

"I was a little careless. I rushed in after the first guy I saw as fast as possible. My tunnel vision was so focused on him that the thought of a second shooter didn't even cross my mind until he started shooting at me, which a second later I definitely regretted." Merrick smiled. He could still see the concern on Indiana's face. "I'm not perfect, bud. No one is. That's why we train in teams. With teams you watch each other's back, and they can help pull you back out of your tunnel vision. If you were there going in with me, I don't think either guy would have gotten a shot off."

"Damn straight," Indiana said confidently.

"Indiana, you will watch your mouth or I will wash it out for you." Lydia scowled. Indiana, at twelve, was already much too big for Lydia to handle and he knew it. Reese, the older and wiser of the two boys, had already learned that his parents were not to be trifled with. Indiana was still learning that lesson.

Indiana grinned at Lydia and tilted his head slightly, as if he was questioning the fact that she could do it.

"Don't give me that look. You don't think Reese would be dying to help me do it?" said Lydia.

"Anytime, Mom, anytime," Reese said, smiling at Indiana and stretching his arms as if getting ready. Indiana responded by sticking out his tongue at Reese.

"Dad, have you heard anything about what the president is going to say tonight? The news has been going crazy with all sorts of guesses," asked Reese. Merrick had almost completely forgotten about the presidential address, and he looked at his watch. He had a little less than thirty minutes before it was scheduled to start.

"I heard just a few things. They're closing the borders for a little while. There's going to be a temporary curfew, and last but not least, no school for a week." Both boys were airborne when they heard the news.

"Dad, that's perfect. I was going to ask if we could stay home anyway," said Reese.

"Well, don't think you're on vacation or that you're going to sleep in all day. Tomorrow morning we're going to get some work done around here."

"Like what?" asked Indiana.

"Don't worry about it right now. I just want to finish my chili that's getting cold and relax while we wait for the broadcast. You two can tell me if you heard anything interesting on the news in the last couple hours."

The boys took turns telling Merrick about what the news anchors and their panels of experts had suggested. Both boys shared the same talking points that every came with every school shooting. They seemed the most excited about the talks on gun control.

In Merrick's opinion, people who had been shot at naturally thought the person who had done the shooting should not have been able to get that gun, and they were right. Others not only had this same thought but also wished they had a gun to shoot back with. Merrick didn't blame cars or alcohol for drunk drivers, he didn't blame cell phones for people who texted and drove, medications were not to blame for overdoses, and he didn't blame guns when someone was shot. All he knew was that he felt he could defend himself better when he carried a gun, and it made sense to him that other law-abiding citizens might feel the same way.

CHAPTER 16

The Albright family was part of an ever-increasing portion of the population that did not have any kind of TV subscription. With Netflix, Hulu, Amazon Prime Video, YouTube, and the Internet, there were plenty of things to watch without the hassle of commercials. Reese found a YouTube channel that was a live feed from the White House, and it had a countdown timer indicating the broadcast was only minutes away. As the timer wound down, the family gradually moved to the couch and anxiously watched the last few seconds tick away as they waited to see what the president was going to say.

"My fellow Americans, today our nation has been wounded deeply. We mourn together with the thousands of families who lost someone today. We must not let this wound fester, and we cannot let something like this ever happen again. I want all of you to know that at this very moment, every resource of this government is being used both here and abroad to find these terrorists and bring them to justice. Nothing can ever bring back those we lost, but we cannot afford to lose anyone else. Enough is enough.

"Three hours after the attacks of this morning, we bombed twenty-five known terrorist camps in ten different countries. The days of terrorists finding safe harbor in countries like Libya, Pakistan, and Venezuela are over. We are on the hunt, and there is nothing that will get in our way of rooting out this evil. Russia, China, and most of our allies have already confirmed that they are with us in rooting out and destroying terrorism in the world for good. The United Nations are going to be holding an emergency meeting to discuss to what degree they will be involved in eliminating terrorism worldwide, but with or without the UN, it will be done, I assure you.

"These changes abroad are only half the answer. The House and the Senate are holding emergency meetings starting tomorrow to enact ways to deal with this threat on our soil. As of right now, I am enacting Executive Order 140021 to ensure the safety of our nation until Congress can agree on how to do it by law. Remember, these are temporary and essential for our national security.

"For the next forty-eight hours, our borders will be completely closed. No one will be coming into or out of the country.

"All gun sales are suspended for one week.

"All schools are suspended for one week.

"There will be a curfew for one week for nonessential travel from 10 p.m. to 7 a.m. If you have a nonessential job and can take time off from work, we encourage you to do so.

"Today, like 9/11, will become a day we will always remember. Let us remember it as a day we came together and became a stronger, more united America. We cannot and will not let those who died today pass away in vain. They will be the spark that helps ignite us to build a stronger and safer America than ever before. God bless you all, and God bless America."

The broadcast ended. The Albright family sat silently for a moment. Merrick found the remote and turned the TV off as the news broadcasters started to talk.

"It was better than I expected. What did you guys think?" asked Lydia.

"It was pretty good, and I liked that they took out those terrorist camps," Reese said.

"Yeah, with the US, Russia, and China working together to hunt down the terrorists, they will wipe them all out in no time," Indiana added.

Merrick sat still and silent, deep in thought. He suddenly felt everyone's eyes on him, and he could tell they wanted him to say everything was going to be okay. He was never one to deal out false hope, even if it offered temporary comfort.

"I agree that terrorism is a horrible thing and we should try to stop it where and whenever we can, but terrorism is designed to use fear as a weapon, and they aren't the only ones who use fear. Dictators and authoritative governments use fear to control their own people. I fear more and more Americans are willing to gladly hand over their rights if the government can promise a little more security. We just keep giving them more and more power, and I think it will eventually blow up in our faces."

"What do you think they're going to do?" asked Reese.

"I have no idea, but when the president said that Congress is getting together to make laws that will ensure this never happens again, it scared me. Think about it. There will always be crime, there will always be murders, and to say you are going to stop something that will always exist sounds a lot like absolutism. Do you remember that movie *V for Vendetta*?"

"Yeah, I love that movie," said Indiana.

"Do you remember in the movie how that crazy Nazi-like government got into power?"

"Not really."

"There was a terrorist attack. The people were afraid of the terrorists, so they handed over their freedom to the government for protection, but pretty soon the people were afraid to go outside—not because of terrorists, but because of their own government. The famous saying in that movie was that 'People shouldn't be afraid of their government; governments should be afraid of their people.'"

"I don't get it. Why would a government fear its own people? The government has all the big weapons like missiles and tanks. Normal people wouldn't stand a chance," said Indiana.

"Have I seriously not taught you anything about guerrilla warfare? Destroying a standing army is simple, but trying to fight an insurgency that is supported by a population is nearly impossible. The US military couldn't stop it in Iraq, Afghanistan, Vietnam, or Korea. Lots of governments have been brought to their knees by their own people. Even the Roman Empire, which ruled with an iron fist, feared the voice of the people."

"Sweet, so you're saying there's going to be a revolution?" said Indiana.

"No, no, I am not. But trust me, you don't want one either. A revolution is a type of civil war, and it's a bloody, ugly mess. Trying to put a country back together that you just ripped apart is not that easy. Plus who's to say the new government is guaranteed to be any better than the last one?"

"So we are just screwed is what you're saying? That sucks balls!" Indiana said, overdramatizing.

Lydia opened her hand and, while looking directly at Indiana, said very calmly, "Reese, grab a bar of soap for me." Reese instantly was up off the couch and running to get the soap. Indiana looked puzzled, and it wasn't until Reese returned with a bar of soap, his mouth wide open and practically drooling with joy, that the situation dawned on him.

"No, no, no. Mom, no. I didn't mean it." Indiana pushed himself up to his feet. Reese plopped the bar of soap in Lydia's hand and sat down next to her. Merrick couldn't help but laugh at the whole thing—not because Indiana was about to get a bar of soap in his mouth, but because Reese reminded him of a well-trained dog waiting patiently for the order to fetch the ball, but this time Indiana was the prize.

Indiana looked at Lydia, but her face was unsympathetic. He turned to Merrick. "Dad, come on, it wasn't that big of a deal. Help me?"

Merrick felt a little sorry for Indiana but knew better than to step on Lydia's toes. "Sorry, bud, but your mom's told you a few times in the past few weeks to watch your mouth, and I guess she thinks you're not getting the message."

Indiana looked back at Lydia, then made a dash toward the garage. In the same calm tone she used before, Lydia simply said, "Reese," and he took off in pursuit. She got up and followed both boys.

Merrick got up and filled another glass of water from the fridge, then turned around to see, through the window, Reese tackling Indiana on the front lawn. Then, as if on cue, Lydia arrived with the bar of soap. Merrick couldn't hear what she was saying to Indiana, but as she made him open his mouth to accept the bar of soap, he thought, *Thank goodness she's on my side.*

CHAPTER 17

Merrick rarely slept in, mostly because his insomnia wouldn't let him. This morning, though, even though he was awake at 5:30 a.m., his warm bed and the dark room made him feel like sleeping in was exactly what he needed.

After lying in bed for a little longer than normal, he decided it was time to get up. He stretched and got dressed, then headed downstairs to make himself some of his famous oatmeal. Anyone who heard about it thought it sounded disgusting, but anyone who tried it had to admit it wasn't half-bad—everyone except Lydia. She never admitted to liking it and stuck with traditional cinnamon oatmeal.

Merrick scooped some oats into a bowl and mixed in milk. (He could eat oatmeal made with water if he had to, but thought it tasted ten times better when made with milk.) Once the oats were cooked, he poured in a little bit of powered Tang and a few frozen blackberries along with some Craisins, then topped it off with a sliced banana. It was a heaping, warm, tangy bowl of goodness, and he loved it.

As he finished preparing his oatmeal, Merrick could hear the TV on in the basement. He walked down the stairs in no big hurry, savoring the relaxing start to the day. Both boys were downstairs, sitting on the couch and totally focused on playing the latest *Call of Duty* video game.

"You guys eat already?" he asked.

Both boys responded without taking their eyes off the TV: "I ate a bowl of cereal about an hour ago." "I ate an English muffin with peanut butter."

Merrick enjoyed his oatmeal as he let himself zone out watching his two boys save the world. The level ended at about the same time Merrick was finishing his last few bites. Both boys then looked over at what he was eating for the first time since he had been downstairs.

"Is that Daddy Oatmeal?" Reese asked. Merrick hadn't named the oatmeal creation when he invented it, but when the boys were little and they wanted the oatmeal he had, they asked for "Daddy Oatmeal" and the name stuck.

Merrick looked down at the contents of the bowl as he put another spoonful in his mouth. "Why yes, yes it is."

"Dad, can you make me a bowl, please?" asked Reese.

"It's not rocket science. You can make it yourself."

"But it's not as good when we make it."

"Can you make me some too, please?" added Indiana. Both boys looked at Merrick and grinned.

"So you want me to make both of you a second round of breakfast so you can continue playing video games?"

"Yup, because you're the best dad in the world."

Merrick got up to take his dirty bowl back upstairs and said, "Remind me to beat your spoiled, ungrateful butts later." He made two more bowls of Daddy Oatmeal and brought them down to Reese and Indiana. He loved those boys and found it hard not to spoil them.

"Okay, you two. Scoot over and eat while I play," Merrick said as he handed them their bowls. He wasn't a gamer, but he enjoyed playing occasionally. After he sat down, he moved his player forward through an open field. The grass was long and moved with a gentle breeze, creating a perfectly natural rippling effect over the top. He crouched lower as he got closer to the enemy position, and he could see the details of the grass blades and the occasional leaf on the ground. He couldn't believe how amazingly lifelike games were today. Technology had come a long way since the days of Wolfenstein 3D.

Lydia came downstairs, looked at all three guys sitting on the couch, and then looked at the TV. "I thought you wanted to get a bunch of stuff done today. You get us all excited that our country is on the breaking point, and Mr. I Am Always Prepared is going to play video games all morning."

"Honey, I just sat down . . ." Merrick tried to argue, but Lydia cut him off.

"I don't want to hear it. I've been cleaning all the bathrooms and doing everyone's laundry all morning. This next week, we're not going to be spending all our time vegging out in front of the TV." With that, Lydia leaned down and turned off the TV. "You two, I want clean sheets on your beds, rooms picked up and vacuumed, and laundry put away. Then Reese, I want you to clean out the chicken coop, and Indiana, you're going to scrub your shower."

"Mom! The chicken coop is way worse than the shower! That's not fair," complained Reese.

"Fair? Who's been cleaning all morning while you play video games?" She gave Reese a look that said, "If you want to argue, you'll be doing even more."

Both boys got up and started walking toward the stairs, but they moved slowly, like they had lead feet.

Lydia then turned toward Merrick. "Mr. Albright, you'll be scrubbing our shower." During the first couple of years of their marriage, Lydia and Merrick, like most couples, divided up the workload around the house. Each naturally fell into doing their part of the work. Showers were Merrick's thing to do in the bathrooms. He didn't enjoy scrubbing the shower, but he had become pretty good at it.

They both went upstairs to the master bedroom. "Can you grab our laundry on your way up?" Lydia asked on the way.

"Yep," Merrick said as he grabbed the full laundry basket that was sitting by the stairs. He walked into the master closet, set down the basket, and started to put the laundry away. Lydia came into the closet and said, "I can do that. Why don't you get started on that shower?"

Merrick turned and walked into the bathroom. He removed all the cleaning products he was going to need from under the sink and then looked at the shower for the first time. It looked like it had already been cleaned.

He turned around, and Lydia was standing in the doorway with her shirt unbuttoned.

CHAPTER 18

After a nice shower and a great start to the day, Merrick was feeling pretty good. He grabbed his phone, which was still on its charger, and powered it on. His phone had died last night, and he had never bothered to turn it back on. He unlocked it and saw he had received 147 new text messages. Part of him just want to throw the thing right into the trash and go back to the days of not having an electronic leash. He took a deep breath, sat on the edge of the bed, and started to scroll through the messages.

A bunch of the texts were from cop buddies giving him their support. Some of the texts were chain texts from family members trying to verify if they were all okay. Luckily Lydia had answered that they were fine but left out that he was involved in the shooting. He didn't even want to think about how many texts he would have gotten if she had told them he'd shot those guys. He kept scrolling and saw another group text with all the group members.

Mark: "FYI, I tried to buy ammo after the president spoke and EVERYTHING is sold out. EVERYTHING!"

Bruce: "Wow, how is that even possible?"

Ryan: "I bet someone in the GOV leaked the gun ban and there was a big gun and ammo grab."

Merrick felt a little ping of guilt that he hadn't let them know about the gun ban when he heard the 9-1-1 dispatcher put out the informational broadcast. He wasn't surprised by the reaction because every time any politician said the words "gun control," the sales of gun and ammo spiked. The best friend of every gun manufacturer had always been the threat of increased regulation. Merrick guessed that if gun sales opened up again in a week, gun stores would run out of their stock as soon as they opened. Merrick continued reading the thread.

Lori: "Bruce told me not to go, but I just went to the store to stock up on a few things and people were going crazy. I saw three heated arguments with cashiers vs. customers at WinCo. There were empty shelves and everyone was loading up full shopping carts of stuff. I can't believe this is really happening. When are we going to all get together at the Albrights'?"

Lydia: "Lori, I am so glad you're okay. It's probably best not to go out right now. As you all know, Merrick was involved in the shooting yesterday, and with everything going on in the world, decompressing is not going to be easy. As long as nothing big happens, I would appreciate it if we could give Merrick a day or two before we decide anything."

Mark: "Lydia, of course we'll give you all the time you need. People are just overreacting like they did after 9/11 and nothing happened then. All the emergency services are still operating. We're on edge, but we still need a good shove to push us over. Can we bring you guys dinner sometime?"

Lori: "Lydia, I feel horrible, and I wasn't asking for us to intrude on you, especially with what Merrick has been through. I just wanted to know at what point we should all get together."

Lydia: "Thank you all for understanding. I'm sure Merrick is fine, but I want to give him a little time. Don't worry about bringing us anything right now. Just stay safe and keep in contact."

Merrick had always seen himself as the protector in the relationship with Lydia, and thinking about Lydia protecting him made him smile. He continued to scroll through his messages, skipping past people he barely knew. Then he saw a message from his sergeant.

Sergeant Nash: "Hey Merrick, hope you are well. Command wants you to schedule your psych interview ASAP. They said for you to take the time you need, but with everything going on, they want all hands on deck. To tell you the truth, things are dicey out there—people are on edge and I would feel better if you were out there with us. Here's the number: (503) 555-1267. Dr. Burke. Keep me updated."

Merrick responded: "Hey SGT, I do feel a little bad having you guys out there without me. But I was looking forward to some paid time off. I'll call today and let you know."

Sergeant Nash: "FYI, Portland is expecting riots tonight with the curfew and is activating their MRT teams. They requested our team, but Admin said no, because we can't spare anyone from the road."

With everything going on, Merrick wanted to be home and make sure his family was safe, but there was another part of him that hated thinking of his cop friends out there without him. He felt torn—not because he put his cop friends on the same level of importance as his family, but as he saw it, currently his family was at a fairly low level of risk while his cop friends were at a very high level of risk. They needed him right now even more than his family did. He copied the number from the text and called it.

"Dr. Burke's office."

"Hi, my name is Merrick Albright, and I'm with the Clark County Sheriff's Office. I need to schedule an appointment with Dr. Burke."

"Is this in regard to an officer-involved shooting?"

"Yes."

"Please hold," the secretary said as the phone clicked. Merrick waited for a bit.

"Okay, are you still there?"

"Yes."

"I'm going to schedule a time for Dr. Burke to call you, and she is going to do the interview over the phone."

"Seriously?"

"Yes. Since the whole terrorist thing, there have been multiple officer-involved shootings in the Portland area. Dr. Burke and the local agencies have agreed that it's important to get officers back on the road, and with the increasing number of shootings, it's the best we can do at this time. Once things settle down, we'll try to follow up with everyone. Does today at 4 p.m. work for you?"

"Yes, that should be fine."

"Okay, and is the best number to call the 360 number that's on the caller ID?"

"Yes, it is."

"Okay, thank you. The interview will last for about an hour, and please be somewhere where you're free from distractions."

"Okay. Thanks."

Merrick hung up and put his phone in his pocket. He didn't even care to look at the rest of the messages; they could wait. He went downstairs to let Lydia know that he would need to be on a call later. He also wanted the boys' help with getting some work done around the house. All three of them were downstairs in the kitchen getting a snack.

"Hey guys, can I talk to you for a minute?" Merrick said as he walked down the stairs. "I got a few texts from my sergeant, and I guess it's getting worse out there. I don't know for sure what's going to happen, but I want to be ready for the worst. Let's brainstorm some ideas of things we need to do to be ready if everyone comes over."

"Should we go to the store again and stock up on more stuff?" Indiana asked.

"No, I think it is too dangerous out there," Lydia said. "Lori texted me and said she went to the store yesterday. People were getting crazy out there and the stores were already going empty, so I don't think it's worth it."

"Well, what if we could stock up but not have to leave home?" Reese suggested.

"What are you talking about?" asked Merrick, confused by how they could accomplish that.

"We could shop online and just order a bunch of things. With Amazon the stuff will be here in two days."

Merrick and Lydia looked at each other and shrugged.

"I knew there was a reason we kept you around. Not a bad idea, not bad at all." Merrick rubbed the top of Reese's head. "We'll pull up Amazon in a little bit and order stuff together. It'll be like Christmas. Okay, what else do we need to get done?"

"If there's even the possibility of everyone from the group coming here, then I think we need to de-junk some of our rooms so they're ready for people to move into," Lydia said.

"You want us to move totally out of our rooms?" asked Reese.

"I don't think you need to move totally out," Merrick said. "Why don't you guys pack up anything you don't want anyone messing with and don't think you'll need in the next two weeks? We'll box that up and store it in the attic. Then pack a suitcase with camping-style clothes and put it in our room. I also think it's not a bad idea to get your bedding all set up and figured out in our room."

"That's going to suck," Indiana added.

"I know, but it's better to do it now when you have time than when people are trying to move in," Lydia said. "We know that having a bunch of people move into our house is not going to be fun, but we need them and they need us, so just make the best of it."

"Okay. Well, honestly I think that'll take us pretty much to the end of the day, unless there's anything else you think we need to do," said Merrick.

"What about talking to the neighbors? You know, checking in with them and having everyone on high alert," Reese suggested.

"That's a good idea. I just don't want to go around too early and freak them out unless I have to. Let's wait a little bit longer on that one," Merrick said.

"I think we need one more thing: a popcorn and movie night tonight," Lydia added. The two boys cheered in happy agreement.

"The real question is, what movie are we watching?" Merrick asked.

CHAPTER 19

The whole conversation with Dr. Burke took thirty-five minutes from start to finish. Merrick was getting tired of telling the story. In the last two days, he'd told the story more than five times. In the military and as a police officer, Merrick had had the pleasure of talking to shrinks on multiple occasions. He knew it was always a formality, and he didn't mind going through the process because he knew there were people who needed help working through what had happened to them.

In his experience, most people with PTSD were exposed to a very specific mixture of circumstances. The person had normally been in some kind of intense situation and wished he could change the way things had happened. Merrick's theory was that PTSD was the brain trying to replay the event in an attempt to come up with a different outcome than what had really happened. As a police officer, he saw it all the time in victims, both men and women. Most felt scared and powerless after an incident where they had been victimized. They would then go through years of counseling, trying to come to terms with what had happened. In his opinion, there was a better way to go about it because redemption was always better than absolution.

Most good military commanders understood that if they had a young, inexperienced soldier who froze during a firefight, the worst thing you could do was pull him off the line, and make him sit in the barracks for a few days and think about how he had screwed up. A good leader would try to get him back in a firefight as soon as possible—not as a punishment, but as a chance to redeem himself and prove he could do it. A soldier whose last act had been negative focused on nothing else, and likewise, a soldier who had just acted bravely reveled in that. In Merrick's mind, people who had been victimized needed to be empowered and focus on a positive, not a negative. Taking a self-defense class could be worth years of lying down on a shrink's couch talking about what happened. The icing on the cake, to him, was that they were less likely to be victimized again.

In the end, Dr. Burke gave him a clean bill of health and the green light to go back to work. Merrick texted Sergeant Nash to let him know that he was good to return to duty. He had two days left in his work week, then he would be off for four days. He walked downstairs to let Lydia know.

"Hey honey."

"How did it go?" Lydia asked.

"Doc gave me the go ahead to return to work."

"But you don't have to go back right away, right?" Lydia knew that normally an officer would have a couple of weeks off while an incident was investigated.

"Yes, I can take some time if I need it, but . . ."

"*But* nothing! You were just in a shooting; people are acting crazy out there. You more than deserve a few days off."

"You're right, and if the world wasn't going to crap, I would totally take advantage of some time off, but we need cops more than ever."

"I know, and we need you *here* more than ever. You're not going to leave. You were shot the other day, and I've been pretty good about not freaking out about it, but so help me, Merrick Eugene Albright, if you leave us here . . ."

"Please just hear me out. First, I don't want to leave you here alone. I think I'm going to call Ryan and Amy and see if they can come here and stay with us at least for a few days."

"Not good enough," Lydia interjected.

"Please, let me finish. The main reason I feel like I have to go back is if something happened to one of the guys on my squad, I'd always wonder if I could've stopped it if I'd been working. I feel like I can't abandon my guys right now when they need me the most. I know you need me too, but right now you're pretty safe out here. We are away from the city with two hard-core Rambo Juniors. If Ryan and Amy are here too, even more so. You need me, I get that, but right now the guys at work need me more. The second I think things are unsafe at home or things have gotten so bad that I'm not safe as a cop, I'll be on my way home as fast as lightning. I promise."

"I still don't like it."

"Duly noted."

Lydia had tears in her eyes as she gave Merrick a big hug. Reese and Indiana had heard the argument, but had enough sense not to walk in until it was over.

"Dad, what if I came along with you tomorrow? You know, to watch your back," Reese said.

"Reese, good idea, but I would feel better if I knew you were here taking care of things, and it's a little too dangerous right now," Merrick said. He appreciated his son wanting to keep him safe, though.

"With Mom, Indiana, Ryan, and Amy being here, everyone will be totally fine. You're the one that needs some extra protection," Reese argued.

"Reese, I don't want be constantly worried about you while I'm out there. I need to be focused, and if I'm constantly worried about you, I can't do that."

"But Dad, you just talked about how if something happened to your guys, you would blame yourself for not being there. If you don't come home . . ." Reese's eyes welled up with tears. "Do you think I'll ever forgive myself?"

Merrick hugged Reese tight. Inside he was starting to rethink whether going to work was the right decision.

"Take him," Lydia added suddenly, with surprisingly little emotion in her voice.

"What?" asked Merrick in shock. All three guys were utterly confused that Lydia would agree to allow Reese to go into what was potentially harm's way.

"Take him with you," she said. "If you take him with you, I know you'll make an effort to be a little more cautious, and if things get really bad, you'll decide to come home sooner than if you were by yourself."

"Honey, I think it is too dangerous. What if he gets hurt?" Merrick argued.

"Too dangerous for a mini Rambo Junior, you mean? No, no. If it's *so* dangerous that he isn't safe, then you shouldn't be going either. This is exactly why he should go, and Reese is right; with Ryan and Amy here, we'll be fine."

Merrick loved to debate, and one of his favorite strategies was to turn a person's own words and concepts back against him. He wondered when Lydia had picked up that same strategy because she was throwing his words right back in his face. He racked his brain trying to think of a logical argument out of taking his son to possibly one of the most dangerous days ever at work, but his mind was blank.

"Okay," he finally said.

"Seriously? Yes!" Reese jumped with overwhelming excitement.

"I don't know why you're so excited; it's not going to be a picnic out there tomorrow."

"Ha, are you kidding? You just totally got owned by me and Mom in that argument. I don't care what we were arguing about—I have never seen you been owned that easily. Ha! WE . . . OWNED . . . YOU!" Reese proceeded to do a victory dance that looked like a cross between a rock star playing the guitar and a chicken spazzing out and bobbing its head. The rest of the family started laughing, and the more Merrick tried to fight the smile on his face, the harder everyone laughed.

"Okay, okay, that's enough. If you're coming with me tomorrow, then you're going to have one of my vests on under your shirt, and you can put your AR with your full kit with plates in the back of my car. Go get it done now, because 4:30 a.m. is going to come sooner than you think. Then we'll see who's laughing then, smart guy."

CHAPTER 20

At 4:30 a.m. the alarm sounded. Merrick was skipping his normal workout this morning, but he dropped and did a few sit-ups and push-ups before jumping in the shower. He went to his closet and started his ritual of getting all of his equipment on. The sheriff's office issued Kevlar body armor that was rated to stop handgun rounds, but rifle rounds would go straight through like butter. SWAT team members were issued plates that would stop rifle rounds, but the regular road guys had to pay for them out of their own pockets and they were not cheap. A couple of other drawbacks to plates was that they were heavier, which definitely made chasing down people on foot harder, and definitely less comfortable, especially after a twelve-hour shift. With the current state of things, though, the added weight felt comforting to Merrick today.

Once Merrick was dressed, he went downstairs to see if Reese was up. The thought crossed his mind that if Reese was still asleep, he'd sneak out and leave without him, but he knew that would be a very poor decision and one he would suffer from for a long time. To his surprise, Reese was already up and dressed. Merrick laughed when he saw Reese wearing all black: black cargo pants, a black shirt, and a black jacket. If he had a black beanie on and some paint under his eyes, he would look ready for some covert operation.

"Let's grab some breakfast," Merrick said. "We're leaving in ten."

The sound of Merrick and Reese pouring cereal into their bowls echoed in the quiet house. Merrick preferred his oatmeal, which was warm and filling, but on days he worked, he normally had cereal because it was quick and easy. He like combining cereals like the Frosted Mini-Wheats and Honey Bunches of Oats he was having this morning.

"Under normal circumstances, I would never do this, but I'm going to have you wear my Glock 43 today," Merrick finally said. "Leave it in the glove box when we go into briefing, and keep it holstered unless it's life or death. You know what? Even if it is life or death and it doesn't include you or me, just let me handle it, okay?"

"Yeah, okay, Dad."

"You okay with this? If you're not comfortable with it, you don't have to carry it." Merrick brought Reese in for a half hug.

"I'm good, but you must think it's pretty bad if you're going to let me carry a gun."

"Honestly, I'd let you carry every day if it was legal. I trust you with a handgun more than I do most adults. Right now the country is in a panic, and people don't always think rationally when they're panicking. So let's just hope you don't need it."

They finished their cereal, and Merrick gave Reese the Glock 43 out of the safe before going outside to his patrol car. Merrick signed in as David 81 on his way to the precinct. At 5:30 a.m. on a normal day, the county was pretty quiet. A couple of calls max, maybe an early morning collision, especially if the weather was bad. This morning there were forty-eight pending calls already. Merrick scanned through them as he drove. Most looked like they were patrol info calls. As he read through them, he realized that yesterday must not have gone well.

The county was on stationary patrol and responding only to priority one calls, meaning someone's life had to be in immediate danger for the police to go. One said all supermarket and grocery stores were closed until further notice and police would not respond to any calls of looting or property damage. Merrick looked over at Reese, who was looking out the window, and wondered again if he had made the right choice by allowing his son to come with him today.

The route he drove to his precinct every morning was very rural. There were miles of pasture lands and nice residential homes on larger lots. This morning it seemed basically the same as it always did, which was comforting. It was still dark out, and in the distance Merrick could see the glow of the city of Portland to the south. He enjoyed living next to a city with a major airport, and he even liked the option of being able to go into Oregon and buy things tax free. As far as he was concerned, cities could be nice places to visit, but he would never want to live there, especially not in Portland.

Portland, Oregon, had a famous bumper sticker that said "Keep Portland Weird," and anyone who had walked the streets of the city, including Merrick, knew why it rang true. There was a huge population of hipsters, hippies, goths, and people so odd they probably hadn't figured out what to call themselves yet. And the city government had attracted one of the biggest homeless populations. The homeless definitely didn't stay in Portland because of the nice weather, but because the city leadership let them go and do whatever they wanted. They spent millions of dollars in handouts that didn't get people off the street, but kept them happy in their current homeless state. Full-on naked marches and naked events were also allowed right in the middle of the city, in total view of the public.

A few years after the "Keep Portland Weird" stickers became popular, the people of Vancouver came out with a sticker of their own that read "Keep Vancouver Normal." While Portland was known to be ultraliberal, Vancouver was more moderate. Like in most communities, there was a stark difference in Clark County between those who lived in the downtown area and those who lived in the rural outskirts. It seemed like more and more city people had begun to move into Merrick's small town. Merrick felt the town he had once known and grown up in was slowly losing its personality and becoming just another big city like all the rest.

The Albright family sometimes talked about moving to a smaller town or somewhere a little more remote, like eastern Washington, Idaho, or Montana. But in the end, they had too much in Vancouver to leave. They had family and friends, and the boys were in the middle of their schooling—not to mention the huge pain in the butt that moving all their stuff would be. Merrick didn't even want to know how many U-Haul truckloads of stuff he would have to pack up and drive hundreds of miles in order to clear out their house. For the time being, the family decided to stay in the area, at least until Indiana graduated from high school, and then they would reevaluate things.

They pulled into the West Precinct parking lot that was reserved for emergency vehicles only and then walked into the briefing room. Sergeant Nash did not look good. In all his years of working at the Clark County Sheriff's Office, Merrick had never seen Sergeant Nash like this. He looked frazzled and unsure of himself, which was completely the opposite of what he normally looked like.

"Merrick, thanks for coming in today. We really need you," Sergeant Nash said, but as he did, he noticed Reese walking in behind Merrick. He immediately stood up.

"ARE YOU OUT OF YOUR MIND? YOU BROUGHT YOUR KID WITH YOU?! Today is *not* a good ride-along day. Take him home right now, and then get back here. Seriously, Merrick, I thought you had more sense than that."

"Sir, I totally agree that today is not the day to have him with me, but this is the only way my wife would let me come in. She figures that I won't get myself in too deep of trouble if I have him around," Merrick explained.

"We are responding to priority one calls only. That means every single call we go to today is going to be pretty effing bad. Thirty years of law enforcement, and I never thought it could be as bad as it got yesterday." Sergeant Nash sat back down in his chair and looked at the ground for a second. "Just go home."

"I came in because I want to be here to make sure everyone on my squad makes it home tonight. Unless you give me a direct order to go home, I plan on staying."

Sergeant Nash sighed. "You're a moron and a good friend, but definitely a moron. Take a seat, and don't make me regret this."

"How bad is it?" Merrick asked.

Sergeant Nash looked at Reese before answering. "Last night there was a riot in Portland. They broke through the lines and started attacking the officers. Fifteen cops are in the hospital. They had to shoot into the crowd. It's estimated about sixty-five people were shot before they had to pull the entire riot team off the streets. Portland police are protecting a few key sites, but are not responding to any 9-1-1 calls."

"I didn't see any of that in the news. I had no idea it was that bad."

"It's happening all over the country, I guess. The government's keeping it off the news right now because they don't want to start a nationwide panic. All the county bigwigs are getting together for a big meeting today. My guess is we're going to do something like Portland."

"Wow." Merrick paused. "I'm just trying to process all of that. I'm not surprised that the government wants to try to prevent a panic by controlling information, but I *am* shocked that they can keep a lid on something this big. How do you stop everyone with a cell phone and social media from spreading the news? It seems almost impossible."

"No idea. I'm not a techie, but the news is the last thing I'm worried about right now. I'm not sure how many guys are going to show up today, but who can blame them? No one is going to leave their home if their family is at risk."

"I agree. The only reason I'm here is that I got some good friends at home with the rest of my family. Is that one of the things the county leaders are going to talk about?

"You kidding? The sheriff's been telling those guys for years that we're completely understaffed and they've just turned a deaf ear. Even if they try to do what Portland is doing and just protect critical sites, I doubt we'll be able to get enough people, especially not when their families aren't safe at home. With no help from the National Guard or the Army, it feels like the whole system is about to go down."

"They aren't calling in the National Guard or military to help with this?"

"Nope. If this was isolated to just one part of the country, I'm sure they would, but because this is everywhere, they don't want to deploy all their troops and leave the entire country vulnerable to attack. They're all spun up on high alert at the bases, but aren't going be helping with law enforcement or anything. That's probably why they haven't declared martial law already."

"So we're on our own."

"It's five minutes to six in the morning and look around. Hopefully you're not the lone ranger today."

"Lone ranger," Merrick said under his breath. "That's what we need to do. We need to go to old-school law enforcement."

"I don't get it. How do we go old-school?" asked Sergeant Nash.

As if on cue, Joe walked into the briefing room. "You guys talking about me?"

"No—well, maybe a little bit. Do you remember how law enforcement was back during the Wild West?" Merrick said half-jokingly.

"Ha ha, an old guy joke?" Joe said with a not-so-impressed look on his face.

"No, seriously. We're talking about how more cops are going to be staying home to make sure their families are safe and not coming to work, so we need to adapt or we're done," Merrick said.

"Bunch of pansies. I'm here."

"Joe, I think you're so hard-core you wear cop pajamas to bed at night," Merrick said, and everyone in the room laughed. "Anyway, back in the Wild West days, people would go knock on the door of the sheriff's house if something was happening. If he needed some backup, he would either deputize someone or get a posse together to deal with the issue. I think we should do exactly that. Have deputies stay at home and help keep the peace in their neighborhoods. They could cover one square mile or so around their homes, and enlist friends that live nearby to assist them. At least then we would have pockets of law and order versus deputies going home and just trying to barricade themselves in their homes with their families."

"That's not a bad idea," Sergeant Nash said. "They can make sure their families are okay and serve as a local leader at the same time. Not bad, but I see a small problem. What are you going to have the deputies do with someone who *is* a problem? They can't take them to the jail. Only half of the jail staff showed up yesterday, and they released something like six hundred of the lower-level offenders. They're even talking about what to do with the hundred or so violent criminals that are left. Some of them are pretty hard-core murderers and rapists. If they release them, it would be like a bomb going off downtown."

"I didn't even think about the jail," Merrick said, surprised he hadn't thought of it.

"What they should do is just shoot them all and do the world a favor," Joe said as he sipped his coffee.

"It sounds messed up, but Joe's right. Letting them go into the city is crazy. They're not stupid. They'll know that the only reason we're letting them go is because we don't have the resources to keep them all locked up. They'll figure out pretty quick that they can just rape or kill anyone in their path and we're too overwhelmed to do a thing about it." Merrick was glad he was a good distance away from the downtown area, but the idea of a hundred of the most violent criminals being released together in one big mob made him think of the movie *Mad Max*. Then he remembered there was a correctional facility closer to his home. "What about the minimum security place on Larch Mountain? What are they doing with their people?"

"No idea. That place is state run, and I don't disagree with you that all those violent criminals should be shot rather than being let go, but you and I both know that'll never happen. No admin person is going to make that call and risk going to jail for the rest of their life for murder," Sergeant Nash explained.

"I know, but we're in a state of emergency, so we don't have to follow the normal legal and court procedures," Merrick said. "Like right now, we're letting petty stuff go to hell and we're even releasing convicted people from jail. With anything big like a rape or murder, you either let the deputies be creative, or, I think in the current situation, you could make an argument that you were in enough fear for public safety to shoot them. If all these inmates are going to get released, someone should at least warn the neighborhoods so they can start gearing up now. That way, there won't be so many of them by the time they get to my place."

"Seriously, your idea is not bad considering the mess we're in," the sergeant said. "I might call the sheriff and try to pitch that idea about having deputies at home and rallying the locals. I may even sell it with a little bit of a lie that deputies would be more likely to respond to something big if they've prepared their neighbors and know things are under control at home. It's just a matter of time before we either don't have enough officers to do anything or no one even shows up. Something is better than nothing."

"Say the magic words, and I'll go home right now." Merrick joked.

"Shut up. You got the day off yesterday when we were all here busting our butts."

"Well, I would at least give the sheriff a call now so when he goes to that meeting, he has a few ideas."

CHAPTER 21

Six deputies and one sergeant ended up coming in for duty for the entire county. Sergeant Nash didn't even bother calling the ones who didn't show, and he didn't call anyone to try to fill the spots. The previous night on graveyard, only four deputies showed up, and when they called everyone who wasn't working the next day, no one answered. Merrick didn't blame them. If he thought his family was in danger, there was only one place he would be. As he looked around, he didn't think it was a coincidence that most of the ones who didn't show up today were the deputies who had kids at home. He wondered how soldiers during the Revolutionary War and the Civil War could leave their families and go fight when they knew their families might be in danger themselves.

Sergeant Nash left the briefing room to go call the sheriff. Everyone else stayed in the briefing room drinking coffee and telling stories about what had happened the day before. They said that once the stores couldn't stop people from running out with shopping carts full of merchandise, they couldn't shut their doors fast enough. The stores were already packed full of people who were trying to grab whatever supplies they could. After the first dozen people walked out of a grocery store without paying, the entire store of people followed. Then it spread to other stores and shops. Banks, ATMs, and even fast-food places were hit. It was as though a wave of looting washed over everything, and there was no way to stop it. A few stores tried to lock their doors or put barricades in people's way, but the crowds became aggressive and the frenzy got even worse.

"You missed a few crazy shootings yesterday, Merrick," Tom said.

"Officer-involved shootings or citizens?"

"Both. First one was a couple of morons who thought they would steal a bunch of guns from that gun store off Fourth Plain Boulevard. The owner and another employee were inside packing some of the weapons up to take home, I guess, and two guys drove their car right through the front of the store. Luckily the owner was in the back, but he came running when he heard the crash. He ended up shooting both of the guys. Detectives didn't even come out. They just wanted the details over the phone. They didn't even go to the scene. They just wanted us to get the details and snap a few pictures."

"Is the medical examiner still picking up the bodies?" asked Merrick, wondering if any other department in the county was working.

"I think so. I called them, but they said they were backlogged and it was going to be at least three hours. I couldn't wait, so the sergeant said I could leave. Joe shot someone yesterday and got no time off. There weren't any detectives at the scene, either. It's just a phone call and a regular report for a shooting now."

"Joe, you didn't say anything about that when you got here." Merrick looked at Joe in surprise.

"Wasn't a big deal. There's really not too much to say. I got a call that a crazy guy was breaking into someone's house. When I arrived, he came after me with a knife. End of story. Plus you were busy telling your old-guy jokes."

"It seems impossible that two days ago things were normal, and now things are falling apart so quickly," Merrick said. He looked over at Reese, who hadn't said a word since they had stepped into the briefing room. He had just sat quietly, soaking it all in. Merrick was proud that he had taught Reese right and that Reese was respectful enough not to jump into adult conversations.

"You okay?" Merrick asked Reese.

Reese leaned over and whispered, "Yeah, I am good. It's super interesting to hear everything. None of this is in the news." He leaned forward to continue listening.

"Do me a favor and text Mom. Tell her to contact everyone and tell them to pack up and come over."

"Okay. You sure?"

"No, but it's a lot worse than I thought it was an hour ago, and apparently if it gets worse, the news won't be telling us a thing."

CHAPTER 22

BEEP, BEEP, BEEP. "West units: shots fired at Ghims Village Apartments, 1304 NE 88th Street. Multiple callers saying that they heard arguing and then heard shots from Apartment 202. The caller thinks the male is Vitali and that he shot his wife. Additionally, there are two kids that live in the apartment: a three-year-old and a one-year-old."

Sergeant Nash walked into the briefing room as everyone was standing up and getting ready to go. "Hold on, everyone. Let's take a minute to come up with a plan before we go anywhere. Merrick, can you pull up the location on Google Maps and put it on the big screen?" It took Merrick just a minute to center the satellite image on the address they had just been dispatched to.

"Okay. Helmets on, everyone, before you even roll out of here. We only have six people, and none of you are allowed to get shot today," Sergeant Nash said. "We need to approach nice and easy so this guy doesn't see us coming. If we go in there with lights flashing, it'll just give him something to shoot at. Merrick, why don't you and Joe come in from the east? Steve and Brad, do the same coming in from the west. This apartment complex is U-shaped with two buildings in the middle of the U. Can someone pull up the apartment and see where 202 is at?"

"Number 202 is just south of the northwest corner of the U." Steve got up and pointed to the spot.

"All right. Dave, go with Steve and Brad. Jeremy and I will stay mobile in our vehicles on 88th Street so we can respond to wherever we're needed or if we need an officer rescue. I don't like this anymore than you guys do, but I'll be damned if I just sit here while those two little kids are in danger. If this guy has a gun in his hand and is doing anything aggressive when we arrive, then we put him down. If he's hunkered down inside or shows no sign of violence, then we watch for just a minute, then try and loud-hail him from one of our vehicles. If he doesn't come out . . . I don't know. I don't think we have the resources to go in there after him. I'm not going to risk you guys getting shot, especially when we don't even know if there's anyone to save. Any objection to that?"

"Sounds good, sir, but I think we should make that decision on the ground after we get a feel of things," said Joe.

"Okay, but If at any point I call 'pull out,' then we're done and I want everyone to get out of there as fast as possible and get back here. Any questions?" Sergeant Nash looked around to everyone in the room.

"Shouldn't we get the armor?" Brad asked.

"I was just on the phone with the command staff and found out that the armor trucks and some of our specialty unit guys are being pulled downtown to provide security for a big meeting they're having today. They'll not be available today to back us up, so we're on our own. Let's go get this done, and I'll fill you in on more details when this call is over. We'll roll out in a convoy all together—lights but no sirens. When we get off the freeway and onto 99th Street, we'll split up and approach from different directions."

Once everyone was lined up in their individual rigs, they rolled out together. On I-5 traffic was almost nonexistent. As they got off the freeway and started to roll through Hazel Dell, Merrick got his first good look at the city. Storefront windows and doors were smashed. Shopping carts and debris were scattered all over. He could see a few people moving around in the stores, but they ducked down in response to the convoy of flashing lights that passed by. Merrick couldn't believe that this amount of damage had happened in one day.

He parked off 88th Street just down from the apartment complex where the shooter was. He grabbed his rifle and his go-bag from the back of his rig, then walked back up to the passenger side of his car and opened the door to talk to Reese.

"Why don't you sit in the driver's seat while I'm gone? Keep the doors locked and your eyes open. This is not the best part of town. If you need anything, just pick up the radio and call for me, okay?"

"Okay. Be safe, Dad." Reese gave Merrick a worried look.

"You too, son. Hopefully this won't take too long," Merrick said as Joe walked up from behind. "You ready, Joe?"

"Yep, let's bag this turkey. Yeah, kid, you see anyone messing with my car, you run them the hell over, okay?"

"Um, okay?" Reese looked to his dad to determine if Joe was serious.

"If you see anyone coming up to the vehicles, just push the air horn and that should scare them away, but if not, you do what you have to do to protect yourself," Merrick said, looking down at his waistline. Reese nodded that he understood. Merrick knew that years on the job had given Joe a kind of morbid sense of humor. Most people in extreme professions deflected some of the harsh reality of their jobs with a little humor. It was harmless, but from the outside it made them sometimes seem callous or even a little perverse.

Merrick and Joe walked away from the car toward the apartment and could see the team about three hundred yards away approaching from the other direction.

"Merrick and Joe are in place," Merrick said over the radio. "You guys see anything from your side?"

"We have a pretty good view going all the way back to the target apartment, but no visual yet. We can hear some faint yelling, but we're not sure if it's coming from the apartment we are looking for. You guys go up your side first, and once you're set, we will move up," said Brad on the other team.

"Copy. We're moving." Merrick and Joe moved up along the east side of the complex using vehicles for cover as they went. It was still pretty early in the morning, so almost everyone was still inside. As they neared the corner of the building that was in the center of the complex, they could hear faint yelling. Merrick slowly moved around the corner, carefully scanning for anyone. Eventually he scanned all the way over to where Apartment 202 should be. On the second floor of the complex, a door to an apartment was open, but Merrick was too far away to see if it was 202. "You want to radio that we are set?" Merrick asked Joe.

"We're all set on the far side of the complex," Joe reported over the radio. "There's a door open on the second floor. It might be 202, but we can't read it from here. No sign of anyone outside, but we can hear yelling coming from that direction. Other team, you can move up."

After a minute of waiting for the other team, Merrick and Joe heard, "Okay, second team all set. We can see the open door and it is definitely 202. We can also hear what sounds like crying coming from inside along with a male yelling."

"Sir, I think we need a vehicle in here to use the loudspeaker and try to call this guy out," Merrick said.

"Okay, moving up," Sergeant Nash reported. It took only a few seconds for Sergeant Nash to get in position with his vehicle and key up the loudspeaker.

"This is the Clark County Sheriff's Office," the sergeant announced. "Occupant of 202, you are under arrest. Exit the apartment now with your hands up and nothing in your hands."

After a long minute, Sergeant Nash repeated, "This is the Clark County Sheriff's Office. You are under arrest. Exit Apartment 202 now with—"

"He's coming out!" the second team reported. "He has the baby in his arms and a handgun. Repeat. He has a baby in his arms!" Joe said.

A white male in his mid-thirties walked out of the apartment holding a baby in his left arm. Merrick could see a silver handgun in his right hand. The male did not look good. It looked like there was blood on both of his arms, and he was half sobbing and half yelling in rage. Merrick couldn't understand a word he was saying.

"Put the baby down. We do not want to hurt you or the baby. Put the baby and the gun down!" Sergeant Nash yelled from the loudspeaker. The male then pointed the gun toward the baby and then to his own head.

"Do you have a clean shot?" Joe asked Merrick.

"I think I could manage a head shot if he stayed still long enough, but with him moving around, I don't want to risk it."

The male walked over to the balcony and held the baby over the edge. Merrick could hear Joe mumble a string of curse words under his breath. The male suddenly walked back into the apartment with the baby. Seconds later he emerged with no baby in his hands.

BANG, BANG, BANG, BANG, BANG. A barrage of gunfire rang out suddenly. No deputy had to speak; they all knew they couldn't let the man get his hands back on the baby.

"We're moving in to check on the children," radioed Brad. "Merrick and Joe, can you cover us?"

"We got you covered," Merrick said into the radio. He knew it was pointless; there was no doubt the guy was dead. Merrick guessed that he had been shot ten to twenty times, and with that kind of trauma, he would not be putting up much of a fight. The other team moved up the stairway, and one deputy went directly to the shooter. The other two went inside the apartment.

"The two kids in the apartment are okay. The mom, not so much," Steve said over the radio.

Merrick saw movement out of the corner of his eye on the north side of the apartments, and a man with a shotgun was opening the door to an apartment.

"Police! Drop the gun! Drop it!" Merrick yelled as he turned and brought his rifle up and sighted in the threat. The man was African American and looked like he had just woken up. He didn't drop the gun; he just looked at Merrick like he was frozen in shock.

"Drop it! Drop it now!" Joe added forcefully. The man dropped the weapon and put his hands up.

"I heard a lot of gunfire. I was just checking," the man said, sounding terrified.

The gunfire definitely would have awakened anyone who was still sleeping in the complex. Merrick looked around and could now see people peeking through their blinds to try to see what was going on. He wanted to get out of there.

"Sir, we are dealing with a situation out here. Use your foot to push your weapon back inside your apartment and shut the door and stay inside, please. FYI, next time, take a peek outside before walking out with a gun," Merrick said to the man standing in his apartment doorway.

"Okay, yeah, sorry about that," the man said, and he closed the door after pushing his gun inside.

"Sarge, we woke up the locals," Merrick said into the radio. "I suggest we get this show rolling and get out of here, or things are going to get dicey."

"I'm working on it. Steve, grab a bag of clothes for each kid. We're going to have to drop them off at the hospital or something. Brad, once the kids are out, drag the male's body back into the apartment. Collect the weapon for safekeeping and shut the door."

"Sir, if we're going to transport these kids, I'm going to have to have car seats or something for them," Steve said.

"Okay, right. Joe and Merrick, start knocking—"

"DIE, YOU PIGS!" came a yell from an unseen person. Sergeant Nash paused for a moment to listen and look around.

"Joe and Merrick," Sergeant Nash continued, "start knocking on their neighbors' doors and try to find out what car is theirs or if anyone knows a family member in the area we can drop these kids off with."

Merrick walked over and started knocking on two doors at a time, hoping at least one would answer. A young Hispanic lady came to the door of Apartment 200. She said the family's car was the red beat-up Nissan.

"Joe! I got it. It should be this Nissan over here." Merrick broke the passenger window and opened the car door. He handed the baby car seat out to Joe and collected the toddler seat. They put both seats in Jeremy's car since it was the closest. Steve and Brad came down the stairs, each toting a kid and a bag.

"Okay, I'll go to the hospital with Jeremy to drop off the kids. You all go back to the precinct and we'll see you there in a few. I don't care what the call is; you guys don't go out until we're back, okay?" Sergeant Nash said.

"Got it. See you back there," said Merrick.

As the officers left, people started coming out of their apartments and more voices could be heard yelling. They even started to throw random garbage at the patrol vehicles as they drove away.

CHAPTER 23

Back at the precinct, everyone sat around the briefing table and topped off their magazines. The atmosphere felt very somber. Everyone knew it was just a matter of time before the next call would be coming, and none of them were looking forward to going back out there. All of the normal joking and small talk that would have lightened the mood was completely absent.

With the relative quiet of bullets going into magazines, Merrick began to think about what had happened, and it weighed on him. He knew he made the right decision to shoot the guy and protect the kids, but seeing the kids had affected him. They were now without a mom and a dad, and in part, that was thanks to him. He wondered what would happen to them with the current crisis. He wasn't sure if CPS was available or if any foster family would take the kids right now, given the state of things. He forced himself to push the thoughts out of his mind.

Sergeant Nash walked into the room. No one asked any questions; everyone just looked at him, waiting for him to say something.

"First of all, you all made the right decision. I know that doesn't make it any easier, though. I called and reported the incident to major crimes on my way up to the hospital, so none of you have to. Sometime over the next few days, all of you try to give the psychologist a call about this incident. I'll email out her phone number to everyone, and if you could email me back once you've talked to her and let me know it's done, I would appreciate it.

"Second thing is just before we left to go to this thing, I got off the phone with the command staff. They understand the limits of what we can do given the situation and our numbers. They also acknowledge that there might come a point that we'll no longer respond to any kind of calls because of the danger to officers. They would like us to continue as long as we're able, and they left it up to the sergeant on duty to make the call for when it's time to pull the plug. I mentioned your idea, Merrick, and while they think it's a good idea, they don't want to take on the liability of authorizing deputies to act when there's no chain of command. So they are going to send out an email saying something to the effect that deputies, while at home, should be unofficial leaders of their communities and to check their email daily for when to return to duty or other important information." Sergeant Nash sounding fairly displeased.

"So when are we going home today, Sarge?" Steve asked, half joking, half-serious.

"I don't know. I don't like being forced into this horrible situation of having to decide when to stop responding to people who need us and putting all of you at further risk. I just thought I'd wait until that one call comes out that makes me say 'Hell no.' I got no plan beyond that, and if you got any ideas, I'm all ears."

BEEP, BEEP, BEEP went the 9-1-1 tones from the radio.

"F—" Sergeant Nash cut himself off before muttering, "Seriously?"

"Central units: multiple shots fired at 10805 NE 67th Street. This is a known biker house. Caller said there's a shoot-out between a green vehicle that pulled up in front of the residence and the people in the residence. Caller believes there to be three gunmen in the vehicle and at least three shooting from inside the house."

"Control X23. We will not be responding to that call."

"Copy," the dispatcher said slowly, sounding confused.

"So, home then?" Steve asked with a smile. Sergeant Nash looked at him with a fairly stern look.

"No, Steve, not yet. I'm not going to send you guys into something like that, but I'm not ready to pull the plug, either."

"X23 Control," Dispatch said.

"Go ahead."

"There's more information coming in about that call. Do you want to hear it?"

"You can put it out as info, but we will not be responding."

"Copy. Updates are that a few of the shooters that arrived at the residence have now entered and they can still hear gunfire from inside the home."

"X23 copies."

"X23, can you call Dispatch, please?"

Sergeant Nash walked over to the telephone and made the call. Merrick and the others around the table listened to Sergeant Nash explain that they did not have the resources to respond to something like that and that from now on, all calls would be evaluated in regard to whether they would be responding. The sergeant really dropped a bomb on Dispatch when he said there might even come a time when he'd send all the deputies home.

The dispatcher on the line tried to ask if all dispatchers were supposed to stop and go home too, but Sergeant Nash said that was not his call and that they were dispatchers for more than just their agency. Then he hung up the phone.

BEEP, BEEP, BEEP. The 9-1-1 tones sounded again on the radio. "County units: shots fired at Legacy Hospital, 2211 NE 139th Street. A white male in his forties wearing a blue jacket is in the ER with a pistol. He's demanding that his wife be treated after waiting more than two hours without being seen. Apparently he shot off a few rounds into the ceiling."

"X23 copies. We will be en route," Sergeant Nash said over the radio. He then turned to the team. "Okay, same thing as before: helmets and rifles for everyone. Just know we're going to be in a crowded hospital, so if you have to fire, make sure it's a clean shot and isn't going to hit anyone else. Let's do the same teams as before. Steve, your team goes to the main ER door. Merrick, you and Joe go the back way through the ambulance entrance. Let's roll."

When he arrived at the hospital, Merrick couldn't believe how packed the place was. He'd been there a thousand times, and it had never looked like this. Cars were parked in every spot, and the roads around the hospital was crowded with vehicles. There were about 150 people all scattered along the entrance to the ER. Most were smart enough not to stand in front of the glass entrance doors, but a few were walking up and trying to see what was going on inside. Merrick pulled up to the ambulance entrance with Joe and told Reese to sit in the driver's seat again.

Merrick typed in the code to the sliding doors and walked with Joe into the ER from the back. The nurses and doctors looked relieved to see them. They all pointed in the same direction toward the ER main reception area. As Merrick went through the hospital, there were more patients in the hallways on gurneys than he had ever seen, but there was almost no hospital staff. Merrick guessed it wasn't just the first responder jobs that had been affected by people deciding it was more important to stay with their families than to come to work.

As he and Joe neared the front desk, Merrick heard gunfire. He started to move faster. All he could hear now was people shrieking in fear. He got to the outer door that lead to the ER waiting area and crouched down next to the door.

"Steve, I heard shots, but I don't have eyes on. Are you guys in position?" Merrick asked over the radio.

"We are Code 4, gunman is down. He came out the front entrance when we were arriving," Steve responded over the radio.

"I copy. We're coming out to you."

Merrick and Joe walked out to meet the other team. As he neared the doors, Merrick could see the gunman on the ground just outside the sliding glass doors. As he was about to walk out and join the rest of his squad, he turned and saw Joe talking to a male who was wearing business clothes. He walked over to them.

"Merrick, this is Mr. Boyle. He's the hospital administrator. He said he's about to shut down the hospital." Joe looked at Merrick and raised both his eyebrows. "Most of their unarmed security didn't show, but the one or two that did are worthless and can't handle anything like this. He said that if we stay, he'll keep the hospital open, but if we go, he'll be forced to shut it down because he can't keep his staff safe. I guess they've had a few guys come in demanding drugs. Can you get the sergeant and have him come this way?"

"Sure thing, Joe." Merrick walked outside to find Sergeant Nash, who was standing off to the side of a large crowd and talking on his cell phone. A few of the crowd members were arguing with deputies about not being able to be admitted to the hospital.

"Sir, the hospital administrator is inside and needs to talk to you," Merrick said, knowing the horrible position Sergeant Nash would be in.

"Let me guess: he wants us to stay and be their security," Sergeant Nash said.

"Bingo, but the rub is that he'll have to shut down the hospital if we don't stay."

"What? Come on! If he does that, these people are going to rip this place apart before his staff even gets out the door. Doesn't he know that?" Sergeant Nash said in frustration.

"Sir, go inside and talk to him. It sounds like they've had people stealing drugs and assaulting the staff already." Merrick did not want Sergeant Nash to bite off the head of the hospital administrator before he heard him out.

"How can you shut down a hospital that's full of patients? What are they going to do with all of the patients?"

"Hey, you're talking to the wrong guy. I got no answers for you. Go inside, and I'll help clean this up out here."

"Okay." Sergeant Nash started walking away, but then stopped and turned toward Merrick. "They're releasing all the inmates over the next few hours. They're trying to avoid a mob of criminals by releasing them sporadically a few at a time." Sergeant Nash shook his head. "It's the final straw. I was going to send everyone home."

CHAPTER 24

"Okay, everyone, I need to talk to you inside for a minute." Sergeant Nash motioned for the team to follow him into the hospital. Everyone followed him to the employee-only area in the ER. "As far as I am concerned, you guys are released to go home to your families. But the hospital said they can't stay open without some type of security here. Joe has already volunteered to stay. You're under no obligation, but would any of you be willing to stay here to help out? I don't know if I will be able to get anyone to relieve you, so it will be up to you to leave when you need to."

"I will stay," said Steve.

Merrick thought about the thousands of patients in the hospital, many unable to care for themselves. Guilt filled him, but his need to go home and protect his own family trumped his guilt.

Sergeant Nash waited just another moment before saying, "Okay. Thanks, guys. I am going to stay as well. All of you take care of yourselves, and hopefully I will see you soon."

Merrick walked back to his patrol vehicle, kicked Reese out of the driver's seat, and secured his rifle.

"Well, that's it; we are going home. You okay, bud?"

"Yeah, I am good. What happened?" asked Reese.

"Guy with a gun wanted his wife to be treated and then he walked out with the gun toward the deputies that were getting ready to come in."

"Just a normal guy?"

"Yeah, he looked pretty normal. You don't need to use the bathroom or anything?"

"No, I went in the bushes just a few minutes ago."

"Perfect. You want to call Mom and let her know we are on our way while I go to the bathroom?"

Merrick relieved himself, then got back in the car and started driving toward home. "Was Mom happy we are headed back?"

"Oh, yeah. I think she half thought you wouldn't actually go in today if you had to take me." Reese smiled at Merrick.

"It almost worked. If I had known how bad it was out here, there is no way I would have risked you coming out here. You guys mean everything to me."

"Are you upset you had to bring me?" Reese asked.

Merrick looked over at Reese. "There is no one I trust more to have my back. I just can't bear the thought of losing you guys. I think I would just fall apart." Merrick had to look away from Reese to keep from crying.

"Yeah, you are kind of a wuss in that way," Reese said with a grin and leaned away, knowing what was coming.

Merrick playfully punched Reese a few times and said, "Where did you learn to be so sassy? More comments like that will definitely help me miss you less." They looked at each other and smiled. Merrick punched Reese's arm one last time.

"Did Mom say who was at the house already?" Merrick asked.

"Everyone is there except the Hales, and she just got a text that they just left their house and are headed that way."

"Good. It's going to be nuts with everyone there, so I am going to need your help keeping everything together."

"Honestly, I think it is going to be awesome. No school, tons of time together. It is like we are all camping out at a cabin together."

"Well, I don't want to be the one to burst your bubble, Mr. Positive, but you have had your own room your whole life. After a week or two with a full house, we will see how awesome you think it is."

Danger Zone started playing, and Merrick pulled out his phone thinking it was Lydia wanting an ETA. But when he looked, it was Bruce calling.

"Bruce, what's up? You guys okay?"

"No, not really," Bruce said with definite stress in his voice. "We were on our way to your place, but there is a truck blocking the road and a line of cars waiting to get through. It didn't feel right to me, so I pulled off the road as soon as I could. We are waiting just down the road now. It doesn't look like an accident; it looks more like a checkpoint or roadblock or something. But the people who are stopping and checking cars look like a bunch of hillbilly morons with guns."

"Okay, good job pulling over. Where exactly are you?" Merrick said, trying to boost Bruce's confidence.

"88th Street, almost to 212th."

"Sit tight; I am on my way. Try and stay out of sight as best as you can while still keeping an eye on them. It's probably a good idea to have your rifle, just in case," Merrick suggested.

"Okay, thanks. See you soon." Bruce had slight relief in his voice.

Hillbilly roadblocks were not a good sign. Merrick could see the very fabric of society beginning to fray even before it was public knowledge that there would be no police response anymore. He knew it wouldn't be long before people lost all respect for what his patrol car and uniform represented, and they would just be a big target. Too many people already hated cops, and if they thought they could get away with taking a cop out, they probably would.

Merrick didn't like the fact that the only way to his house was right through the roadblock. He and Bruce could park their vehicles and try to walk around it, but going through random people's backyards to get to his house wasn't going to be a whole lot safer. Merrick decided he wouldn't get himself worked up too much until he saw it for himself. He even hoped that if he showed up in his cop car, it might completely dissolve the situation and he could hightail it out of there.

The siren on the patrol car was off but the lights were flashing as Merrick drove. People were not just looting; it seemed like traffic rules had become optional as well. People were speeding by and blowing through intersections all over the place. He had his lights on hoping that people would instinctually slow down or at least notice him so he wouldn't get T-boned.

As he neared 88th Street and 212th Avenue, he turned off his lights and eventually spotted Bruce in his charcoal van about 200 yards west of a string of five cars that were stopped because a large navy blue pickup was blocking the road. He could see about five guys in their mid-twenties taking items out of the cars they had stopped.

A vehicle in the rear started to back up in an attempt to leave, and one of the hillbillies shot a round in the air before pointing his shotgun at the vehicle. Bruce's van was pulled into a side road and sticking out just enough to see the roadblock down the roadway. Merrick pulled into the side street, then turned around and pulled up parallel to Bruce's van. Merrick could see Bruce's whole family in the van, which was completely full of their stuff.

"Bruce, have you seen anything in the last few minutes?"

Bruce didn't respond right away; he instead walked over to Merrick's window and leaned on his car.

"These are bad guys, Merrick. They have been taking whatever they want out of the cars and threatening to shoot anyone that tries to drive away." Bruce leaned in closer and whispered, "They roughed up a couple of guys, and dragged a woman off to the side." Bruce raised one of his eyebrows.

Merrick understood what Bruce was suggesting without saying it and turned to Reese.

"Reese, grab your rifle and gear. Make sure you are locked and loaded; this ain't no drill. Bruce, why don't you get geared up as well?" As he spoke, Merrick kept his eyes on the group down the road.

Bruce and Reese quickly got ready and returned to Merrick's window, each with a vest on and rifle slung.

"Okay," Merrick said. "Bruce, you are going to follow us in your vehicle, but I want you to pull in behind the last car in the line and then park your car there. I want you to jump out and get to the right side of the roadway as fast as you can. They will be focused on me pulled up in my patrol car, so you should be able to make a beeline right into the woods over there without any issues. Get in a good prone position so you can see as many of them as possible. Get your sights locked on the guy who is the farthest away from me or the one that would be the hardest for me to get to.

"Reese, I want you in the back seat behind me. Get as low as you can so no one can see you when I pull up. Once I contact these guys, slip out nice and easy. Get down on the ground and move up to my front tire. If I start shooting or if you think someone is going to do something, drop them. Are we clear?"

"Wait, Dad, you're going in alone? I don't think that's a good idea," Reese objected.

"I am not alone. I have the two of you," Merrick said with a smile.

"That's not what I meant. They will see you walking up there alone. They will think it is five against one and that they can take you. We shouldn't look weak or they will try something."

"I understand your concern, but this is not the time to debate this. There are times when you want to appear weak. There are times you want to appear strong. Showing up there with a fifteen-year-old at my side isn't going to cripple them with fear. Right?"

"But Bruce could go with you and I—"

"Reese, this conversation is over. Get your crap ready and get in the car. Bruce, are you good?" Merrick asked as he watched Reese get into his patrol car's back seat. He didn't like raising his voice to Reese, but he didn't have the time to explain the advantages of deception and diversion played in tactics.

"I am nervous, but yeah, I am ready," said Bruce with a nod.

"You will do fine. Just start shooting when we do. It is just like the target shooting you have done a thousand times before."

Bruce nodded again and got into his car.

Merrick rolled down the back window by Reese and said, "Just remember you can't open that door from the inside. You will have to pull the outside handle to get out."

"Okay," Reese said.

Reese was a good kid and a great shot, but he still had a lot to learn when it came to group tactics. If the situation involved simple force on force, Reese was fairly competent, but when it came to unconventional warfare, he was lost. Merrick had tried to get Reese to read *The Art of War* by Sun Tzu and a few other books on unconventional warfare, but they weren't exactly page-turners for a fifteen-year-old.

The best strategies in warfare, in Merrick's opinion, were not direct force on force tactics but instead based on exploiting the enemy by using their perceptions and assumptions against them. Merrick knew the dangers of playing chess with his life, but how dangerous was it really to play chess with a bunch of hillbillies who didn't even understand the game?

"Here we go, Bruce, follow me in," Merrick said as he rolled forward onto the road. He waited until Bruce was behind him, and then turned on his lights and his siren and sped down the road toward the roadblock. He figured the lights and the siren would be hard to miss as he pulled up. He figured that if all the attention was on him when he stepped out of his patrol car, it would be easier for Bruce and Reese to get into their positions.

The siren really did the trick. Once he turned it on, the hillbillies were practically falling all over themselves to get back to their pickup truck and probably trying to figure out what to do. Merrick drove in the left lane, passing the cars that were being held hostage, and parked evenly with the front of the first vehicle in the line. He wanted to try to give Reese the best line of sight possible. He grabbed his rifle as he stepped out and slung it around him.

"Hey guys. Deputy Albright with the Clark County Sherriff's Office. Can I get you to come over here for a second so I can talk to you?" Merrick motioned them to gather closer. The five armed hillbillies glanced at each other, considering their options, but eventually they all shuffled in around Merrick in a loose half circle. They were awkwardly keeping about twenty feet away from Merrick, no doubt in an effort to make sure all of them could engage with their weapons if necessary. Merrick didn't argue because it allowed for just the right angle for both Reese and Bruce to be able to shoot just about any of them without Merrick being in the direct line of fire.

He looked at the five relatively young guys standing before him. Three had shotguns, one had a hunting rifle, and the one in the middle had an AR-15. The kid in the dominant middle position appeared to be the default leader. As he looked at them, Merrick couldn't help but wonder which of them was the animal who had raped the girl.

At least that was what Merrick assumed had happened, and based on what Bruce had seen, it was a fair assumption. As far as Merrick was concerned, rape was a much more sickening crime than even murder. He compared rape to a kind of both mental and physical torture. Pulling a random woman out of a car and raping her was a huge psychological boundary to cross. If a man was able to do that, there was no telling how far he would go. Merrick knew that people like that tended to steadily increase their violent behavior over time, especially when they were not suffering any consequences, but today he would ensure the guys' actions had consequences. To him it didn't matter who exactly had raped the woman; they all were guilty for letting it happen. Either way, Merrick would feel better if none of them were even remotely close to his home ever again.

"I wanted to thank you for protecting our community. Having these checkpoints and making sure criminals are not coming into—" Merrick quickly drew up his rifle on his shoulder, firing immediately once the front of the muzzle was raised past the pavement and onto the leader's legs. The bullet hit the leader in his right hip, causing him to lean forward slightly at the waist. Merrick fired again, his second round hitting the leader in the middle of his chest.

Merrick's rifle didn't stop moving for even a split second. He swung his barrel right, transitioning to the next hillbilly. He was almost centered on the next guy and squeezing the slack out of the trigger when he heard Reese begin to engage from his left. He felt a wave of relief wash over him, even though the gunfight was far from over.

Merrick was confident that if he drew first, he could probably take out two, maybe even three, untrained guys by himself. Humans, he knew, needed time to process what they were seeing and then decide what to do, and they needed even more time to react. That was why action was always faster than reaction. The problem was he was facing five guys, and as fast as he was, he wasn't fast enough to fire on all of them before at least one of them got a round off in his direction. All he needed to know in order to even the odds was that Reese was shooting. He had seen Reese shoot five 300-meter targets in three seconds at a competition. These guys were standing within fifty feet; he had no doubt Reese would hit his mark.

Merrick buried two more quick rounds center mass into his second target and started to move slightly backward and to the right at a forty-five-degree angle. The shock of his surprise attack was wearing off and moving targets were harder to hit than ones standing still, so he decided to make it a little harder for them. He saw the last two guys had the same idea and were moving in different directions, one to the right and one to the left. Both of them were starting to bring their weapons up in his direction, which was not good.

Merrick hedged his bets and chose to focus on the guy on his right because his weapon was already going in that direction and the other guy was running in Reese's direction. Merrick knew that guy had seconds to live before Reese put him down, and he bet that Reese would make his shot before the hillbilly did. His rifle raced to the guy on the far right, but that guy ducked around the engine block of the pickup truck.

BANG, BANG, BANG. There was a quick succession of rounds from Reese's direction, and while Merrick didn't see it, he knew they were now down to only one guy left. Bruce had not shot yet, and if this had been a few years ago when he had first met Bruce, he might have guessed that he wouldn't shoot at all, but Bruce with a little bit of training had proven to be quite aggressive in most circumstances.

Merrick was confident that Bruce would take the shot if he had the opportunity, but that didn't mean he was just going to sit around and wait for it. He dropped onto his right side and lay down on the pavement, which gave him a clear view of the feet of the last guy, who was standing on the other side of the pickup truck. He aimed his rifle and was about to take out the guy's legs when he heard a couple of shots fired from Bruce's direction. He saw the guy fall to the ground.

Merrick was quickly back on his feet and double-checking to make sure all the threats were neutralized. Three were dead; two were struggling to breathe and barely conscious. They would soon succumb to their wounds, but their last few minutes alive would not be pretty. Merrick hated seeing an animal in agony—it didn't matter if it was a bunny, a deer, or a human. He understood the need to kill an animal for meat or because it was a nuisance, but he thought it should be done as quickly and as painlessly as possible.

On the job, Merrick had to put plenty of animals out of their misery. It was considered the humane thing to do, but when it came to humans, it was a different story. The Geneva Conventions prohibited what were considered mercy killings, and for good reason. They didn't want any uneducated soldier deciding at what point a wounded, unarmed person needed to be put out of his misery.

However, almost every World War II movie depicted some soldier or medic giving a lethal dose of morphine to someone who was critically wounded. In the end, Merrick believed that mercy killings were not morally wrong, but they were administratively illegal. The thought of it didn't feel right, so he left the hillbillies alone and turned away. When he did, he saw the faces of traumatized families staring back at him and was grateful he had chosen not to shoot any more.

He dragged the guy Bruce had shot toward the back of the pickup to clear the right side of the roadway, then waved the cars forward. They slowly drove past him one at a time, looking both grateful and deathly afraid. Eventually only three cars remained: Merrick's police car, Bruce's van, and the blue pickup.

"Reese! Help me check the bodies for the keys to the truck. Then let's get them loaded them in the bed of the truck."

Reese started with the far left guy and moved right, searching their pockets. The problem was they all had keys, just not the keys to an older Chevy pickup. Bruce walked over and stared down at the bodies that Reese and Merrick were searching.

"Got them, I think," called out Reese to Merrick.

"Try them and see if the truck still runs; we put a few rounds into it."

Reese ran around to the driver's seat, and the truck started up. Merrick grabbed the guy closest to the back of the truck and looked up at Bruce, who was still just staring down at the bodies. He felt bad for Bruce. Taking life was never easy, and the fact that these guys were pretty young made it harder. There would be time to talk about it and console him, but it wasn't here and it wasn't now.

"Bruce, help me load these bodies so your kids don't have to see them when we pass."

Bruce didn't say anything; he just walked over and grabbed the legs of the guy Merrick was lifting. Bruce was a doctor, so he had seen plenty of wounds and bodies in his career, but this was different. Seeing something in a sterile environment was a far cry from witnessing carnage. Bruce, to his credit, was powering through.

Reese seemed surprisingly unaffected by the whole thing. Merrick wasn't sure if that was totally a good sign or not. They finished loading all the bodies in the back of the pickup, but it was not easy or pleasant work. Every one of them was more than 150 pounds of warm, dead weight.

CHAPTER 25

As they were loading the bodies, Merrick noticed that in the back of the truck were a few items that the hillbilly crew had liberated from people at their roadblock. He could see gas cans, a generator, liquor, and random food items.

Merrick had already decided to bring the bodies home and bury them for a couple of reasons. If the family members of these guys found them sprawled across the road shot up and bloody, they would want to hunt down whoever had done it. The last thing Merrick needed was a blood feud with a local lowlife family. So he would remove and bury the evidence to protect himself and those he cared about.

He also wanted to take the bodies back to give them an ounce of dignity by burying them. For generations the military taught trainees to dehumanize the enemy. The logic was that it would make soldiers less likely to hesitate to kill when they had to. Their dehumanizing propaganda had worked, and soldiers killed the enemy without so much as a second thought. One of the unintended consequences of having soldiers see the enemy as less then human was that it created incidents of misconduct like soldiers pissing in the mouth of a person they had just shot or the events that happened at the prison of Abu Ghraib. Merrick thought it was a bit hypocritical of the military to demonize the enemy and then arrest soldiers when they treated the enemy as less than human.

Police officers, like the military, trained long and hard to shoot when it was necessary. However, police were not trained to dehumanize people but still managed to take the shot when they had to. In fact, most departments trained their officers to start giving first aid to the person they had just shot if it was safe to do so. During his military career, Merrick tried to instill in his soldiers that it was possible to respect a person, his culture, and his country and still shoot him if necessary.

"Bruce, why don't you get back in your van and follow me to the house. Reese, if you could, bring up the rear in the truck."

Reese looked at Merrick like he wanted to ask a question, but didn't. "What is it?" Merrick asked.

"The bodies—do you want to drive into our neighborhood like that?"

Merrick looked at the back of the truck and saw the five shot-up bodies sprawled out and thought maybe Reese was right. Maybe that wasn't the best thing to drive through the neighborhood.

"Good call. I have a blanket in the back of my rig. Let's cover them up as best as we can, then we will roll out." Merrick started walking to his patrol car. "And I have a favor to ask."

"Sure, what is it?" Reese asked.

"Let's try and keep most of the details of today to ourselves. Otherwise I might be sleeping in the doghouse for quite a while."

"Sure, but you know Mom is going to find out; she always does," Reese said, hinting that being open might be the better way to go.

"Not always," Merrick said. Reese raised an eyebrow. "Okay, sure, she finds out most of the time, but by the time she does, usually the whole thing has blown over enough that she is not nearly as mad as she would have been."

Reese didn't say a word, but still didn't look very convinced. Merrick secured the blanket and turned to Reese. "Reese, you're a better man than me. I can see it in you. One day when you find a girl, you do the right thing and tell her everything, okay?"

"So are you going to tell Mom or not, then?"

"Fine. We will do it your way, but if she keeps you locked up in the house for the next month to keep you safe, I don't want you to come crying to me." Merrick smiled at his son, who was becoming a man right before his eyes.

Merrick, Reese, and Bruce got into their vehicles and drove off—no lights or siren anymore. They had only a few miles to go, and Merrick was hoping to go unnoticed. On the way, he saw a few frantic families in their driveways, packing their things in their vehicles and preparing to go somewhere else. As the vehicles turned onto the Albrights' dead-end street, Merrick felt relieved and promised himself not to go anywhere for at least a few days.

One of the many perks of living in the country was seeing your neighbors only when you wanted to. Merrick loved the peace and privacy of having space between him and other homes. Too many times Merrick had to respond to 9-1-1 calls involving overactive neighbor associations, annoying neighbors, and sketchy door-to-door salespeople. He had no such problems here. His large metal gate prevented any unannounced guests from even being able to knock on his door. His home was his fortress of solitude, and as he pulled up to the gate, all he wanted to do was go inside and shut out the craziness of the world.

Merrick saw all the vehicles and knew that his home would probably be anything but quiet for a little while. He backed his police car in and jumped out to motion Bruce to pull right up to the front door so they could unload. He directed Reese toward the shop. The front door of the house swung open, and a dozen people came piling out. They swarmed around Merrick, Reese, and the Hale family, giving hugs and consoling words.

Lydia came pushing through the crowd and ran straight past Merrick and hugged Reese. "I am so glad you are home," she said as she held Reese.

"Don't worry; I am okay too, babe," Merrick joked. He knew he would have done the same thing. He and Lydia loved each other, but there was no love like parents for their children.

"I am glad *both* of you are home," Lydia said as she playfully swatted Merrick's arm. "Lori called us and told us you guys had to fight your way through the roadblock."

Merrick wasn't sure how Lori portrayed the guys fighting through the roadblock, but the fact that Lydia wasn't super pissed at him at that moment left him guessing that Lori had left out at least some of the details. Part of him wanted to abandon Reese's plan, but he decided to go for it.

"It got a little dicey there for a minute, but we got through it. I will tell you more of the details later if you want," Merrick said as he gave Lydia a hug and a kiss. She looked at him and nodded in approval.

Merrick then turned toward the group and yelled, "Hey everybody, listen up for a second!" Everyone quieted down and turned to look at him. "Tonight at dinner, we can visit and swap stories but right now we need to get a few things done while it is still light out. Most of you have heard that we had to shoot our way here. Even though the people we shot were definitely in the wrong, we are going to do the right thing and lay their bodies to rest. Ryan, do you feel comfortable using the backhoe on my tractor?"

"Yeah, it's been a while, but I have used it a couple of times," Ryan answered.

"If you can dig two large graves down on the lower property: one for the guys we have in the back of the pickup truck and one extra just in case we need it at some point." Merrick then turned to the rest of the group. "Indiana, Will, and Jake: I want you guys to unload all the gear out of the truck Reese drove in. There are loaded guns back there so be extra careful and just put everything off to the side in the shop for right now. If there are any food items, bring them into the house. Mark and Miranda, would you guys mind just keeping your rifles close and an eye on things while everyone works? . Lydia, can you handle getting everyone settled in and get started on dinner? I am going to go shower and change, then I will meet you guys in the shop. Questions, anyone?" Merrick looked around and there were none.

"The world out there has fallen apart, and we need each other more than ever. Us having to fight to get here is a perfect example of that. We have a lot of people living in a small space, and if this is going to work, we all need to do our part. Okay, let's get it done." Merrick clapped his hands together.

He went back to his patrol car and grabbed his rifle, computer, and water bottle. Then he went inside and took a nice, hot, long shower. He put on some clean work clothes and then slung his rifle on his back. He stopped in the kitchen for a quick bite and a drink of orange juice. Feeling refreshed, he went outside to find Miranda and Mark.

Merrick found them separated; Mark was over by the boys at the shop, keeping an eye on them, and Miranda was leaning against the wall to the garage. He walked over to Miranda.

"Miranda? I got a question and you might not like it."

"What?" Miranda asked.

"We are going to bury the bodies of those guys we had to shoot at the roadblock. I know it sounds morbid, but I think it might be good for your two older boys to help move the bodies and bury them. I think it might let them know how real this whole thing is. What do you think?"

"As long as I get to do it with them."

Merrick was shocked. He hadn't known what to expect, but he wasn't expecting that. He still hadn't said a word when Miranda said, "You're right; it would be good for them, but it would be good for me too. I have never seen a dead body before. I know it is bad out there, but this just feels so unreal right now that maybe it would help."

"No problem, and I am impressed you would want to," Merrick said, still a little taken back.

"Thanks, but can I tell you something?"

"Of course."

"You are a great leader, Merrick, and you do a great job, but you're a bit sexist," Miranda said bluntly.

"What? Why do you say that?" Merrick was now truly shocked. He couldn't even think of anything he had done that would be misunderstood as sexist.

"You want the boys to see and handle the bodies, but you didn't even think to ask the women to do it. You, Reese, and Bruce shot your way through the barricade and left Lori in the car with the kids. You definitely shelter women, Merrick."

Merrick felt himself suddenly turn red with embarrassment, and he started to sweat a little bit. He didn't think of himself as a sexist guy, but everything Miranda said was undeniable. What made it worse was that he had done everything without even being conscious of it.

"Don't beat yourself up about it; a lot of guys do it," Miranda continued. "Why do you think I am over here and Mark is over there by the bodies? I don't think you're sexist in that you think of females as being lesser, but maybe you're old-fashioned, or chivalrous. Either way, I think you need to trust us women a little bit more."

"Miranda, I am sorry. I honestly didn't even know I was doing it, but I will try to be more conscious of it now, but just in case I forget, you remind me anytime you think I need it, okay?"

"Deal," Miranda said, shaking Merrick's hand.

Merrick smiled at Miranda and asked, "Want to mess with Mark a little bit?"

"Like I would give up an opportunity to do that. What are you thinking?"

"Well, I was going to bring these latex gloves over to the boys in the shop and have them go through all the bodies and remove anything in their pockets, and then I was going to drive them to the lower property and put them all in just one of the graves that Ryan is digging. If you want, I will take your place on guard duty while you go over with the boys and take care of it. I got a feeling it will drive him nuts knowing what you are doing while he is on guard duty."

Miranda smiled. "I like it, and you're right; it *will* drive him nuts." She took the box of latex gloves from Merrick and started walking toward the shop.

"Oh, Miranda? Can you send Reese over? He has already done enough. Oh, and if you could say some words or a prayer when you bury them, to pay some respects."

"I will take care of it," Miranda said.

Merrick watched as Miranda walked into the shop and Mark began to protest. He couldn't hear what they were saying, but from the look of things, Miranda schooled Mark just like she had schooled him. Merrick chuckled to himself as he watched Mark squirm outside the shop as he paced back and forth for minutes. He felt a little sympathy for the guy, knowing he would probably do the same if Lydia was in there.

Merrick thought more about what Miranda had said about him being overly protective of women. He had known plenty of very capable women, especially in the military. Over the years he had a few very good female commanders, and it had never bothered him at all. Still, he had to admit that when he had a female in his squad, he was more protective of her than the rest of the soldiers, and if he was being completely honest, the last soldier he wanted to see wounded in battle was a female soldier.

As Merrick searched his soul, trying to figure out why he was more protective of women, the only thing that came to him was that he didn't view them as weaker, but he just couldn't bear seeing women and kids hurt. He wondered if his protective instincts were really selfish acts to protect himself emotionally.

"DAD!" Reese yelled.

"Jeez!" Merrick was startled.

"Some guard you are, right now," Reese joked.

"Shut up. I was deep in thought."

"What about?" he asked.

"You," Merrick lied.

"Me?"

"Yeah, you did really good today and saved my bacon."

"Thanks, Dad." Reese's smile showed a little bit of pride.

"Well, it got me thinking that your skills as a rifleman are top-notch, and don't let this go to your head, but you might be the best marksman we have in the group," Merrick said.

"Can you say that around Indiana later?" Reese joked with a big grin.

"No, but what I was getting at was even though you are not an adult, you're going to be a leader around here in a lot of ways. I need to start training you to lead and to come up with plans of attack as a leader. What do you think about that?" Merrick had always trusted Reese, but in the last few weeks, there had been multiple instances when Reese showed incredible maturity and clearheaded thinking in a crisis.

"I don't know. I like the sound of learning all that stuff, but honestly I don't know if I am ready. Like today—I am not sure I would have ever come up with a plan like you did on the fly." Reese shook his head and sounded a bit unsure.

"Bruce is three times your age. Do you think he feels more ready to come up with a plan?" Merrick asked.

"Probably not."

"That's right. You've got tactics stuff wired tight, and a lot of people in the group are still trying to understand the basics of that. We just need you to start thinking outside the box a little bit, and you would be a great leader."

"How do you do that? How do you train yourself to think outside the box?" Reese pinched his eyebrows together.

"Do you remember the *Matrix* scene where the kid tells Neo that trick to bending the spoon?"

"Yeah. There is no spoon," Reese said, quoting the movie.

"The trick is not to try and think outside the box, but to realize that there is no box. The only box in any situation is the one you create for yourself. If you hand a soldier a rifle and tell them to solve a problem, they just think about using that rifle; they don't even think to use other options. We limit our own creativity when we think of a problem. It won't be easy to change how you think; your brain's going to fight it at first. I will give you a bunch of different scenarios, and you will have to come up with different ways to solve them. The brain likes having very simple responses—like if this happens, then I do this—but after a little while, you won't be able to stop yourself from seeing things differently."

"I am way too tired to understand what you just said; you totally lost me." Reese had an overwhelmed look on his face.

"Don't worry about it. Why don't you go take a shower and change? You've had a long day too." Merrick patted Reese on the shoulder.

"Yeah, I think getting a decent shower is going to get a bit tougher with all these people."

"Yep, I will add a shower schedule to the list of things we need to do. Get going; I'll see you in a bit."

CHAPTER 26

It didn't take long for Miranda and the others to bury the bodies. With the tractor moving dirt, it was easy enough work. They put all the bodies in the same deep grave, and for now it was unmarked. The pickup and all the other nonperishable items were tucked away in the shop. When everyone returned from their grave duties, Lydia ordered them all to wash up in preparation for a rather chaotic dinner.

The scene reminded Merrick of a big family Thanksgiving. At first he was hoping to hear about everyone else's experiences over the last few days while they ate dinner. It didn't take him long to realize that was not going to happen. There was way too much noise with the number of people moving around and trying to take care of all the kids. The sharing of stories could wait.

Once the kitchen was cleaned up, everyone gathered together in the family room. Merrick looked out at the people in front of him and thought about how for the foreseeable future, they all needed him and he needed all of them. They had an official election every year, but he had always been the leader of the group; in fact, there hadn't been a whole lot of movement at all between positions in the group once they had all their members. He had formed the group one couple at a time. Above all, he wanted people he could trust and enjoyed being around. After that, as long as they were willing to train and learn, he could work with them.

Merrick had written most of the bylaws, standard operating procedures, and group strategies himself in his spare time. The other group members each had a specialty to contribute. There were times when he wished there was someone else in the group more qualified who could take the reins, but there wasn't; he was stuck with it.

He knew from experience that being a leader was a lonely position, no matter the organization. It was impossible for any leader to make everyone happy; no matter what a leader did, it was going to upset some people. With nearly twenty people living in one household and the nation falling apart around them, he knew there would be plenty of hard decisions to come. He hoped that there wouldn't be too much unnecessary drama and that he could live up to everyone's expectations.

While everyone was gathering together, Merrick asked Will to keep an eye on things while they had their meeting. Will stood by the front window watching outside, but was close enough that he could hear everything the group talked about.

"Well, welcome, everyone. I think most of us were hoping we would never need to get together like this, but here we are. With all of us living in the same house, there are bound to be issues and hurt feelings about something. Let's be open with each other about how we are feeling and maintain our perspective that this arrangement is keeping us all safer. Ryan, would you mind reading off the current roles and duties?"

"Sure. Merrick, commander. Mark, second-in-command and logistics officer. Ryan, third-in-command and sergeant at arms. Bruce, medical officer. Miranda, maintenance officer. Lori, educational specialist. Amy, food procurement. Lydia, logistical support. Will and Reese are members, but as of yet are unassigned."

Planning and scheduling were preparedness 101. Too many people, when they considered being prepared, thought of having gear and gadgets, but that was not preparation at all. Merrick believed that the first thing anyone should do to prepare for any event was simply to plan for it. He was a planner, and for him, not having a plan in a situation was like nails on a chalkboard. He enjoyed planning vacations and researching what kind of things a place had to offer so the family didn't miss anything. When he and Lydia had gone on a trip to Europe, he had researched the history of the different sites they were visiting. By the time they had left, he had learned enough that he could have been their own tour guide.

Merrick had a younger sister named Emily, and in terms of personality, they were very different people. She was an easygoing, fly-by-the-seat-of-her-pants kind of person. Her carefree attitude caught up with her every once in a while, like when she had waited until the last day of college registration to sign up for her classes. Then she had wondered why she hadn't gotten into the classes she wanted. Once she had asked Merrick and Lydia to go to Hawaii with her and her husband. It was a nice gesture, but Emily wanted to leave in two days and didn't even have a hotel reservation. She was very giving and fun to be around, so her quirks never really bothered Merrick, but he knew he couldn't live that way, and it would have killed him to be married to someone like that.

When it came to the group, Merrick had tried to think of the possible situations they might face and planned what he thought would be the best way to deal with each one. To help them stay organized, they had multiple three-ring binders dedicated to different topics and tasks.

Merrick had put together a logistics notebook with hundreds of inventory sheets. He had a security notebook with SOPs and plans for different maneuvers and situations. He had an intelligence notebook with details on people and places in the area he had already identified as possible threats or areas of interest. He had a notebook to record any new information the group might get and to record movements of people. There was a medical book with tables of medications and their uses, and a how-to section with instructions for certain medical procedures. An entire notebook was dedicated to scheduling: daily, weekly, and monthly.

Merrick now pulled out a prefilled week one schedule. "Once we are done with this meeting, I think one of the first things we need to do is have a posted schedule of who is doing what and when. That way people know when they are supposed to be cleaning, cooking, doing laundry, on guard duty, or whatever. Mark, Lydia, and Miranda, if you can get a rough schedule together for the week before we go to bed tonight, that would be great. Amy, if you want to make adjustments to the food calendar so we are using all the fresh stuff in the fridge and the freezer items first, that would be great. Ryan, you're the head of security. How do you want to do guard duty?" It didn't matter that Merrick knew more about security then Ryan did. Having someone else take point on security, food, and medical care helped so everything didn't have to be on his shoulders.

"Based on what we know right now, I think the threat is fairly low, and we can get away with just one person on guard duty at all times," Ryan said. "You don't have to *be* outside all the time, but your focus is always on what is going on outside, like Will right now. If everyone is okay with it, I think we should walk around the house at least once during the guard duty shift. When the next person comes on shift, there should be a casual brief of anything that happened during your shift—where people are and what they are doing. I think we should work it so the person that is getting off guard duty goes and finds the person who is up for guard duty in four hours and gives them their radio. That person is kind of in the bull pen and they can do whatever they want, but they should be dressed and have their gear close so they are ready to respond if needed.

"Anyone coming or going from the property should check in and out with me. Anyone wanting to come onto the property also needs clearance from me or whoever is in command. Everyone should try and have their weapon and gear no more than fifty feet away from them at any given moment. We are not a large army, so we can't afford not to have people ready if needed. Merrick, is there anything else I missed?" Ryan turned to Merrick.

"No, you explained it well. I think tomorrow you and I should go around and try to get the neighbors onboard with some kind of neighborhood security plan and warning system. Do you want to go over rules of engagement real quick?"

"Sure. First thing is we don't want any friendly fire, so make sure you identify all your targets. The property is totally fenced in, so no one should be just walking in by accident. Anyone trespassing on the property gets detained; if they run or don't respond to commands, then they are a threat. Hopefully we can get to know the neighbors and get them onboard with a security plan, but for right now, casually contact anyone outside the gate and ask who they are and what they are up to. Anyone armed and walking down the road should likewise be contacted and identified, but with your sites on them. If it were me, I would ask them to keep their hands off their weapons as they walk by. Any person or vehicle seen outside the property should be radioed in and recorded in our intel notebook."

Merrick was impressed. Ryan sounded very knowledgeable and confident. He guessed that Ryan had brushed up on the group SOPs and rules of engagement recently because he was practically reciting them verbatim. It made him smile to hear so many military terms used by average citizens. He was surprised that military and police terminology were becoming more well known to the average citizen.

Merrick knew that some people in America were very concerned that the police force was becoming more militarized, or a "police state" as they sometimes called it. A variety of factors had pushed the country to change some police tactics and to upgrade gear and equipment, but there was no credence to the wild accusation that somehow the federal government was preparing average police for some kind of coup against its citizens. One of the circumstances that had propelled this change was the explosion of the drug trade. Police were now faced with extremely violent, well-armed criminals who had access to military-grade munitions.

There were also events like the famous Los Angeles bank robbery shoot-out. Two criminals with high-powered rifles and body armor robbed a bank and got into a shoot-out with police. At the time the average police officer had just an issued handgun. Being outgunned, cops in the middle of the gunfight ran to local gun stores to arm themselves with rifles and shotguns to even stand a chance. Police agencies all over the United States, in an effort of pure survival against an enemy who was better armed than they were, had to upgrade their arsenal. Now an AR-15–style rifle was considered standard equipment for a road officer.

Merrick knew it wasn't just the police who continued to expand their weapons and tactics. Mixed martial arts fights, TV shows, and gyms had popped up everywhere. Average citizens, even if they did not regularly practice MMA moves, had become more skilled fighters. With games like *Call of Duty*, the average high school student also knew more about weapons and military tactics than any generation before.

As Merrick sat and listened to these civilians talk about and understand military terms, he realized his group was another example of how commonplace the lingo had become.

"Merrick, do you have a copy of the example week one schedule?" asked Mark.

"Yes." Merrick took it out of the three-ring binder and handed it to Mark. "Use it as a guide, but not everything might be applicable to our situation. If you can, let's try to make doing a complete inventory of all our assets one of the top priorities. Once we have that up, we can figure out where we stand with our supplies and ration accordingly. We can also keep a running tracker of critical items so we know how many days' worth of each thing we have. That way, we can identify any shortcomings far enough in advance to deal with it. Two other things that I want to ensure make it on the schedule are training time and fun decompressing time."

"We will make it happen," said Mark.

"Can anyone think of anything else that needs to be on the schedule for everyone?" Merrick asked the group.

"I don't think it needs to be on the schedule, but I would like to do a quick health evaluation of everyone. That way, I know if there are any special needs, allergies, or things like that," said Bruce.

"Good idea," Merrick said. "Can you also figure out a suggested hygiene plan for rotating showers and bathroom use?" Everyone groaned in response. "I know, I know, I get it. No one loves a nice long shower more than me, but with this many people, it isn't feasible for everyone to shower every day. Right now we are lucky that the power is still on. If it goes out, we are going to have to be a lot more careful with energy use."

"I might need some help, but I will come up with a plan," said Bruce.

"Thanks. Anyone else?"

"What about the kids and education? What do you want me to do with them?" asked Lori.

"I was going to leave that totally up to you. With all of them in different grades, I am not sure how to tackle that one, but Lori, don't feel like you need to figure it all out right away. There is no rush. The kids will be fine just playing for a few days while we figure out a plan."

"Well, I am not concerned about the younger kids—they are mostly mine anyway—but I did have an idea for the twelve-and-up group," Lori said.

"What is your idea?"

"Well, I was thinking we could have all the kids twelve and older help me teach the younger kids and do some self-directed studying one day. Then the next day, they shadow one of you. Whatever project or assignment you have for that day, they are your helpers. That way, they learn both the bookwork and the practical, real-life side of things too. I thought we could rotate who the kids shadow, giving them all a chance to learn from each adult and not just a parent. What do you think?" Lori asked excitedly.

"Lori, I think that is genius," Merrick said. "I was thinking the kids should be included with cooking and a lot of the other chores, but it would be good for them to see all the other things as well. I am for it. What does everyone one else think?"

The group consensus was positive. "Okay, Lori, great idea. Anything else?" Merrick looked around the room to make sure he wasn't missing anyone. "I know there are a lot of other things that we can talk about, but I think we have enough on our plate for tonight. Let's try to get that schedule out so people on guard duty tonight can know when their shift is going to be, and maybe tomorrow night or tomorrow afternoon, we will try to sit down all together again and figure out a few more things."

CHAPTER 27

For someone who normally didn't sleep well, Merrick was surprised by how deeply he'd slept last night. It was a little shocking for him to sleep better under these circumstances than he did when everything was normal, but he wasn't trying to look a gift horse in the mouth. He was up and dressed around seven o'clock and jumped in to help Amy make breakfast for everyone. Pancakes and sausage were on the menu today. The pancakes were made from a box of Krusteaz mix; Merrick thought it tasted way better than other brands. One of the best differences, though, wasn't the taste; it was that all the mix needed for delicious pancakes was water. Most other mixes required milk, eggs, and oil. At a few bucks for a twenty-pound reseal able bag of the stuff, it was the gold standard when it came to breakfasts stored in the pantry.

"How are you holding up, Amy?" Merrick asked as he whisked the pancake batter.

"Good. I know it's silly, but I just worry about our house."

"That's not silly. I think it's perfectly normal."

"Yeah, I guess. Do you think we'll be able to maybe go back and get a few more things?" Amy asked, but from the sound of her voice, she knew the answer.

"I don't think it'd be a good idea for a while," Merrick said, remembering that he had forgotten to tell everyone about all the inmates being released. He decided he would wait to tell everyone at the same time. "We had to fight our way just to be able to get home yesterday. My guess is that it'll get a little worse before it gets better. I will explain why to everyone after breakfast." He put a hand on Amy's shoulder and said, "What were you hoping to get?"

"Nothing much—just little things."

"Whatever you need, let us know and your chances are pretty good we've got it," Merrick offered. "Lydia says she's a couponer, but she's kind of a closet hoarder."

"I can hear you talking about me, mister, and you better watch yourself," Lydia said as she came down the stairs.

"Morning, babe. I was just saying if Amy needs anything, you could hook her up."

"Uh-huh, sure," Lydia said as she slapped Merrick on the arm playfully.

"Hey, easy! That assault," He grabbed his arm dramatically, acting like he was hurt.

"Oh, is it? Call the cops then. Oh, wait, there are none. Too soon?"

"Ha ha." Merrick leaned over and kissed Lydia.

"Okay, easy. Let's keep it G-rated around here. We have children present," Mark said as he walked into the kitchen from the basement.

Everyone else slowly woke up, filed into the kitchen, and enjoyed a filling breakfast. Merrick was happy that everyone seemed to be okay with the sleeping arrangements, or at least that was what they said. Each family was assigned one bedroom of its own. Merrick had a few extra mattresses, so no one had to sleep directly on the floor. Once he knew all the adults were present and most had eaten, he got everyone's attention.

"Morning, everyone. I forgot to give out some important info last night, but it's something I think you should know about. The Clark County jail, like everyone else, was having issues with people not showing up for work. So as of yesterday, they shut it down. How that relates to all of us is that they released all of the inmates. Most of the low-level criminals were released the day before yesterday, but even the most violent criminals were released sometime yesterday afternoon."

"How can they do that?" "Seriously?" "They're going to burn the city down!" were just a few of the comments Merrick heard.

"I know it's messed up, but this is just another reason why we need to get the neighborhood onboard with a security plan. I was hoping to take Ryan, Miranda, and Indiana around with me this morning to visit with the neighbors. I'd like to talk to each one individually today and hopefully have all of them get together this evening at one of the neighbor's houses."

"Don't you want to have that meeting here?" Mark asked.

"No, I would prefer it not to be here. We already have an overly full house, and to be honest, I don't want everyone asking why so many of you are here. Ideally I'd like to do it at the Freemans' house on the corner. It's centrally located and it's pretty big, so it'd fit everyone better.

"We've talked about this before, but I want to make sure we're all on the same page before I commit us to anything," Merrick continued. "I'm going to try to make a mutual aid agreement where if anyone in the neighborhood is threatened, the whole neighborhood will respond. It also might mean patrols in the area to be able to identify any threats. The further we go from this house, the more dangerous it is for us, but the further out we go, the less likely it is that we'll be fighting from our front door. I know this isn't what you wanted to hear first thing in the morning, but it's a reality we have to face. Everyone in favor of the mutual aid agreement with the neighbors?"

No one shouted in excitement, but everyone nodded in agreement.

"For those that I talked to last night about going with me today, be ready to roll out in twenty minutes," Merrick said. "Have your rifles and your kits with you."

Merrick's team congregated in the family room minutes later, and he filled everyone in on his plan. He would be in his police uniform and use his patrol car to approach his neighbors. They all knew he was a police officer and had seen his patrol car countless times. He knew that if his neighbors saw a random vehicle pull up in their driveway, they might freak out, so he was hoping the familiar vehicle would be enough to give them a little bit of comfort. He had everyone leave their kits with their extra mags in the car with the exception of Indiana, who had his kit on him. Miranda was the designated driver, and Indiana would be dropped off by each driveway entrance while Merrick and Ryan went to the front door.

Merrick decided to start at the Freemans' house. That way, if they agreed to host the get-together tonight, he could tell everyone else when and where. He knew everyone pretty well, and while there were some interesting characters, all the neighbors were pretty nice. Merrick brought his intel notebook with him, which had some information about his neighbors. He was good at remembering faces but had a hard time remembering everyone's names.

Most of the neighbors appeared happy to see Merrick in his police uniform, but that soon changed once he broke the news that the police were no longer functioning and all the inmates at the jail had been released. Almost everyone thought the mutual aid agreement was a good idea, and only one household flat out refused and thought it was an awful idea: David and Karen Patterson, who were hippie, liberal types in their early sixties. Even though they refused, Merrick invited them to go to the meeting that evening just to listen.

Of the twenty-five homes in the neighborhood, three homes appeared vacant. Merrick guessed from the missing vehicles and messes inside the houses that the residents had left in a hurry to go somewhere else. He was also happy to hear that none of the neighbors had seen any activity in the area.

It took four hours to visit all the homes. When the team finished and returned to the Albrights' house, it was lunchtime and they were ready for a break. Amy and Lydia had a whole stack of freezer meals for people to choose from. Merrick didn't like the premade meals, but he was happy that someone was finally eating them. Lydia had gotten a bunch for free by couponing, and they had just taken up space in the freezer.

"Hey honey," Lydia said, "Amy and I were looking in the outside freezer, and we have a ton of meat in there. We were thinking we should probably can a bunch of it so if the power goes out, we don't have to use it or lose it."

"Sounds good to me, but check with Mark since he's the logistics guy. I only hope that we try to wait on the frozen turkey out there. Thanksgiving is only a couple weeks away, and it would be nice to have it then." Merrick made a pleading motion with his hands.

"You do love your Thanksgiving turkey and pumpkin pie," said Lydia with a little sympathy in her voice.

"Pumpkin pie! Oh, make it two requests. We got to make pumpkin pie, or it's not even Thanksgiving," Merrick said seriously.

"Being grateful might be an important part in it too, Mr. High Maintenance. I thought I married a tough guy," Lydia mocked.

"If I have to choose between being a tough guy and pie? I choose pie," Merrick responded with an extra big smile.

CHAPTER 28

At 7 p.m. the whole neighborhood gathered together at the Freemans' house. Merrick arrived early with the same crew that went out with him earlier that day. The Freemans were some of his favorite neighbors. Keith was a retired pilot who liked to come over and shoot his M1 Garand with Merrick, and Trish was a retired nurse and the friendliest person you'd ever meet.

As everyone entered the home and greeted each other, Merrick noticed that his crew was getting stared at a bit. He was pretty sure it had something to do with them each wearing a kit with extra magazines and whatever personalized items they chose to carry.

"Thank you all for coming tonight," Merrick started. "I realize I talked to most of you already today, but I wanted to get everyone together so we realize we are not alone and hopefully come up with some kind of security plan for the neighborhood. It's official that all police action has stopped in Clark County. All of the jails have released all their inmates, and they are now running around with no one to stop them. There will be no federal or military assistance because they're being held in reserve to secure the country against foreign threats. Look around you because for the foreseeable future, the people here are the only people we can count on for help." He looked to the left and right to emphasize his point.

"As days turn to weeks, things are going to get worse. People are going to become more desperate, and people are going to become bolder in what they think they can get away with. Almost every store has already been looted. Anyone who has been out in the last few days knows how bad it is." A few heads nodded in agreement with what Merrick was saying.

"The looting will soon turn to the neighborhoods. We're further away from the city, so it'll not be quite as bad out here, but it is coming. I don't like being the bearer of bad news, and I'm not trying to scare you, but I feel like if I don't give it to you straight, I am doing you and your families a big disservice."

"We understand, Merrick, and we appreciate it. The news isn't telling us anything. Please keep going," said Keith.

"The power is on for now, but with no one working the lines, it's just a matter of time before it'll go out. We all have well water out here, but that means eventually we'll have no running water. Our fridges and freezers will stop working. We need to start now while the power is on to get ahead of this. The only way we'll survive this is if we come together and help one another. We're ten times stronger together than we are if we try to survive this all on our own. Each of us brings different skills and knowledge to the table. We're going to have to make our resources stretch. It may be months before the stores can get up and running again. I really think that if we put our heads together, we can come up with some creative solutions to whatever problem we may face.

"Security right now is our biggest problem, and it's one area where I think I can offer some guidance. Since we're all each other has, we first need to agree that if any of us are in trouble or gets attacked, we'll all come to their assistance. If attackers are at your neighbor's house, it'll only be a matter of time before they come to yours, so we're all in this together. Two things are critical: a good communication plan and intelligence.

"We can use cell phones while the power is on, but even then they have their limits. Right now let's say someone sees a person sneaking around their property. Just text out what you see and where they are to the group. That way, everyone will be aware. What will most likely happen is I'll text a place for a few of us to meet up close by, and then I'll lead the team and try to make contact. Of course, if any of us feels immediately threatened, then defend yourselves, but let's avoid shooting at shadows. The last thing we want is an accident. If people are in imminent danger and can't text, I think a good secondary plan is to use the panic alarms on your cars. When you hear a neighbor's car alarm sounding, then whoever can hear it should immediately send out a text making sure everyone knows there's an issue. I would be happy to visit with any of you to help you go over how best to defend your individual homes. At some point, I also want to meet anyone who is able to carry a weapon and would be willing to help.

"The next thing we should do is close off our neighborhood. We can park some spare cars or trailers to block the entrance. It will at least slow people down or make anyone coming in continue on foot. I think we should also park a car on the bridge. We can always move it if we need to get out, but it would slow anyone down a bit, hopefully giving us time to react.

"For intelligence, we just need to reach out and warn the other neighborhoods around us. If they do something similar and band together, then if they see anything, we can share information both ways. With that said, we need to commit that we won't break into houses or steal anything from those around us or each other. If we do, it'll start falling apart and piss people off at the same time. If we can regularly communicate with everyone around us, we'll be able to hear about problems coming our way. We don't want to wait until the looters are at our doors to take action. Ideally, if a neighboring community has a looting problem and we help them take the guys out before they even have a chance to become a problem for us, we'll all be a lot safer."

"Merrick, I have to stop you right there. I can't believe that you, as an officer of the law, can talk so casually about killing people for minor crimes and then advocate for us to do the same. I think that's appalling," said Karen Patterson, the only person who had told him earlier that she didn't want anything to do with a neighborhood security plan.

She was a petty, annoying woman on a good day, but she had an ax to grind with Merrick. While shooting in the area was legal, she didn't like it, so she had once asked Merrick not to shoot. She'd walked down the fence line and yelled at him from her property. She whined about it being amazingly loud and asked if he wouldn't shoot anymore on his property out of respect for his neighbors. She had the gall to add that he had to get plenty of practice at the sheriff's office and probably didn't need to shoot anyway.

Being somewhat new to the neighborhood then, Merrick had tried to let her down easy and be respectful, but she didn't get the hint. He was blown away when she asked him to construct some kind of barrier to block the sound so she didn't have to hear it. At this point, he was done being nice and flat out told her that building a barrier was a great idea and that if the noise bothered her, she should build it on her property. She stormed off looking not too happy, and he kind of figured that she never got over it because she'd avoided talking to him for the last few years. That avoidance had never bothered him. In fact, he was hoping to see how long he could stretch it.

"Karen, thank you for coming tonight, even if you don't want to be a part of helping secure the neighborhood," Merrick said. "You'll still be living in it, so it'll still affect you. When our society is working like it should and we have the resources to put people in jail, you're right, but right now they just released convicted murderers onto the streets. The justice system you're holding on to doesn't exist right now. I don't like talking about killing, but in the past three days, I've had to shoot multiple people while working as a police officer and that was before it got so bad and chaotic they sent all of the police home. Karen, I hope the days of law and order soon return, but right now we're living in the Wild West days and we are only as safe as we can make ourselves."

"Surely you don't expect us to go around shooting people for simple theft. Even if we wanted to, we're not police officers or trained soldiers, and none of us are prepared for that. We wouldn't stand a chance against a bunch of armed vagrants," Karen said.

"Well, Karen, I don't think you know your neighbors as well as you might think. Paul Jacobs over there was a Marine, and if you know anything about Marines, once a Marine, always a Marine." Merrick looked at Paul.

"Semper Fi," Paul said softly with a slight smile.

"You probably only know Kenneth as a guy who owns a machine shop, but he's very active in a gun club up on Larch Mountain, and he shoots every week. Keith's a gun lover and a decent shot, and Dale and his boys are avid hunters. Tom's an old combat vet from Vietnam that I wouldn't want to mess with. Alone we are venerable, but if we can work together with a little planning, I'd say our chances are pretty good against—what did you call them? A bunch of armed vagrants."

Merrick paused and took a step closer to Karen. "To me, this is our only option. We either fight and defend our neighborhood, or we just open our doors when they come and let them take whatever they want, then hope and pray they don't hurt us or rape us in the process, but there's no way in hell I'm going to put my family at that kind of risk. I, for one, am going to fight. Karen, all of your life you've benefited from soldiers and police officers sacrificing their blood to keep your little slice of the world safe. The great news for you is that the same thing is going to happen again. Everyone else here is going to risk their lives to keep this neighborhood safe while you sit in your house comfortably and benefit from it. Just do me a favor: Since you are incapable of showing an ounce of gratitude, kept your self-righteous comments to yourself."

It was obvious that Karen was not accustomed to being put in her place. She didn't say a single word for the rest of the night. Merrick kicked himself for letting Karen get him all riled up. The last thing he wanted to do was belittle someone in public while he was trying to bring people together. He figured he should cut his losses and bring the meeting to a close.

"It's getting late, and there is no way I can cover everything tonight. So I'll wrap this up. I think we should meet again soon to talk about more details of how we should react to threats to our individual homes and how we're going to fight together if it comes to that. Keith and Trish, I hate to impose, but would you be okay if we meet back here every Sunday night till this thing is over?"

"Of course. All of you are welcome in our home, and if I might say so, I feel better already knowing we're going to help each other," said Keith.

"Thank you, Keith," Merrick said. "The great thing is we'll not only *feel* safer, but we'll *be* safer when we band together."

CHAPTER 29

"Remind me again why you thought it would be a good idea to invite that woman tonight?" Ryan said as he got into the car to drive back to Merrick's house after the meeting.

"I'm not going to invite everyone in the neighborhood and then not invite her. I can't believe I did that. Sorry, guys. When she started talking, all my past history with her came back to me, and she just has one of those voices that can drive you nuts, you know?" Merrick said sounding disappointed in himself.

"I thought it went well," Miranda said with a smile on her face. Merrick glanced at her and guessed she was being sarcastic.

"What meeting were you in? It was stone silent in there after Merrick reamed that chick. I love you, man, and God knows she deserved the wake-up call, but it was a bit harsh when we're trying to foster some diplomacy," said Ryan. Merrick was beating himself up about it already, but it didn't make him feel better to hear someone else had the same thoughts he did.

"I disagree," Miranda said. "I think when you said that for years people have been skating free while the military and law enforcement spill their blood to defend us was powerful. When you added that now the neighborhood would have to defend itself and she was going to skate free was brilliant. You totally guilted all of them into being a part of the security plan. Oh, and I loved how you publicly listed a bunch of your neighbors' tactical skills, giving them all a confidence boost. I even think the public harshness and putting someone in their place was good. It showed your authority and probably cemented your place as a leader. Seriously, I think you're beating yourself up for nothing."

"Thanks, Miranda, but I'm mad at myself because chewing her out was a knee-jerk reaction, not a calculated one. I wasn't careful with what I said, and that frustrates me. Hopefully you're right and it pans out, but Ryan's right too; diplomacy is difficult, and I need to be a little more careful with what I say."

Everyone who had stayed at the house was curious how it went, so Miranda recounted the story, and with her positive outlook on it all, the group members thought that Merrick had done the right thing.

"Can I talk to you for a minute?" Lydia asked Merrick once they were done going over the meeting.

"Yeah. What's up?"

Lydia motioned Merrick to follow her into the laundry room, away from everyone else.

"My parents called while you were gone." Merrick hadn't noticed it before, but he could now see worry in Lydia's eyes.

"What did they say? Are they okay?"

"They're okay, but they're scared and mentioned possibly coming over here," Lydia said while looking at the ground.

"Babe, I am sorry to hear that. It's super dangerous out there right now, and I don't think it's a good idea for them to try to drive all the way across town." Merrick remembered that they had already had conversations about friends or family who might want to just show up at their house. He didn't know exactly what Lydia wanted.

"I know, but we're talking about my parents. Hearing them ask if they can come over here and then not being able to say yes made me feel like my heart was being ripped out. Is there *anything* we can do to help them?"

"I'm not sure how much we can do from here—they're on the other side of town." Merrick looked at Lydia; her eyes were tearing up. "I'm not sure how much it'll help, but I can call them and give them some advice. Your dad used to be a cop, and he knows what he's doing. I am sure they will be fine."

"I would really like it if you would call them, but—and this is just a hypothetical—what if they *were* able to make it out here?" Lydia asked hesitantly.

"Our house is pretty full and I don't want to get your hopes up too much, but there is a possibility that they could stay in one of the empty houses in the neighborhood or even with one of the neighbors. There are a couple of older couples that might be interested in having another couple stay with them that are trustworthy and have some firearm experience, but I would need to do some checking before we do either."

"That sounds perfect. They have done so much for us, and I know that they've never really been interested in the whole 'being prepared' thing, but I just feel like we have to try to help them."

"I agree. I'll give them a call them tomorrow."

Lydia didn't respond; she just smiled at Merrick.

"You want me to call them tonight, don't you?"

Lydia nodded shyly.

"Fine," Merrick said as he exhaled loudly.

Lydia gave him a big hug. "Thank you. This makes me feel so much better."

Merrick liked his in-laws, Frank and Debbie. They were great people who were easy to get along with. They had always been willing to watch the boys when they were younger or help them in any way they could. Over the years, they thought Merrick was a little paranoid for being into preparedness and dedicating so much time to it, but they never gave him too much grief about it. He had tried on more than one occasion to get them more into being prepared, but they never took much interest. Already he felt like he had talked more today than he normally did in weeks, but he pulled out his phone and called Frank.

"Hey Frank, it's Merrick. How are you guys holding up out there?"

"We're doing okay, but this whole thing feels a bit unreal," Frank said. Merrick could hear the nervousness in his voice.

"Yeah, no kidding. I'm half expecting to wake up at any moment."

"We just feel so alone, and everyone around us is freaking out. I'm trying to tell myself that it'll be okay, but my mind keeps focusing on the worst things that could possibly happen. I have no idea what to do."

"I think just about everyone feels that way right now," Merrick agreed.

"Not you. You knew something like this was going to happen and have been getting ready for it for years. I doubted you and thought you were wasting your time, but man, was I wrong."

"Frank, you're giving me too much credit. It's just like when you were a cop and you investigated a burglary where someone had their door kicked in. It's natural to go home and think about 'How can I make sure that doesn't happen to me?' We've all seen countries on the news that have been brought to their knees over riots or an economic collapse, or a national disaster devastating entire regions and it takes the government weeks to respond. I just didn't want those things to happen to me or my family, so I tried to think of things that I could do to protect them."

"Yeah, but like you said, we've all seen that stuff and you're the only one that I know who did something about it. The rest of us morons just see the news and think 'sucks to be those people.' How did you see this coming?"

"I was in Boy Scouts my whole life growing up, and their motto is 'be prepared.' I guess it kind of stuck with me. I would always carry a pocketknife and a first aid kit in my car. After needing it a few times, I added a few other items from time to time, and before you know it, it practically became a way of life, but I definitely didn't know this would happen; no one knew it would. The entire US government wasn't prepared for it and didn't see it coming, so you shouldn't feel too bad about it."

"Well, if we make it through this, count me in. I feel so helpless right now."

"I get it, but you're probably not as bad off as you might think. Can I give you a few pointers?" asked Merrick.

"Please do," Frank said.

"Ok, grab a pen and paper. Let me know when you're ready."

"Ready."

"Being prepared is all about prioritizing. You have to worry about the biggest problem or threat first. Safety and security are always number one. You should be armed at all times with a handgun, and always have a rifle close. You should also do what you can to train Debbie just in case she needs to use one. Get all your first aid stuff together in a backpack. With only the two of you, I would also have an escape plan just in case you get overrun. I would back your Pilot into your garage and have it loaded and ready to go. Load your extra weapons, ammo, sleeping bags, extra clothes, food, and water in the car. That way if you need to, you can just jump in and go."

"But where would I go?" asked Frank.

Merrick knew what he was asking. "Our house is pretty full right now, but there are a few empty homes in our neighborhood and there are people around here who would probably take you in. If something happens, you can head toward our place and we'll figure something out, but I would use it as a last resort. Driving right now is risky. Did Lydia tell you about the roadblock we hit on my way home yesterday?"

"Yes, she did. I still can't believe it."

"Well, I think it's going to get worse before it gets better. I'd try and contact as many of your neighbors as possible and get them ready to fight any threat that might come into the neighborhood. Just tell them that all of you will work together to protect each other."

"You really think we're going to have to defend the neighborhood against a large group? I figured it might be a couple guys going around looting, but you make it sound like we're being overrun by an army or something."

"I don't know what we're going to face. All I know is the hundreds of criminals that were in our jail yesterday are now back on the streets, and that's not even including the thousands of criminals that live around us every day. Just think what people would do if there were no laws and no cops. That's the world you and I are living in. My gut tells me that with no police to stop large groups of criminals from amassing, they're going to get larger and bolder."

"Jeez, you're not making me feel better."

"That's because I'm trying to warn you, not comfort you. Did Lydia talk to you guys about food and water at all?"

"A little bit. She said we should start eating what's in the freezer first and save the stuff that'll last longer."

"That's good. I would fill up some empty milk cartons and put as many of them in the freezer as you can. As you get more room, put more in. That way if the power goes out, you can put the frozen milk cartons in a cooler or your fridge to keep things cool. What about water?"

"Lydia had us fill up the bathtubs we aren't using, and we have a couple cartons of bottled water around, but even when the power goes out, we've always had water here," Frank said.

"I know, but that might not last. When the power goes off, the public water system can function for a little while off the water towers and backup pumps, but not forever. I doubt anyone is still working at the water treatment plant or at the power company. Once the grid goes down, it's just a matter of time before public water goes as well. I'd get a large container, like your big recycling bin, and clean it out and cut off one of the gutters in your backyard so the gutter drains into it."

"Okay. I'm pretty sure I can manage that. I remember seeing the rainwater system you have at your house, but can you drink that water?"

"I wouldn't, at least not without adding some bleach, but that water you can use to flush your toilets and wash with if you need to."

"Okay. Wow, this sounds like we are living in a third world country."

"Without regular grid power, yeah, that's exactly what it's going to be like."

"I hate to even ask it now, but will our natural gas eventually run out too?"

"I don't know as much about natural gas, but that would be my guess. I know you have a barbecue, but do you have a camping stove or anything?"

"We have an old one that we haven't used in years."

"I would try to see if you can get it working. Frank, I know I'm probably freaking you out and you're feeling overwhelmed, but I just wanted you to be mentally prepared if the power goes out. Right now the power's on and you're doing great. If you just do a few things now while the power is still on, then if it goes out, it won't be the end of the world and you will know you can still make it."

"I know, Merrick, and thank you. We're a bit clueless with this kind of stuff. Take care of your boys and Lydia."

"I sure will. We'll keep in touch, and call us if you need anything or have any questions," Merrick said, feeling sorry for his in-laws.

"All right, we will. Bye."

"Bye." Merrick ended the call and sat looking at his phone. He wondered how his parents and siblings were doing with all this craziness. He was tired and his other family members were states away, but he decided to spend the rest of the night calling each of them.

CHAPTER 30

The last few days had been a bit overwhelming, and this morning Merrick was looking forward to a fairly low-key day. He was busy helping Mark, Braydon, Sessile, and Reese inventory their supplies in the basement. It was simple, mind-numbing work with minimal conversation. They were taking turns picking songs for everyone to listen to.

"Hey Merrick, we have a small issue upstairs. Can I steal you for a minute?" Bruce asked. Merrick could tell from Bruce's tone that it wasn't an urgent or life-threatening issue, but it also seemed like he didn't want to wait. At the moment, Merrick was very relaxed and he didn't want to leave, but duty called.

"Yeah, of course." Merrick stood up and made his way through the maze of supplies to get to the door. Once they were outside the door, he asked Bruce, "So what's going on?"

"Lori and Lydia kind of got into it a little bit," Bruce said with a concerned look.

"Really? About what? I know Lydia's a little spitfire, so I can understand that. But Lori's so easygoing." Merrick was curious about what the issue could be.

"I don't know the whole thing. I kind of walked into them arguing about it and said that I'd get you. From what I could tell, Lori had some extra snacks in our room that she brought from our place, and she was giving them to the kids in between meals. Lydia didn't like Lori having a private food stash and got upset about it."

"Drama, drama, drama! With this many people in a small area together, I'm surprised this is the first issue we've had. All right, let's go and see if we can keep our wives from killing each other."

"You want me to come with you? I was sort of thinking I would stay out of it."

"Ha! You and me both. But I think if we both do this, it will be better. We'll talk to each of them separately and hopefully come up with a solution that makes everyone friends again. You being there the whole time will help prevent your wife from thinking I'm being biased, and you being there will keep my wife from biting my head off."

"I don't know how you do it, with all the hand-holding and being careful not to hurt people's feelings at the same time. Keeping us all alive and making sure we don't kill each other."

"Well, I feel like the hand-holding thing comes from my years of experience as a police officer. I've been to hundreds of calls where people were fighting over the stupidest things and I had to try to find a way to settle everyone down again."

"So who do we talk to first?"

"Let's start with your wife. Lydia takes a bit longer to cool down." Merrick and Bruce walked up to the main level. Lydia was in the kitchen with her arms folded across her chest, waiting for them to come up the stairs.

"Babe, we're figuring things out. Just give us a few minutes to talk with Lori and we'll be right back to talk to you. All right?"

"Fine," Lydia said with some definite sass. Merrick guessed she was already upset that she was being talked to second. He followed Bruce to one of the bedrooms, and Bruce knocked on the door.

"Honey, it's me and Merrick. Do you mind if we come in?" Bruce asked as he peeked into the room.

"That's fine. Come on in." Lori was sitting on the bed with a pillow on her lap and tears in her eyes. Bruce moved to sit beside her, and as he did, she said, "Merrick, we are so grateful to be here with you guys. I didn't mean to cause any trouble."

"Lori, you and Bruce have some of the biggest hearts of anyone I've ever met in my life. You didn't cause any trouble. Misunderstandings happen all the time, and I'm sure that's what this is. Bruce and I are going to hear you both out, then try and figure out where the misunderstanding was. Then hopefully we can fix it. Why don't you tell us what happened?"

"Well, I was just finishing up some school time with the girls, and River asked if they could have a snack and I said sure. So I walked into our room and picked out two chocolate granola bars from our snack stuff I brought with us, and I gave them to the girls. I think Lydia saw me go into our room and get the snacks because she walked in a minute later holding our bag of snacks and accusing me of having a private food horde. I didn't even think about putting these little snack things with the group stuff. I'm sorry, but I didn't even think about it."

"It's okay," Merrick said. "Not even close to a big deal, and I've been so busy I haven't noticed. Do you know if Lydia and Mark have a snack bin or something set aside for people to snack on in between meals?"

"Not that I know of, but they might. I feel awful," said Lori.

"You shouldn't feel bad at all. You were solving a problem yourself without having to go ask someone else if your kids could have a snack. No one's used to living like this, so there are going to be some little adjustments that need to be made as we go. Eventually your snacks were going to run out, and I'm sure you would have brought it up then."

"Yes, exactly."

"Okay. Is there anything else before we go talk to Lydia?"

"No. Merrick, she seemed pretty upset with me. Is it really going to be all right?"

"She definitely has some Irish spunk in her, and she's been pissed at me more times than I can count. Don't tell her I said this, but she normally figures out pretty quick that she was wrong and might have overreacted a little bit. I'm sure you guys will be perfectly fine. Just give us a minute to go talk to her. Okay?"

"Of course," said Lori, looking a little bit better.

"You are pretty smooth, you know that?" Bruce said as he and Merrick walked out of the room.

"Well, my wife might not be so easy, so don't jinx me now."

Merrick and Bruce walked back to the kitchen, where Lydia was still waiting. "Sorry about the wait, love," Merrick said. "Can you tell us what happened?"

"First of all, don't talk to me like I'm one of your police calls. I am your wife, and I think I have a right to be a little upset."

Merrick allowed himself a slight glance over at Bruce, whose eyes were wide with shock at the tone of Lydia's voice. It was obvious that Lori did not talk to Bruce like this. Merrick couldn't help but smile just a little.

"You think this is funny!" Lydia said, sounding even more upset. Apparently she noticed Merrick's little smirk.

"Honestly, no, I don't think this is funny. I think it's unfortunate. Little issues like this are bound to come up, but we need to find ways to make this work, not ways to drive us apart." Merrick gave Lydia a serious look back.

"I agree, but if we're going to live all together, we need to have people follow some basic rules."

"I agree that rules are very important. What rule did Lori break that you're upset with?" Merrick asked.

"All of our food in our house became the entire group's when this thing started, and everyone's food that was brought here became the group's as well. We should not have private stashes. Having a private stash is basically stealing from the group. Bruce, I'm not saying Lori is stealing; I know she didn't mean anything by it." Lydia shifted into trying to smooth out the harshness in his voice for Bruce's benefit.

"We know you don't mean that, but I don't think Lori does. She's in there crying because she thinks you're upset with her." Merrick paused for a moment, than asked, "Do we have a snack bin or something set up for kids or adults who might want something in between meals?"

"We're working on setting something like that up, but we haven't announced it to everyone yet. It's been busy," Lydia said defensively.

"It has been busy for everyone. Lori didn't know there were snacks available, and neither did I. She was just trying to keep her little girls happy in between meals." Merrick could see Lydia soften, but there was one more issue he had to deal with. "How did you find the snack bag Lori had?"

"When I saw Lori go into their room and come out with the snacks, I went in right after and found the bag," Lydia said.

Merrick didn't say anything at first; he just nodded and waited for Lydia to put together exactly what she did. "You went into the Hales' private room without their permission, searched around in their private stuff, and then took something out. Is that right?" Merrick's tone emphasized that what Lydia had done was far worse than anything that Lori had done.

"Yes, but . . . I was just . . ." Lydia stumbled to find the right words.

"Honey, we're all making adjustments, including both you and Lori. This is your house, and you're not used to having areas in your own home that are off-limits. Why don't we just get Lori out here so everyone can say they're sorry and you can tell Lori about the snack bin so there aren't any more issues?"

Lydia, now with tears in her eyes, nodded and said, "Okay."

"Perfect. Thanks, honey." Merrick gave her a hug. "Bruce, can you get Lori?"

"Sure," Bruce said. He came back a few moments later with Lori slowly walking behind him.

Both Lydia and Lori started to sob when they saw each other. Lydia moved toward Lori, and they hugged. Merrick couldn't comprehend what they were saying among their sobs. He wasn't even sure if they could understand each other, but he was pretty sure they were making up. He started walking back downstairs to get back to work and was stopped by Bruce on the stairwell.

"Hey, thanks for smoothing everything over."

"Of course. They're both great people, but in the moment, it can be hard to see the other person's perspective. Do me a favor. If I'm ever out of line, make sure you help me see the light?"

"I'll try," Bruce replied.

"Do or do not. There is no try," Merrick said in a funny voice. Bruce looked like he had no idea what Merrick was talking about. "Yoda . . . *Star Wars* . . . come on, man."

CHAPTER 31

Tom lived in the first house at the entrance of the neighborhood and was, like many Vietnam vets, a crusty old man who didn't take crap from anyone. He was also one of Merrick's favorite neighbors. He had retired years ago but still operated a side business of selling bees. When Merrick showed interest in the bees one day, Tom was more than happy to show him his setup and explain the process of beekeeping. He sold starter bee kits that shipped all over the country. The kits came with a queen and an entire colony of workers that had not hatched yet. They would come out in the spring, and then, if cared for, they would become a fully functioning hive.

Merrick received a text from Tom to everyone in the neighborhood at 3:52 p.m.

Tom: "Just ran off two guys at my property. They were looking through some of my stuff. They took off pretty quick when I came out with my 12 gauge. I think we need to do some of the suggestions Merrick talked about the other night to secure the neighborhood. Sooner rather than later would be good."

Merrick: "Tom, I'm glad you are okay. If everyone can meet tonight and Keith's okay with it, let's try meeting in a few hours. Did you happen to see what kind of car they were driving by chance? Or how old the guys were?"

Tom: "They were driving a white, beat-up, large SUV. Might have been a Tahoe. One of the guys looked like he was in his forties, the other guy looked a little older, maybe in his fifties, and he had a beard."

Keith: "We can meet at our place tonight at 6 p.m. if everyone can make it."

Dale: "Tom, I thought you were a better shot than that ;) We can be there at 6."

Merrick: "We'll be there as well."

Dan: "Thanks for scaring them away, Tom. I'll be there."

Almost everyone responded that they would make the meeting. Merrick pulled everyone in the group together and told them about Tom and the meeting that night. He then asked, "What security measures should we try and push for tonight?"

"I definitely think blocking off the street is first priority," Ryan said.

"Good, I agree. I'd also like to create squads and assign squad leaders. If each house can provide one person, we can have a leader for every four houses or so. We should also incorporate them into a regular training program. I know they're not going to be pretty, but a few basics would go a long way."

"How often and how long are these training sessions going to be?" asked Mark.

"I don't know. I was thinking once a week for maybe two hours or so," Merrick said.

"Weekly training is a lot to ask for," Ryan said skeptically.

"In their normal lives, sure, but most of these people are sitting around not doing a thing right now. I think they'll love having a purpose and some direction once a week. We can even encourage the squad leaders to practice with their people separately if they want. If they don't spend time together, they won't become a team. The more we invest in their training, the more we'll be able to count on them if something happens."

"Who is going to be in charge of their training? We're talking about at least five separate training sessions a week. That's going to suck up a lot of our time," said Ryan.

"Well, that is a fair point. I was thinking you and I should be the trainers for now. We might be able to train two or three squads at the same time. That should cut it down to a manageable level. We could even try and focus their training on defending their part of the neighborhood."

"That sounds good. We'll have to get together later to come up with a training plan."

"Absolutely."

"I have a question. Are we going to station some kind of security detail at the front of the neighborhood?" Amy asked. "It just doesn't seem right to leave this Tom guy out there with no help."

Merrick agreed, but he knew that manning such a station would be hard to sustain and potentially dangerous for whoever did it. "I'd like to, but we'd need the support of the entire neighborhood to have the man power for that. Tom would also have to be okay with sharing his home with people coming and going every day. For a crotchety old man, that's going to be quite a sell," he said.

"What if each squad took one day a week?"

"Being away from your family for a full day? I don't even want to do that right now," said Merrick.

"Could we have each squad split up a twenty-four-hour shift any way they want? That wouldn't be too bad."

"That might work," Merrick said. "We could even sell it that they can sleep during their shift or play a board game, but they need to be armed and in the area. Okay, we'll try to sell that tonight then. I'm thinking it might be good for the same crew we had before to come again. New faces might make people feel uneasy or prompt questions. What does everyone think?" Everyone nodded in agreement.

That night Merrick and the same group members got to the Freemans' house a few minutes early. Merrick didn't like asking questions in a group setting that he didn't already know the answers to, so they went to the meeting early to corner a few people as they arrived and get their input. Tom was one of those people, but he was swarmed with people wanting more details about what had happened. Merrick waited for a pause in Tom's storytelling and then jumped in.

"Tom, could I talk to you for a moment?" Merrick gestured for a side conversation.

"I suppose." Tom followed Merrick to a corner of the room. "This can't be good."

"What do you mean?" asked Merrick.

"A police officer wanting a private conversation. Seems like I'm in trouble," joked Tom.

"You certainly are not, sir. In fact, I wanted to ask what you thought about something."

"You want to turn my house into an observation point," Tom said bluntly.

"For an old man, you're pretty sharp."

"I was in the military for a minute or two, and it doesn't take a rocket scientist to figure out that you would want to defend the main access point to the neighborhood. Tell me what you had in mind."

"Tonight I'm going to suggest that we block off the entrance to our neighborhood. The gist of it is that the odds are if trouble comes knockin', your place is going to be hit first. We want to have rotating people come hang out at your place as a kind of quick reaction force. They don't have to be stationed at the barricade or on guard constantly, but they're there to back you up and raise the alarm if there's trouble. Would you be all right with having a few armed people come hang out with you each day?"

"The real question is, do you think they can handle hanging out with an irritable old man like me?" Tom asked with a smile. "I heard what you said the other night about it getting worse before it gets better, and I reckon you're probably right. In my younger years, I would tell you that I could do it myself, but I'm not the young man I use to be, that's for darn sure. You can count me in, Colonel."

"Thanks, Tom. I'll bring it up once the meeting starts." Merrick patted Tom on the shoulder.

Merrick made his rounds to a few other key people he was hoping to get support from before it was almost time to start. He then noticed a face he was not expecting: Karen, the annoying neighbor he'd chewed out at the last meeting. She was sitting and not talking to anyone, and she seemed different somehow, timid maybe. He really didn't care for her, but he still felt a slight pang of guilt when he saw her.

Merrick made his way over to Karen, thinking he should apologize for last time. He could tell that she'd noticed him walking toward her, but she was making a real effort not to look in his direction. He had a second thought that maybe he was about to make things worse, but he hated leaving things unsaid and wasn't sure how much worse things could get at this point.

"Karen, I am sorry. I was a little harsh last time and . . ."

Karen stood and put up her hand, stopping him midsentence. "Merrick, it's fine. You don't need to say anything. I've been thinking a lot about what you said and doing some self-introspection. Hell, I have nothing else to do. Anyway, I hate violence, plain and simple. I think it's childish in our civilized world. Those who resort to using violence just haven't evolved yet from the caveman days. The military and law enforcement are, of course, different from criminals, but they're still violent people. People who learn to solve their problems with violence tend to lean in that direction whenever there's a problem. You were in the military; wouldn't you agree that soldiers get in more bar fights than the average person?"

"Yes, I guess they do." Merrick had to agree that a large percentage of soldiers had a tendency to drink and got into more than their share of fights.

"Right. Well, I think the only way we're going to make the world less violent is not to respond to violence with violence. It's like a parent who spanks their child for hitting their sibling. The intent might be to stop violence, but we're really just promoting it." Karen grew more animated with each sentence.

"That's an interesting way of thinking about it, and I agree the world would be a much better place with less violence, but I can't see us ever getting rid of it completely. I think you're an idealist wanting to live in a perfect world, but the hard fact is that world doesn't exist. Human nature prevents it. The only reason the voice of America is so influential is because we're a superpower holding a big stick. If there was a country that was more powerful, they would have more influence."

"Yes, but power doesn't mean military strength; it can be economic power. You don't have to bomb or shoot everyone to get them to comply. You can do sanctions and things other than violence."

"Do you remember the genocide of Rwanda?" asked Merrick.

"Yes, vaguely," Karen admitted.

"There were something like 800,000 being massacred. Who do you threaten with sanctions to stop that? How many do you let be killed while you wait for their response to the sanctions?"

"I don't know." Karen looked down.

"It's not what you want to hear, but sometimes violence is the only language some people speak, and it's the only way to stop them," Merrick said.

"Maybe you're right. Maybe when dealing with violent people, there are times when violence must be used to stop them immediately. What about nonviolent behavior? Can you agree that violence has no place in nonviolent issues?" Karen was clearly trying to come to a compromise.

Merrick thought about just agreeing to end the conversation, then decided to answer honestly. "I wish I could, but no, sometimes it is necessary, even against nonviolent people."

"Merrick, come on. I'm trying to be open-minded, but how can you believe you need to be violent with nonviolent people? That's crazy." Karen put her hands on her hips.

"Suppose a crazy guy walks into your house and thinks it's his and he refuses to leave. You call the cops. We show up and try to talk him out, but he refuses. The guy is not violent, but to remove him from your home, we're going to have to put hands on him and use force to remove him. Once diplomacy has failed, what can you do?"

"You could have a doctor or psychologist come out and talk to him to get him out of the house. They're trained for that," Karen offered.

Merrick laughed. "You'd think so, right? But that isn't what happens. In real life, the doctors and shrinks are calling the police. We get calls nonstop to go and help the hospital with out-of-control people. I have literally stood right next to a psychologist in the hospital who had a patient that was freaking out. It's easy for doctors to sit back and say what should have happened in a certain case in hindsight, but to be standing there toe to toe with a guy yelling in your face is a whole new reality. The shrink at the ER didn't even want to try to talk with the guy anymore, so he asked me to try to talk him down. He said they don't get that kind of training to deal with people in a crisis, just how to help people who have had a crisis."

"That's interesting. You've given me a lot to think about," Karen said, and sighed. "I think I'm just really scared. When you talk about people breaking into our homes and having to defend ourselves, I don't want that to be true because if it was, I know I'm powerless and it would petrify me." Her voice broke slightly.

"It's scary for all of us, but your troubles and fears tend to get bigger if you run away from them. You'll only conquer a problem once you have faced it," Merrick said.

"You get that off a fortune cookie?" Karen joked.

"Probably, but it's still true. Are we good?" asked Merrick.

"Yes. We may disagree on some things still, but we're good."

CHAPTER 32

"How was the meeting?" Lydia asked when Merrick and his group came home.

"Good, but a little less exciting. Merrick didn't chew anyone out this time," Ryan said, sounding slightly disappointed.

"It went well, and they agreed to do all the security procedures we talked about," Merrick said. "A couple people volunteered unused cars for the barricade and we divided everyone up into squads, and each group has a day they are assigned to have at least one person at Tom's house to keep an eye on the entrance. Our day is Monday."

"Nothing else interesting?" asked Lydia.

"Well, Dale and Keith reached out to a couple friends who live in some other neighborhoods in the area. They came to the meeting because they wanted help forming their own neighborhood security plan. Ryan and I gave them a few ideas, and we exchanged contact information. So we can now communicate with them if they have any problems and vice versa. This is really good news. The more news spreads about these neighbor security groups, the safer we'll be," Merrick said. "It's also creating a communication network so if anyone sees anything, we should hear about it."

"Would we go and risk ourselves if another neighborhood had an issue?" asked Mark.

"I think that'd have to be evaluated on a case-by-case basis, but if it was a threat that could come this way, it's usually better to attack than to be attacked. If we can choose when and where to ambush them, then we're much better off," Merrick explained.

"I just think it's dangerous to turn into a police force for the area."

"We wouldn't, and we can evaluate each case. Most of the time, each neighborhood can handle small problems within itself, but if there is a group hitting multiple homes in the area, then maybe we need to help set a trap for them. If there's a large group taking over an entire neighborhood, then we have to pool our resources and deal with it."

"And you really think there're going to be large roving groups like that?" Mark asked.

"Look, I don't have a crystal ball, so I don't know anything for sure," Merrick said. "I feel like every time I even bring up the possibility that such a group may come together, people don't want to believe it. If we are honest with ourselves, that's our biggest threat right now. If the power goes out, the odds of it happening will only go up."

"Why if the power goes out?" asked Miranda.

"Desperate people do desperate things," Merrick said.

"You're just full of good news," replied Mark.

"Hey, you're the one asking the questions. I'm just answering honestly."

"Yeah, but would it kill you to sprinkle just a little hope in there from time to time?" joked Mark.

"I was just saying that more of these neighborhood security groups spreading is a good thing. That sounds positive to me."

"Yes, very positive." Mark deepened his voice and puffed out his chest to imitate Merrick. "Here is the good news, everybody. When a roving band of armed criminals comes into the area, we should be warned of their presence by the screaming and yelling of all the people they are killing before they get to us. Yes, yes. I am Mr. Positive, and I will be here all week." The entire group roared in laughter.

When the laughter started to die down, Merrick said, "Mark, you crack me up, but for the record, that's not what I sound like." Everyone erupted into laughter again, and for the next half hour, everyone tried their own imitation of Merrick. He knew they were just joking around and letting off some steam, but he couldn't help but turn a little red with embarrassment each time he heard someone mimic him.

CHAPTER 33

Merrick woke up out of a dead sleep when he heard the squawks of the chickens in the coop. He had grown accustomed to the sound over the years. Normally a coyote, raccoon, or possum was attempting to get into the coop, and Lydia would practically shove Merrick out of bed in his underwear to go and defend her precious little flock. He had almost crapped himself on one of these occasions. He had opened the door to the coop expecting to find some little critter, and a fully grown owl came flying out right toward his face. Luckily he had fallen backward in surprise, and the owl flew right past him into the night.

Merrick ran down the stairs in his underwear, rifle in hand, mostly out of pure reflex. He could hear Reese getting up and intending to follow, but at a much slower pace. He hit the main floor of the house and started to go down the basement stairs when he heard someone yell. It sounded like "Don't move!" but it was the sound that immediately followed that caught his attention. *BANG, BANG.*

Merrick paused for a half second in shock after hearing the gunshots, then practically threw himself down the basement stairs. The Hales and their kids were just starting to stir when he reached the bottom. The back door to the basement was open, and he could see someone standing just outside the door. He ran over to the door and found Amy standing there with a rifle in the low ready, facing the chicken coop.

"Amy, are you okay?" asked Merrick. She didn't say anything. "Did you shoot someone?" Again, no response from her. He grabbed her rifle and turned it to see the ejection port cover open.

"Merrick, what's going on?" asked Bruce from behind him.

"I don't know; Amy shot at something. Why don't you try and talk to her and see if you can get something out of her. Once we have a couple more people, we'll check it out." Merrick moved Amy inside the house and took up a position at the open back door.

"Dad," Reese said from behind Merrick. When Merrick turned around, Reese handed him his tactical vest with his equipment on it. He put it on quickly as Reese took up a position at his side. "What do we have?"

"Amy's a little shocked so she isn't saying anything, but she fired a few shots. Not sure at what at this point. Can you grab the thermals?"

"Yeah," Reese said as he turned to get them off Amy's neck. The thermals were normally left with whoever was on guard duty.

Merrick scanned the darkness. It was too dark to tell, but he thought he could see one of the side egg hatches to the coop opened. He didn't want to shine his light on it yet and give away his position, so he waited for the thermals.

"Okay, got them. Do you want me to look, or do you want to do it?" Reese asked.

"You go ahead; just scan nice and slow so you don't miss anything."

"Merrick, Amy said she shot someone," whispered Bruce.

"Okay, thanks. Reese, anything?" Merrick was eager to know what was out there.

"There could be someone prone just in front of the coop, but I'm not sure. It's a bad angle and I can't make it out," Reese said as he looked through the thermals.

After rest of the group slowly gathered in the basement, Merrick gave directions. "Reese, Mark, and Miranda, go out the side door and sweep counterclockwise using the thermals as you go. Ryan, you, me, and Indiana will sweep clockwise. Reese, your team will provide 360 security while my team approaches the coop. Bruce, stay with Amy and the kids in the basement. Lydia, stay on the main level and watch the front. Questions?" Merrick glanced back and forth at everyone. "Okay. Be safe. Let's get it done."

Merrick moved nice and slow with his team around the house. They paused at the corner of the house behind some cover to listen and scan the property.

"Reese, are you guys in position?" Merrick radioed.

"Yes, we've got you covered, and I can definitely see a body down by the coop. The way the body is laying, it looks like he's dead," Reese said, half whispering over the radio.

"Copy. We're moving in. Watch your sectors."

Merrick moved down the slight grade toward the coop. As he got closer, he could see what looked like a male lying facedown on the ground. When he got within thirty feet of the coop, he squeezed the pressure switch to his mounted flashlight. The beam of light cut through the darkness. Almost immediately after he activated his light, the rest of his team members turned on their individual lights. The backyard was now lit up like it was daylight.

Merrick stayed fixed on the male on the ground, and in his peripherals he could see his team continuing to scan the surrounding area. He could now see a handgun lying next to the side of the male who was down on the ground. He kicked the gun to the side so it was well out of reach of the male. He slowly knelt down onto the male's back and could feel the body compress to handle his weight. There was no stiffening of muscles or breathing that he could feel. He quickly slung his rifle onto his back and drew his pistol. With the handgun aimed at the male, he reached down with his left hand and checked for a pulse. There was none. Satisfied that the person was no longer a threat, Merrick holstered his pistol and repositioned his rifle into the low ready.

"The male by the coop is down. Hold positions while we check the coop." Merrick turned and nodded to Ryan to check it with Reese covering him.

"All clear," they said moments later.

"Everything seems clear up here. Reese, take your team and do a quick check of the rest of the property with the four-wheelers and the thermals. Radio anything out of the norm," Merrick said.

"Copy," said Reese.

Merrick flipped the dead male over onto his back. He had been shot two times midchest. There wasn't very much blood, but he was covered in raw eggs. The male was young, maybe sixteen years old. Merrick didn't recognize him as one of the neighborhood kids. The boy's pants were soaking wet almost to his waist.

"Reese, FYI. The male's pants are soaked; he probably crossed the creek."

"Copy. We'll check it out," Reese responded over the radio.

"Be careful," Merrick advised. They had already had too close of a call today.

"Always."

This is not good, Merrick thought. Amy didn't do anything wrong, but he knew she would take it hard. He also knew that somewhere out there was a family who would be waiting for a sixteen-year-old boy to come home. It wouldn't matter that the boy was at fault; they would not be happy.

"Dad, Dad. Two other males running away on the north side of the creek by the bend; should we take them out?" asked Reese.

"Do not engage; let them go. Try and yell to them to meet us at the creek at dawn to talk." Merrick felt sick as his gut start to twist into knots.

A few seconds later Reese said, "Okay, I think they heard me. Do you want us to stay down here?" Merrick looked at his wrist, but there was no watch there. Ryan, seeing the gesture, looked at his own watch.

"Zero three forty," Ryan said.

"Two of you can stay down there and set up good LP/OP positions. Send one back here on the other four-wheeler. I'll send a relief down to you guys in just a few."

"Copy. Not a problem."

"Ryan, I need to go get dressed real fast. If you could handle relieving the team down by the creek so they can get some food and gear up? Have the team that goes down there eat and be ready to stay down there for a few hours. I would like the four-wheelers back up here so we can use them to deploy quickly down there if needed," Merrick suggested.

"I'll take care of it, but don't be so rushed to change. You look pretty good in your skivvies." Ryan chuckled at Merrick's boxers.

"Hey, I was the farthest one away and the first one to get there tonight."

"That is pretty impressive; maybe you being so aerodynamic in those tight boxer briefs was a significant factor," Ryan said as he made a quick running motion.

"You know they did, but don't go stealing my underwear just to be cool like me. See you in a bit." Merrick started walking away when Ryan piped up again.

"Are you going to let the neighborhood know?"

"Yeah. I'll text them when I get upstairs. I'm sure there are at least a few of them who heard the shots and are chomping at the bit to know what's going on."

"I got my phone on me, and they already sent out a few texts asking if anyone knows where the shots came from."

"Okay. I'll get on that right away," Merrick said.

"One last thing," Ryan said somberly.

"What?"

Ryan tilted his head toward the dead kid. "What do you want to do with the body?"

"Let's hold off on burying him and maybe get the body ready to give to the family if they show up. Maybe have it on some kind of litter to be transported down if needed. What do you think?" Merrick wanted someone else to share in making sure they were doing the right thing.

"I agree. I'll talk to you in a bit, but we should be prepared if this thing goes bad," Ryan warned.

"Okay. We'll talk later. Just get things moving."

CHAPTER 34

Merrick texted to the neighborhood: "Hey everyone. We just had a guy on our property. He was stealing some eggs from our coop and when he was confronted, he pulled a gun and we had to shoot him. He looks like he was about sixteen years old. We saw a couple others who were with him run over the north part of our property by the creek. We asked them to meet us by the creek at dawn to discuss what happened. Not sure if they will meet us, but either way there's a good chance they won't be happy about their boy being shot. All teams, please be ready at dawn. If Dale and his team can be to the east side of our property and then Paul with his team to the west to ensure no one tries to get behind our position, I would really appreciate it."

Dale: "We got your back."

Paul: "We'll be ready."

Kenneth: "Not to sound morbid, but can you send us a picture of the boy? Maybe one of us will know who he is or his family."

Merrick: "Good idea, Kenneth. I'll send it in just a bit."

Merrick got dressed and carried his full kit downstairs to get some breakfast because it was going to be a long day. He got there just in time to see Mark and Will leave to go relieve Reese and his team.

"I saw your text and it sounded good," Miranda said. "Want me to go get that photo for you?"

"That would be great. Try and make it as tasteful as possible," Merrick said as he sat down on a barstool and rubbed his temples.

"You okay?" asked Lydia.

"Just a lot going on, and seems like I can't get a break." Merrick felt slightly overwhelmed.

"You're doing great, and we're all very grateful to you." Lydia walked up behind Merrick and put her arms around him.

"Thanks, babe. How's Amy doing?" Merrick asked.

"She'll be okay. She's just taking it hard, you know, because it was a kid stealing eggs."

"I understand. Do you think she'll be ready to hold a rifle and help guard the house in a couple hours? It's one of those 'all hands on deck' kind of days." Merrick felt horrible about Amy, but he needed her.

"I think so," Lydia said.

"I'll try and talk to her after this thing's over with."

Lydia nodded and asked, "Are you going to eat breakfast?"

"Yeah. Oatmeal probably." Merrick's phone buzzed, and he looked down and saw that Miranda had just sent out the text with the dead kid's face attached to it. Merrick thought that if no one showed up in a few hours, it would be nice to have an idea of where the kid lived. The group would then at least have something to go off of when trying to contact the family. They'd also have a place to strike if the family decided to try to do something stupid, or at least more stupid than sending kids to steal eggs in the middle of a mass crisis.

Ryan and Merrick sat at the island and ate breakfast in silence. They'd both agreed to wait until after they were done eating to talk tactics about what they were going to do this morning. Merrick was halfway done with his oatmeal when Reese, and Miranda walked in.

"Hey guys. Get some breakfast, and then I want to hear the details about what you guys saw," Merrick told them.

"We didn't see much. There were two guys running northwest from the creek area. Honestly, if we'd been more than a second or two later, we probably wouldn't have seen them at all," Reese said. Mark and Miranda nodded in agreement.

"We've got lots to do, so please eat. If you don't want to wait, we can talk while you eat," Merrick said, motioning them toward the pantry.

"Okay by me," said Reese.

"We're okay with talking about it now, but I'm not really sure what else we can tell you," said Mark, shrugging his shoulders.

"Could you see muddy footprints on the bank where they crossed?" asked Merrick.

"Yes, definitely," Reese said.

"How many sets of footprints? Did the kid come over alone, or were the other two with him?" Merrick asked.

"What do you think, Mark?" Reese asked. "I thought it looked like too many for just the one kid, but it was hard to tell."

"Now that you mention it, I think the freshest prints were facing the creek, meaning they were probably not made by the kid. So I think they were on our side of the creek," Mark said.

"We have to secure that northern area better. I don't like that a bunch of kids were able to get right up on our doorstep without us knowing it," Ryan said.

"We can definitely try and make it less passable and have some trip-wire devices, but if it's unmonitored, there's only so much we can do," said Merrick. "Tell me about the two you saw running away. Anything you can remember: size, age, clothing, the way they ran."

"Man, it was dark, but I think they were young. Under thirty for sure, but clothes I don't know, dark probably," Mark said.

"That's good. Reese, Miranda, anything else you guys remember?"

"When Reese yelled to them to meet at the creek for a meeting, at least one of them turned his head like he heard it," Miranda said.

"Did either of the guys running away look armed?" Merrick asked.

"Not that I could see," said Mark, looking to Reese and Miranda.

"Don't think so," answered Miranda.

"They definitely didn't have rifles," said Reese.

"Well, this is a crap sandwich, but all those things make it sound like maybe it isn't as bad as it could have been. If they had rifles, they probably would have brought them on a night raid. They're young, so hopefully whoever's in charge of them will understand the situation they put us in and won't blame us for what we did. What I don't like is the other two most likely saw a lot of our property and know that we have a decent number of chickens." Merrick looked over at Ryan, who was now done eating. "Ryan and I are going to be downstairs in the war room looking at the map and coming up with some type of strategy. You're all welcome to join us when you're done, if you want."

Merrick and Ryan put their dishes in the sink and headed down the stairs. The war room wasn't anything special. It was just a basement room with whiteboards and maps on the walls. Merrick had used it for reloading ammo and some minor gunsmithing work. He was an armor for both Glock and AR-15s for the sheriff's office. Over the years he'd built at least a dozen or so ARs for the boys and friends, but he had too many other things going on to really get too much into it.

"So what do you think?" Merrick asked.

"I think it sucks," Ryan said.

"Right, well, other than that?"

"I think there's a 50/50 chance they show. If they don't show, it's probably because they think we'll just shoot them. Then if they do show up, I think it's another 50/50 chance that they try to shoot us," Ryan estimated.

"Sounds about right. So if they want to shoot us, we should probably give them the opportunity," Merrick said in a slow, thoughtful voice.

"You mean like bait them?" Ryan asked.

"Exactly. If they plan to shoot, my guess is they'll stay hidden until they see something to shoot at and then they'll take their shot. If we stay hidden, then they'll just continue to wait. If we give them something to shoot at, it'll at the very least reveal their intentions."

"Sounds good. Are you thinking of setting up a scarecrow? Because by the time we can get one together, we can't really guarantee they won't see us set it up, and they could even shoot the people that go down to put it up," Ryan said.

"What if we get a few of our people set up down there right now before they can get out there? Then we drive a truck down there with the scarecrow set up in the driver's seat. At dawn it'll be too difficult to see through the windshield enough to make out any detail, even with binoculars. Whoever drives it down can scoot the dummy into the driver's seat and lie down on the floor. What do you think?"

"Might work, but what happens if they try to make contact and want to talk? What if they want the body?" Ryan asked.

"I don't really want a face-to-face. I think it's too risky. I think I'll just be prone somewhere in the area and yell back and forth. If they want the body, we'll bring it down in the truck and drop it off. They can get it five minutes after we pull our people back."

"There are still a million things that can go wrong with this, but at least it doesn't sound like a suicide mission anymore," Ryan said.

CHAPTER 35

The morning was still cold, so Merrick had to be careful not to breathe too deeply or the white cloud of his breath would possibly give away his position. He was lying on a green workout mat that was giving him some insulation from the ground. He was on the northwest side of the Albright property, about fifty feet from the bank of the creek. Five others were spread out, forming a rough half circle. Even though he felt fairly confident with his team and two of his neighborhood squads close by and able to give support, he was very aware that even one loss or casualty would be devastating. In the dead silence, it was hard for him not to drift off into thinking of the ripple effects of losing any individual in his group.

He glanced down at his watch. It was 6:10 a.m. Sunup was right around 6:30 a.m. or so, but they wanted to make sure they didn't miss their guests, so they wanted to be a little early. It was dead silent, so there was definitely no missing the sound of the V8 truck slowly making its way through the field, and just to make sure it wouldn't be missed, its headlights were on. With the sound of the truck thundering closer, Merrick used the noise to cover his radio transmission.

"Okay, wake up, everybody. Heads on a swivel. If they are out there once the truck pulls up, they might try to make a move. Do not fire unless you have to or they fire first. We're trying to appease these people, not wipe them out. If you see something, call it out on the radio, but do not give away your positions."

A few moments later, the noise of the truck seemed deafening as it pulled up behind him. He felt a slight sense of panic, thinking the person in the vehicle might be crouching low in the truck and not see him. The vehicle came to a stop ten feet to his right, and the engine shut off. The world again returned to complete silence. He scanned and waited a full minute before trying to communicate.

"Hello! I don't know if you're there, but we don't want any trouble with you. Your boy was taking some eggs from our chicken coop and had a gun. We feel horrible about his death and wanted to reach out to you to make amends. Can you hear me?" Merrick had to pause and take a breath every few words because he was trying to yell as loudly and clearly as possible. He didn't know how many times he was going to have to do it, but he hoped not too many. For some reason, the yelling felt exhausting. He made a mental note of the time and decided he would try again in five minutes.

He yelled twice more, each time waiting five minutes in between. Just when he was almost sure the people were going to be a no-show, he heard someone yell back.

"Is he dead?" a male voice yelled.

"Yes," Merrick yelled back.

There was a silence for a few seconds before any response was heard. "We don't want any trouble either. Boys shouldn't have been on your property," the voice yelled again.

"We understand. Can I call you rather than yelling?" Merrick wasn't sure how long he could keep yelling like this and not lose his voice.

"Okay, you ready."

"Ready."

"360-555-3656."

"Got it. I'm calling." Merrick dialed the number into his phone.

"Hello?" the voice answered.

"Hi. My name is Merrick. Thanks again for talking to us."

"Well, honestly we didn't know what to do there for a while. We were afraid you'd think we're all a bunch of thieves and want to shoot us all."

"No, we don't want any trouble with you and just wanted to say we're sorry for your loss. What's your name, sir?"

"I apologize. I'm Jake McGuire. The boy was Sean, my daughter's son. He came out here to stay with us when all the trouble started. Did you say your name was Merrick?" Jake asked.

"Yes, I did."

"I think one of my neighbors was telling us about you."

"Good things, I hope?" Merrick said, half joking and half-serious. He had made plenty of people upset over the years doing his job as a police officer. Normally when someone remembered him by name, it wasn't always good.

"He said you were a cop and started up a neighborhood security team, and he wanted to do the same thing over here," said Jake.

"That's me." Merrick felt a little relieved.

"Let me tell ya, those boys were not supposed to be at your place. There are a few vacant homes in the area, and the boys have been trying to check them for supplies during the day. I didn't know they even went out last night till they came running in this morning yelling and waking us all up. Believe you me, they are in trouble." From the tone in Jake's voice, Merrick believed him.

"Well, don't be too hard on them. They already lost a family member. I have a feeling it's a lesson that'll stick with them for the rest of their lives. We still feel horrible about Sean," Merrick said.

"Okay. So what do you want to do now?" asked Jake.

"We brought Sean's body down with us. We can bury him if it'd be easier for you, but we wanted to give you the chance to bury him and do your own service for him."

"I think we would like to bury him; that is very thoughtful of you."

"We can do this one of two ways. We can leave his body here for you to come and get once we pull back. Or some of you can walk over with your hands up and get him now. Just so you know, we didn't know if you'd be violent this morning, so we had some people in the area just in case things went bad."

"I feel a bit better knowing who you are now, and I don't mean any disrespect, but I think my people would feel better coming over there if they knew you'd pulled your people back," Jake said.

"I understand and would feel the same way. We'll leave him here and you can get him in about ten minutes or so once we've gone. Just do me a favor. Make sure that no one that comes on our property to get him is armed and that none of your people come into our neighborhood again without calling first, okay?" Merrick didn't want to ever have to deal with this family again.

"Of course. Thanks for being understanding," said Jake.

"You too, and again we're sorry about Sean."

"Thanks."

"Bye." Merrick hung up the phone and picked up his radio. "Good news, everyone. I think we have everything settled. We're leaving the body here by the creek, and they're coming to get it in about ten minutes once we leave. Ryan and Reese, you two stay put and keep an eye on them while they get the body. They should be unarmed. The rest of you can crawl out of your positions, but stay low till you make the midpoint of the lower pasture. I'm going to unload Sean, and we'll meet you there with the truck and give you a ride back up. Questions?"

Merrick listened for a few seconds to make sure no one had any questions, then he started to slowly low-crawl in reverse. He low-crawled to the back of the truck and put the mat and his rifle in the back. He pulled Sean's body out of the truck and dragged it to the side so it would be clear of the truck. He crawled in the back and lay down in the bed, then banged twice on the side of the truck. A few moments later, the engine roared to life, and the truck slowly backed up and made its way to the midway point in the property.

CHAPTER 36

"Amy, how are you holding up?" Merrick asked.

"Honestly, horrible."

"I like honest."

"I know you do." Amy looked up at Merrick and asked, "How do you do it?"

"Are you talking about how I make my amazing orange oatmeal or how I cope with shooting people?" Merrick smiled. "I wish there was a secret, but honestly, everyone deals with it differently because everyone has their own moral dilemma they have to work through. You could tell me what you're thinking, and I'll try to help you sort it out."

Amy looked down then up again, but still didn't seem ready to talk.

"Or I could tell you a story about how I dealt some of the messed-up stuff I've had to deal with," Merrick offered.

"Let's start there."

"Okay, but some of this is classified, so if you tell anyone, I'll probably have to kill them."

"I'll take the chance."

"Okay then. So I was on my first deployment to Iraq, and I was a young dumb kid who just got out of basic training. I was in a military police unit back then, and we were doing route clearance and convoy security runs. I was the gunner in our truck turret and had a .50 caliber machine gun. We had only been there for a couple weeks and we were getting shot at all the time, but they were little pop shots and you couldn't always see who was doing it or where the shooter was. The first time I fired and actually hit something was at these guys who were shooting at us from a rooftop. The .50 ripped them apart. When we got back to the FOB, I had a host of hardened soldiers giving me high fives. It was the first time I had taken someone's life, and the whole thing didn't bother me a bit."

"Maybe this won't help," Amy interrupted.

"I'm getting to a point. Give me a chance?"

"Okay, Rambo. Continue."

"Yes, thank you. Well, back to the story. Same deployment, we get word that other units were getting hit when they stopped for random people who were walking in front of their convoys. So we were told not to stop, just run them over. Anyway, a week or two after that, we got this intel. We were out and I saw this woman walking toward our convoy holding a baby. I knew as I saw her that she's getting too close and I have a clear shot." Merrick stopped and then, with some emotion in his voice, said, "But I didn't shoot."

"Of course—you couldn't." Amy reached over and put her hand on Merrick's.

"No, you don't understand. The woman threw the baby in front of one of our trucks and it exploded. It was an IED and it killed two guys—guys I knew in my unit. No one blamed me, but you bet I blamed myself. It bothered me for weeks, and I was second-guessing myself and not sleeping. I kept thinking that if I'd just shot her like I knew I should have, those guys would still be alive. This morning you did the right thing. You shot to protect yourself and all of us. If you hadn't shot and you or someone else got hurt, I bet you'd be feeling a whole lot worse than you do now."

"But why did it have to be a kid? If he was a tattooed criminal, I wouldn't feel like this," Amy said with tears in her eyes.

"You're probably right, and if that woman with the baby was an adult male with a package, I probably wouldn't have hesitated to shoot him either. You faced a hard decision today, and in a split second you made the right choice. A lot of people hesitate like I did. I still remember those guys who died, but I've come to terms with my part in it. From then on, I realized that I needed to err on the side of the safety of those I care about most. People had to die for me to learn that lesson. Everyone here is proud of you. They know that when the moment comes to making a hard decision, you can make it and you won't hesitate to protect us. Even that guy's family today didn't blame you. They knew he was sneaking around on someone's property in the middle of the night when the whole world is falling apart. They would have shot him if he was doing that same thing at their place."

"Thanks. Your story finally did come around."

"No problem."

"How did you get over not shooting that woman?" Amy asked.

"Shooting a few more people."

Amy gave Merrick a questioning look, not sure if he was joking again.

"Yes, I am serious," Merrick said. "Shooting a few regular bad guys got my confidence back. I had to prove to myself that I could make the right decision again. Getting back in the saddle and shooting more of those insurgents was the best medicine I could have gotten."

"You know, you're kind of a messed-up cookie."

"That's the general consensus, I believe."

"Half the time you have these incredible insights and you're kind, then the other half of the time, you're like a machine with no feelings at all."

"Don't try and figure me out. You'll just end up more confused. Ask Lydia. She'll tell you." Merrick winked at Amy.

"Well, thanks again."

"Anytime you need a few more messed-up morbid stories, you let me know. I am here to help."

CHAPTER 37

It was game night at the Albright home. Everyone was gathered around playing a heated game of Catch Phrase. Mark had suggested that an easygoing event might help Amy get back into being social again instead of isolating herself, where there was nothing to do but think about the incident. Merrick was happy that Mark was right. At first Amy seemed quiet, but after a few rounds, she was laughing and totally normal.

"Blue small magical creatures," Bruce said excitedly.

"Smurfs," Lydia guessed.

"Yes!" Bruce said as he passed the game to Ryan.

"Okay, it's a kind of metal that you use to make your clothes less wrinkly."

"Iron," Merrick guessed as the beeping sped up significantly. Ryan quickly passed the game to Amy.

"This is what you call someone who is really tight with their money."

"Cheap," guessed Miranda.

"Yes, but there's more to it," Amy said quickly.

BUZZ.

"Ah, cheapskate. We were so close," said Amy.

"Close, but that's three rounds in a row your team's lost. I don't think you can really say it's a fluke and—" Mark was cut off by the room going dark. Cell phones immediately came out to be used as flashlights.

Merrick walked to the kitchen to retrieve a flashlight from a drawer. He clicked it on and said, "I'll check the breakers. Lydia, can you grab some candles?"

"Indiana, come along and make yourself useful," Lydia said.

Mark followed Merrick out to the garage and waited till they were out of earshot of everyone. "Do you think the power is out for good?"

"I think if it is out, there are definitely no crews out there fixing anything right now. Don't worry, though; we'll manage without it," Merrick said calmly.

"I'm not worried about us, but I am about everybody else. People have been on edge, but they haven't really been hurting for the basic essentials of life. With no power, people's water, freezers, heat, lights, and phones will be gone. I think we're going to see a big shift to people being more desperate," Mark explained.

Merrick finished checking the breakers and closed the panel. He'd known Mark for years and could tell he was getting to some kind of a point. "So what are you thinking?" he asked.

"I think we need to calm the craziness around us before it gets out of control. We should have another neighborhood meeting. We need to discuss how we're going to communicate if we can't rely on cell phones. We need to have a plan on how to address people's needs like food and water if they're running low."

"It's a good idea, but I think we should walk in with a suggested plan and not try to talk it out at the meeting."

"Okay. I think we should spend the rest of tonight brainstorming with everyone, and since people's phones are probably still working right now, it's the best time to send everyone a message about having a meeting tomorrow."

"Well, you convinced me. I'll send the message right now. I'll probably try and have the meeting during the day rather than at night so we don't have to meet in the dark." Merrick pulled out his phone and started typing a message to the neighborhood as he followed Mark back into the house. Lydia and Reese were in the process of lighting a few candles and placing them around the living space.

"Mark, you want to share your idea with everyone?" Merrick said as they walked into the family room, where everyone was gathered.

"Sure. Well, with the power going out, things are going to get a lot harder for most people. We're going to have a neighborhood meeting tomorrow to talk about how we're going to communicate if cell phones aren't a viable option anymore. We're also going to talk about what everyone's going to do for water or food once people run out. We wanted to have a discussion to try and think about possible solutions."

"I'm not sure what kind of solutions we can really come up with for food. We can't buy it or grow it right now, so whatever they have, they have to make it stretch. We can't give away our food to feed everybody," said Lydia.

"No, but we can't stick our heads in the ground and pretend starving people aren't going to be a serious problem. I think we need to be open about it. That way, when someone's running low on food or whatever, we're talking to them rather than shooting them," said Mark.

"I agree. I think it's good to get it all out in the open, and I think there are some temporary solutions we can think of that'll help people, at the very least, last a little bit longer," Merrick said. "Let's start with water since that's probably going to be the most pressing issue for everyone. Mark, do you want lead the discussion, and does someone else want to take to take some notes?"

"I'll take notes," said Amy. Lydia walked over and handed her a notepad.

"Okay, Mark, go for it," said Merrick.

"So how can we help people get drinkable water now that there is no power?" asked Mark.

"Everyone out here is on a well. I think the best option is having people use a piece of PVC pipe on a rope to dip into their existing well. The water is safe to drink as is, and they wouldn't have to waste fuel to boil it or to filter it. It is basically going back to the old-school well-and-bucket method," Ryan said.

"What kind of materials would we need for that, and how much labor would that involve?" asked Merrick.

"We would just need a few feet of PVC per household, some glue, and a hundred feet of rope per house. Then we just need to help open the cap to the well," Ryan explained.

"I think that would supply good safe water, but doing that for everyone is going to be tedious. Drinking water out of a rain barrel system is pretty safe, especially if it doesn't sit for long. With how often it rains here, you can get a ton of water that way," Merrick said.

"I like the rain barrel idea because it solves not only the drinking water issue, but people need water to flush their toilets and wash with," Bruce added.

"It doesn't do a lot of good, though, if people are getting sick from the rainwater. Then we have a whole other issue on our hands," said Ryan.

"What about using bleach to purify the rainwater? The water's pretty clean as is, but it would only take a few drops of bleach to make a gallon of water safe to drink. Literally one container of bleach would purify a year's worth of water for an entire household, and everyone has bleach," suggested Lydia.

"Good point, babe. What materials would we need to setup a rain barrel system?" said Merrick.

"The hardest thing to get is the barrel," said Ryan.

"I know we have a couple barrels, but I think we could get people to use things other than a barrel. We could have them use any large container like a storage tote, and everyone has those. Then they just use a bucket to collect water out of it. Then they can purify water they want to drink with bleach, like Lydia said," Merrick said.

"Done," Mark said. "Let's roll with that. I had a thought about food. What if we get everyone to agree to go into the three homes that are vacant to check for food supplies? These supplies can be stored somewhere safe and be given as needed to families who are in need. What do you think?"

"I think that's great for the food that'll last, but there's probably a bunch of food in the fridge and the freezer in those houses that is going to go bad. We should hand out all that perishable food to people that are starting to run low now," said Merrick.

"I feel like all of this is just a short-term Band-Aid on the problem. Once the food runs out, people are going to be screwed. The only way we can change that is if people start gathering and producing food," said Ryan.

"We are in the beginning of winter, so any producing or gathering is going to be pretty minimal," Merrick said. "Sure, it will help to plant gardens in the spring, but that is so far away right now. We are on ten acres, and I am not sure we could produce enough meat and veggies to sustain all of us indefinitely. We need to help everyone hold out long enough with what we have till the government and society can recover."

"What if that never happens?" Ryan asked, raising his eyebrows.

"Come on; while something of this scale hasn't happened here in the US, it has happened in other places. We'll recover eventually; it just takes time. I even think there could be a silver lining," Mark said.

"This I got to hear. What is the silver lining to the collapse of our nation and so many people dying?" Ryan said sarcastically.

"I'm not saying this isn't absolutely horrible or that we are even out of the woods yet, but having to fight to survive changes people. The United States was broken long before the collapse. Ask anyone; we all know it. For at least fifty years, the level of corruption has been going up and up, while the efficiency of the government has been going down. Washington's asking for more and more money, but never fixes anything. This is a chance for change; that's all I'm saying. Right now people aren't distracted by sports teams or celebrity gossip. They just want to be safe and the people they care about to be safe. People's priorities and political views are being changed by this whole thing. A lot of people were on the fence about guns and thought they weren't necessary and that the government would take care of everything. Once this thing ends, I don't even think it'll be an argument anymore. Hopefully, the country will be motivated enough for real change so we can put an end to the political soap opera crap and get some real leaders in Washington." Mark's voice was full of passion.

"Mark, you surprise me. That's never going to happen. You know that all the top-level politicians are in some undisclosed bunker somewhere eating fresh T-bone steaks and watching TV right now, courtesy of the taxpayers. They'll emerge from this thing without missing a single meal, and they'll go right back to being in power and probably vote in higher emergency taxes to pay for rebuilding and relief efforts. Change will not be coming from them," said Ryan.

"Maybe you're right about the politicians, but mainstream America will be changed, and I hope that it motivates us to put in some good people and make changes," Mark replied.

"If this happened during the generation of the Great Depression, sure, they might be able to bounce back, but not our generation or, God save us, the millennials. Most of them can't even make mac and cheese. That's why they looted everything and the system came crumbling down. People were too dependent on the government and having everything they wanted handed to them on a silver platter. Self-reliance is almost nonexistent, and people don't have the fortitude to endure prolonged hardships. Our system was so fragile that you could have just pulled the pin on food stamps and there would've been riots in every major city in the US. I think we're in this for the long haul. I'm honestly not sure if there's going to be an America when this thing is over," said Ryan.

"Let's try and stay focused here, folks," Merrick interrupted. "We can debate possible theories of the future later. Let's focus on solutions to our immediate problem. It might be a short-term solution, but it's better than doing nothing. If the only thing we did was tell people to ration their food, we'd be in a better position."

Everyone but Ryan nodded their heads in agreement. Merrick looked over at him with one eyebrow raised; Ryan rolled his eyes and then nodded.

CHAPTER 38

It was early in the morning, and Merrick was relaxing in his warm bed and letting his mind drift. The sudden ringing of his cell phone felt more startling then gunfire. He fumbled to answer the phone quickly just to stop the noise.

"Hello?"

"Merrick, it's Chris Richardson." Chris was a longtime friend of Merrick's and had saved his life just a few weeks before by running over a gangbanger who had been about to shoot him. He could tell from the hushed, serious tone of Chris's voice that this was not a social call.

"Chris, what's going on?" Merrick said, sitting up in his bed.

"My neighborhood is being overrun. I just didn't know who else to call." Chris's voice sounded desperate in a way Merrick had never heard before.

"Overrun? What? By who? How many people? Paint me a picture."

"Rough guess, at least fifty armed guys. They're taking homes by force and killing anyone who resists. I heard some serious gunfire to the west a few nights ago and should've checked it out. I was hoping whatever it was wouldn't come my way, or at least I thought I would have some advanced warning and be able to deal with it then. I was stupid."

"Okay, can you get out?"

"That's just it. I'm pretty sure they've got me boxed in."

"What about going through a fence or a yard? Don't just think roads." Merrick was trying to think of a way to help his friend.

"Maybe. The ground's pretty wet, and all I have is our Forester. I don't know if it'll make it all the way through that open field, and even if I don't get stuck, I'll be a sitting duck going through there."

"It's your call, but from what you're telling me, your window is closing pretty fast, and I don't see a whole lot of other options. It is pretty dark, so if you drive with your lights out, they might be too distracted to notice you."

"No, you're right, and I hate to ask this, but is there any way you can come down here and maybe just engage them even for a minute as a diversion? Then I'll make a break for the field," Chris asked.

"Chris, I don't think you don't have time to wait for me to get out there. Absolutely best case, I'm twenty minutes out, but even then it's super risky. I'd be driving out there blind and could run into them or some other trouble before I even get to you. I just can't risk it, not without some kind of security element coming with me. I am sorry." Merrick felt horrible telling this man, who had saved his life, that he couldn't help.

"No, I get it. I think I'm going to try to make a break for it, but we don't have any other family in the area. Do you think I could come to your place just until we figure out where to go?"

"Chris, if you can make it out to me, we'll figure something out. Even if it isn't at our place, we'll find you something."

"You're a lifesaver, man." Chris sounded relieved.

"Just hurry up and get your butt over here."

"Okay, thanks again. See you in a bit." Chris hung up. Merrick put the phone down, got out of bed, and grabbed his pants.

"Dad, what's going on?" asked Indiana.

"A friend of mine at work might be headed here. His neighborhood is being overrun by a group of armed men." Merrick rubbed his eyes.

"Seriously?" Indiana asked in surprise.

"Where does he live?" asked Reese.

"In Orchards, just off of 99th Street."

"I'm surprised you told him he could come here," said Lydia.

"The guy is a friend, he saved my life just a few weeks ago, and he has nowhere to go. Right now the plan is for him to get here, but we can figure out where they will be staying once they are safe. We're having that neighborhood meeting today, and maybe I can get permission to put him in one of the empty houses." Merrick started to get dressed.

"What about my parents? Should they head this way too?" Merrick could hear the slight hurt in Lydia's voice that he was so quick to give his friend Chris a place to stay but not her parents.

"Babe, he has no choice. He has to leave his place; there are guys with guns coming in his neighborhood as we speak. He is in a horrible position and might not make it out of there. Then he still has the trek here. Right now your parents are safe. For them to try to cross now is a big, unnecessary risk."

"Having them wait till there are armed guys surrounding their neighborhood doesn't sound like a great plan, either," Lydia argued. "No matter what, it is going to be dangerous. If they come over now, they at least have time to pack and the immediate area around them is clear."

Merrick felt stuck. He wanted to help his in-laws, but he didn't want to start the precedent of taking in family and friends into their home.

They didn't have the resources or the space for that. He knew Lydia would continue to stress out about her parents, and he knew that he might alienate some group members by telling Chris that he could come to the house, let alone Lydia's parents. "If you want to talk to them about it, that's fine, but make sure you don't sugarcoat how risky it is. I will also leave it up to you to break the news to the group."

Lydia was already on her phone calling her parents before Merrick even finished.

"Reese, Indiana, please go around and knock on people's doors quietly, and tell them that I just got some information that I need to share with everyone. Make sure they know we are not in danger and I will brief them over breakfast at six o'clock. Kids can sleep in if they want."

"Sure," Indiana said as he ran out of the room.

Merrick finished getting dressed and could hear Lydia still on the phone with her parents as he headed downstairs. He knew she would do her best to talk her parents into making the dangerous trek out to their place. If something happened and they never made it, she would be a wreck. Merrick knew that people could work through grief if they knew the details, but with the unknown, it was harder to get closure.

Merrick walked into the kitchen to get started on cooking breakfast, but he found himself just sitting on a barstool and trying to sort through everything. In the last few minutes, he'd made several impulsive gut decisions that had a high probability of coming back to bite him. He had two families headed toward his place, and he hadn't consulted with his group or the neighborhood yet. It'd be a hard sell, and the fact that the families were potentially on their way already wouldn't help his position. The cherry on top of the whole thing was that their worst fears of a lawless horde were real. As hard of a sell as it was going to be to convince everyone to let a few perfect strangers move into the neighborhood, it was going to be even worse convincing everyone about what to do with this new threat.

"Morning! So what's all this hubbub about? Reese is unusually tight-lipped about it," Ryan said as he came into the kitchen.

"Don't get your hopes up; it isn't good."

"Good news from you? We gave up on that long ago, remember. So what is it?" Ryan asked.

Merrick wanted to tell Ryan to just wait and that he would tell everyone at the same time, but he knew that Ryan liked having information a bit sooner than everyone else. He guessed that it made Ryan feel important and gave him a little more time to process everything. He decided to just give Ryan what he wanted; it didn't cost him anything, and if it made him happy, why not?

"A friend of mine from the sheriff's office just called. His place was overrun with a large group of armed men moving through the area."

"Is he all right? How big was the group, and what part of town does he live in?"

"He was okay when he called, but he's not sure if he can get out. He guessed there are more than fifty from what he could see, and he lives in the east Orchards area." Merrick decided to leave out the part that his friend might be on his way to the house.

He started getting all the ingredients out for his world-famous French toast. He wanted to butter everyone up, both figuratively and literally, for the news. As he got things ready, he watched Ryan's face process everything and hoped Ryan would come to the same conclusion he had only a few minutes earlier.

"That's fairly close. I mean, it's a few miles away, but still it's close." Ryan looked deep in thought.

"Yep."

"We're going to do something, right? We can't just let them roll this way. What are you thinking?"

Ryan's stock went up a little bit more in Merrick's mind, and he let himself hope that maybe it wouldn't be as hard of a sell as he thought it would be. Maybe everyone would understand the danger of this looming threat and that they couldn't afford to simply pray that they would be spared. They would have to ensure their safety with the only language a violent mob understood—and that was overwhelming violence.

CHAPTER 39

"Is your friend okay? What's he going to do?" asked Miranda once Merrick recounted the information he got from his phone call with Chris.

"He's going to try and drive out of there and possibly head this direction. He had nowhere to go. I thought maybe we could ask the neighborhood if he could stay in one of the empty houses."

"Does he have any kids?" asked Amy.

"Yes, he has a little girl. Sorry I didn't ask all of you first," Merrick said.

"We understand," Miranda said. "He could have not called at all and just shown up here anyway."

"Yeah, don't feel bad," Amy chimed in. "It's just one family. I'm sure we can get the neighbors to agree to put them up in one of the vacant houses."

Merrick looked at Lydia and said, "Well, it might not be just one family; it might be two. I will let Lydia explain."

Lydia cleared her throat. "Some of you know that I have been talking with my parents, who live in the Felida area. Once I heard Merrick on the phone this morning talking to his friend about this massive group moving around and taking over entire neighborhoods, I reached out to my parents to let them know. My dad is a retired cop out of Portland, but the neighborhood where he lives is pretty liberal and so there are not too many people with guns. With Merrick's friend Chris coming over already, I thought we could house them in the same vacant house and get two shooters at the same time instead of one." Lydia's tone was positive and confident.

"Oh," said Mark.

"Why are they headed over now? Is something happening over there too?" Amy asked.

Merrick jumped in, "As far as we know, there's no significant activity over there, but we are completely blind, and we really haven't seen or heard what has been going on out there for a few days now." He knew that while none of them had family that lived close by, plenty of them had friends in the area they had to be concerned about. He hated even thinking that maybe his position was allowing him to get away with things that other group members wouldn't be able to.

"If the neighborhood doesn't want to let them stay in the empty houses, do you have a backup plan?" Merrick's heart sank a little when he heard Miranda ask this question. She was asking in a nice way if Merrick and Lydia were planning on letting all these people stay at the house. Miranda knew full well that not even the leader of the group could give the okay for someone who wasn't in the group to move into the house without a majority vote. So her question was more "Are we still following the rules or not?"

Merrick didn't blame her. In the lawless, crazy world they currently were in, the security and stability that came from group rules and schedules gave them all comfort.

"I am pretty confident that we can get permission to move them into an empty house," Merrick finally said. "There aren't too many downsides to having trustworthy people we know living in these empty houses."

"Last night we talked about extending our neighborhood food supplies by using the food in these empty houses. I doubt that either of these families will bring too many supplies with them, and they'll need any supplies that are in the houses. So it will put more of a strain on our neighborhood resources," said Mark.

"That's a fair point, Mark," Merrick admitted. "I know that Lydia's parents had their car prepped and loaded with a good amount of supplies. I have no idea what Chris is bringing, but I can guarantee they are all coming with their own battle rifles and a lifetime of experience. Chris is no joke. He was in a high-speed special operations unit in the service and is on our SWAT team at the sheriff's office. I feel bad that this might put more of a strain on the food supply issue, but right now this roving horde is our top priority. If both of these families make it here—and that's a big if—we'll have two more skilled fighters to add to our fighting force."

"Wait a second. Are we really talking about going head-to-head with this group? When we formed this group, I remember that one of the core values was that it was about defending each other, not about becoming some vigilante militia. I mean, going up against more than fifty people seems crazy, right?" asked Lori.

"That is something we are going to have to talk about, but taking this group out before they can attack us is an act of defense. I don't want to attack this group, but my military instincts tell me we should. I know this sounds scary, but right now we know where they are. If we wait a few weeks, who knows what direction they'll travel or if their numbers will increase. If we do it right, we can take them out with one well-planned ambush. A few stragglers might survive, but they'll be cut down to a manageable size.

Neighborhoods like ours could then defend themselves against anyone that survived." Merrick did not like the idea even as he said it.

"But if we're going to go through all the trouble of setting up the ambush, shouldn't we try to just eliminate them entirely?" asked Ryan.

"Part of setting up a good ambush is anticipating your enemy's retreat and building in additional ambushes to wipe out even more, but the risky part is advancing through the enemy and clearing buildings. That can be costly. Getting everyone is not worth losing our own people. If we can get some good intel, we should be able to pull off this ambush with little risk to our own people," said Merrick.

"How many shooters do we need for the kind of ambush you're talking about?" asked Mark.

"As many as possible is the short answer. The more shooters we have, the more it'll limit any possible counterattack and lessen the chances that they could scatter or slip away. Ideally, I would like to have our neighborhood and the surrounding neighborhoods help us with this and get at least seventy-five shooters."

Everyone was silent for a little while. Merrick felt conflicted about the whole thing and guessed most did too.

"I'm not trying to pressure anyone, but we're under a time crunch if this operation is going to have a chance, and we have to get some things in motion ASAP. So, unless there are other questions, I think we should vote as a group if this is the course of action we want to take." Merrick normally could read his group pretty well, but he was unsure how everyone would vote.

Before Merrick could call for a vote, Ryan spoke up. "I don't want to leave the safety of this home any more than any of you, but we can't let a threat like this just walk away. Just think of what would happen if we got a call right now that this group attacked a house in this neighborhood. Right now we can make our plan and decide where and when we want to attack them. If we don't do this, they could decide to attack us, and it will be us waking up in the middle of the night surrounded and with nowhere to go, just like Merrick's friend."

Merrick was grateful for Ryan's words. He could tell by the look in people's faces that they were more determined than they had been just a minute ago.

"Thanks, Ryan. Anyone else want to say something or have a question?" No one said anything. "Then let's vote. All those in favor of purposing a coordinated ambush at the neighborhood meeting today?"

Everyone raised their hand.

"Well," Merrick said, "it looks like this operation is a go."

"We should totally come up with a cool name like they always do for military operations," Reese said. "Like Operation Desert Storm, Operation Just Cause, Operation Red Dawn . . ."

"Okay, bud, I tell you what. You boys agree on a name, and as long and it's not really stupid, we'll roll with it."

"Seriously, it's going to be something epic like Operation Showdown, Operation Jailbreak Justice, Operation . . ."

"Okay, how about you guys take it somewhere else and let us know when you're ready for the big unveiling."

CHAPTER 40

Merrick knew the saying "A picture is worth a thousand words," but he also knew a thousand words wouldn't even touch the amount of information contained on a single map. Ryan and the others were looking at the biggest map of the Orchards area that Merrick had. They were strategizing and thinking of possible places to plan their ambush.

Merrick recognized that it was a little bit foolish to try to plan too much at this point. They needed two things before they could choose their battlefield: a fighting force and accurate, reliable intelligence on the enemy's location. That was why he was busy sending out a group text message to everyone in the neighborhood and letting the other members pore over the map. He told everyone he had received information about a large, violent group in the area, and he wanted to try to invite as many of the surrounding neighborhood representatives to come to the meeting this afternoon as possible.

He also warned Tom at the neighborhood entrance that he might have two separate sets of friends arriving at the front at some point and that he would prefer if they were allowed to come back to his place with being shot at.

Danger Zone started to play, and Merrick saw the call was from Tom.

"Merrick, one of your friends just showed up at the gate in a red Subaru Forester and is headed your way in a hurry. He has a female who's shot and doesn't look too good."

"Got it. Thanks, Tom." Merrick hung up the phone and jumped into action.

"Bruce! Get the medic bag! We've got one coming in with a gunshot wound. Reese, grab the gate. Lydia and Mark, get the table cleared and prepped."

"Do we know anything about the patient?" asked Bruce.

"It is Chris's wife, Andrea. Tom said she looks like she got shot and didn't look good. Just do what you can and let us know what we can do to help you."

"Okay," Bruce said, but he looked horrible.

"Are you okay?"

"Just nervous out of my mind is all," Bruce said with a fake smile.

"You'll do fine. No one expects miracles; just do your best. You can have whoever you want to assist, but this is your show, doc."

"Merrick!" Ryan yelled from outside.

HONK, HONK, HONK. A red Subaru turned sharply through Merrick's front gate and skidded to a stop in the driveway right next to the front door. Merrick could see Andrea slumped over in the passenger seat with a gunshot wound to the right side of her abdomen. It looked like Chris was trying to hold pressure on the wound as he drove.

Ryan and Reese ran to open the car door and started to pull her out as Merrick arrived with a fabric stretcher. As Chris killed the engine, Merrick could hear the sound of a baby crying from the back seat. Chris got out and, with an unsteady walk, started to make his way around the front of the vehicle. When Chris saw Andrea's limp body being pulled out of the front seat, he fell to his knees and started to sob.

The group left Chris outside and carried Andrea inside, where they were met by Miranda, Lydia, and Bruce. Everyone helped lower Andrea down to the table, which was covered with a large thick piece of plastic. Bruce had laid out a whole display of surgical tools, and he, Mark, and Lydia started to cut off Andrea's clothes, exposing the area around the wound.

Bruce looked up and with a look told Merrick exactly what he was thinking: Andrea wasn't going to make it. Merrick nodded and walked outside to check on Chris.

He found Chris exactly where he'd left him: on his knees at the front of the SUV, sobbing. "I thought we were clear, but they . . ." Chris kept sobbing without looking up.

Merrick noticed he didn't hear the baby crying anymore and then saw Amy walking around the front yard with the eight-month-old, who had calmed down.

Merrick knelt down and put his arms around his friend. He didn't say a word. There was nothing he could say in the moment to lessen the hurt of the loss. All he could do was be there and make sure his friend knew he wasn't alone.

After a long while, the sobbing stopped. Merrick patiently waited for his friend to decide when the silence was going to be broken.

"Is she gone?" Chris asked. Merrick looked at his friend and nodded slowly. Chris collapsed on Merrick, gripping his shirt tightly in his fist and sobbing again. Merrick couldn't help but feel his friend's pain and began crying with him.

After several minutes, Chris pulled himself away from Merrick and fought to compose himself enough to ask a question: "Is the baby okay?"

"She's fine. Amy has her." Merrick gestured to Amy walking with the baby in the front yard. Chris let out a huge groan and sobbed again. Merrick looked at his friend, confused.

"She started crying when Andrea got shot and I . . . I couldn't look to see if she was . . . I just knew I'd break if she . . ." Chris said as he fought back the tears.

Lydia came out with a glass of water and a piece of French toast for Chris.

"Thanks, babe," Merrick said, placing both down on the driveway next to his friend. Lydia silently walked back inside, and Merrick got down and tried to put his hand on Chris's back.

"Just give me a minute, okay?" Chris said.

"Sure. Chris, I can't believe what you are going through, dealing with losing Andrea, but I can tell you that after the Prairie High School shooting, I went and puked my guts out. Just the thought of losing my kid was so consuming that I almost couldn't function."

Chris didn't respond, but after a while his sobs slowed and eventually stopped completely. When he was somewhat composed, he downed the water Lydia had brought in one breath, but didn't touch the food. He sat silently, staring off into the distance at nothing. Merrick could tell there was something building slowly in his eyes. It was a dark, deep rage.

Merrick knew it was perfectly normal during the grieving process to blame someone for the loss of a loved one, even if there was no one directly to blame. Chris had someone to blame, though, and there would be no law enforcement agency that would be holding those who did it accountable. Without speaking a word, Merrick knew what Chris would want to do. He knew because if his wife was lying lifeless inside, he'd want to do the same thing.

"It's a little cold," Merrick said quietly. "I'm going to get your daughter a blanket. Are you going to be okay for a minute?"

Chris didn't say anything; he just kept looking straight ahead. Merrick got up and leaned into the cab of Chris's car. He grabbed a blanket out of the back seat and, as stealthily as possible, removed the keys from the ignition.

"Amy, let's get the baby warmed up and inside!" Merrick yelled and motioned Amy inside. As he walked in, he could see that Andrea was still on the table, but no one was around her. Lydia immediately walked over to Merrick.

"Can you get all our car keys and put them somewhere out of sight along with these?" Merrick handed over the keys to Chris's vehicle.

"Sure, but why?" asked Lydia.

"Just a feeling. Chris is going to want his pound of flesh."

"Could you for once not talk in riddles and speak plain English?"

"Revenge. He's going to want some serious biblical revenge."

"And you think taking the keys will be enough to stop him?"

Merrick thought about it for a moment. "No, probably not, but hopefully it will at least give me a chance to talk to him before he just takes off."

As if to prove his point, they heard a car door slam hard. Merrick gently pushed Lydia away with the keys and turned to go out the door. As he stepped outside, he came face-to-face with Chris. Before he knew what happening, he was thrown onto his back with his friend kneeling on his chest and gripping him with both hands.

"Where are the keys?" Chris growled. Merrick looked straight up into the eyes of his friend and saw the scariest human being he had ever encountered. The remorseless eyes of murderers or the thoughtless rage of insanity was nothing in comparison to the unstoppable, blazing determination to kill that was in Chris's eyes. Merrick knew this was one enemy he did not want to fight.

"Chris, I promise you I will get you your keys. I just wanted to tell you before you took off that we are in the process of planning an attack on those guys. Since I got your call, I've been trying to pull a small army together to go out there and wipe them out." Merrick tried to sound as calm as possible.

Chris didn't say a word; he just kept a white-knuckle grip on Merrick's shirt. Ryan and Reese were standing at the door with their hands on their weapons, thinking about stepping in, but Merrick waved them off.

"Can I give you a radio before you go so you can feed us information on where they are and what they're doing to help us set up the ambush?" Merrick saw Chris's eyes slowly look down and to the left just for a moment, showing that he was thinking about it. Then his eyes came back and centered on Merrick again.

"You could go and take out a few of their scouts or sentries while I get my team in the area." Merrick paused for a second, then added, "Chris, this way they *all* die." He knew Chris wanted justice for his wife and hoped to slowly draw him back from the bloodlust craze he was in.

Merrick felt Chris's grip on his shirt loosen. "Just get me my keys," Chris said in a low voice.

"Ryan, can you get the keys from Lydia and grab an extra ham radio?" Ryan nodded and stepped into the house. Merrick then turned back to Chris. "Do you need any extra ammo or mags? Food? Water?"

Chris looked at Merrick and back at his vehicle, then gave a slight nod. "I'm good on ammo," he said.

"Reese, grab a few MREs and some water bottles," Merrick said, barely turning to look at Reese.

"I'm not going to wait forever," Chris said. "If you're not in position in twenty-four hours, then I'm going to do this on my own." Merrick knew he meant it.

"I understand, but before you go, let's lay your wife to rest, and you need at least a few minutes with your daughter."

CHAPTER 41

"You okay, Amy?" Merrick walked up to her as she stood with tears in her eyes and soothed Chris's baby.

"I am fine, just fine." Amy did not take her eyes off the baby.

"You sure?"

"I am just sad that this perfect little girl is going to grow up without a mother," Amy said.

"Her name is Mia," Merrick said as he stroked the baby's head. "And maybe if Chris stays around, you could help him out a little bit."

"Is he really going to leave?" Who is going to take care of her?" Amy asked.

"I don't know. He seems hell-bent on going, but let him bury his wife and hold his daughter for a while. I am hoping that will clear his head at least a little bit. You okay watching her for a bit longer? I am going to get things moving on this funeral."

"I could hold her all day." Amy smiled. Merrick smiled back, amazed that in a world that was upside down, she seemed to be in her own bubble.

Merrick left Chris and Amy outside and walked into the house. Everyone stopped their conversations and turned to look at him. Andrea's body still lay on the table.

"Lydia and Miranda, could you clean up Andrea's body a little bit for the funeral? And then Mark, can you make sure Andrea's body is loaded up on a truck when they are done? Bruce, would you mind officiating over the funeral ceremony? Chris may or may not want to say something." Merrick was feeling a bit overwhelmed yet grateful he had friends he could rely on.

"I am not one for speeches but will do my best," said Bruce. Merrick patted him on the shoulder. Everyone went into motion, but Lydia walked over to Merrick.

"How are you doing? Lydia asked.

"Compared to Chris? I just don't know what to do about this armed group. I know that something needs to be done, but I don't want to risk our people to do it."

"Even though it has frustrated me countless times over the years, you have always done what you think is right, no matter how hard it might be. It is one of the things I love about you and that make you, you." Lydia drew Merrick in for a hug.

"So you think we should attack this group?"

"I think you should continue to do what you think is right. I don't know much about tactics, but I trust you. I know you will figure this out, and we will support you in whatever that is." Lydia kissed him.

"Thanks, babe."

"Hey Merrick, do you want everyone to go down to the funeral?" Mark said.

"Let's keep at least two up here on guard duty while we are down doing the service."

"Got it," Mark said.

Merrick slowly walked back outside to Chris, who was sitting on the bumper of his SUV, and took the spot next to him.

"Are you getting ready to bury her?" Chris asked, looking over at Merrick.

"Yes. Lydia is getting her cleaned up a little bit, and then we will be ready."

"I don't know if I can bury her right now." Chris shook his head.

"We can wait till you're ready," Merrick offered.

"I don't know if I will ever be ready."

"If you don't want to see her and just remember her like she was, I understand, but you have to be there. It's your wife's funeral."

"What do I even say?" Tears pooled in Chris's eyes.

"You don't have to say anything if you don't want to. You just have to be there. If you want, I can help you write something up, or you can say whatever comes to you."

"I will go, but I don't want to say anything."

Merrick put his arm around his friend and said, "You don't have to say a word." They sat together silently.

The front door creaked open. "Merrick, we are ready when you are," Mark said quietly.

"Okay. Thanks, Mark. We will be right down." Merrick turned to Chris. "You want to walk down with me?"

Chris nodded. Both of them got up and slowly walked around the house.

Just as they started to go down the hill, they heard honking behind them. Merrick looked back and saw his in-laws at the front gate.

"Dad! It's Grandma and Grandpa!" Indiana yelled as he ran toward the gate with his rifle.

"Chris, sorry; it's my in-laws. Let me go let them in real quick, then we will do this."

"No rush—do your thing," said Chris.

Merrick could see Lydia running to her parents and thought he could almost see her smiling from across the yard. He walked up and gave his father-in-law, Frank, a hug.

"Glad you made it okay. Any problems?" asked Merrick.

"No major issues. We took it slow and stuck to the back roads. There were a couple times when we saw something in the roadway, but we'd just turn around and try a different way. That's why it took us a while," Frank said with his hands on his hips.

"Well, we're glad you're here. Let me introduce you to everyone real quick." Merrick went around and introduced the people who had gathered around them.

"What is going on here?" Frank asked as he eyed the blood trail going from Chris's vehicle into the house. Merrick looked in the direction Frank indicated.

"My friend Chris's wife got shot and didn't make it." Merrick gestured to where Chris was still standing on the front lawn. "We were just about to have her funeral service when you arrived."

"Oh, I am sorry. We didn't mean to interrupt," Frank apologized.

"It's no problem. Why don't you go inside with Lydia and we'll be back up shortly?" suggested Merrick.

"If it's okay, I think we'd like to attend the funeral," Frank said.

Merrick nodded. "I am sure Chris wouldn't mind you being there."

CHAPTER 42

Andrea's funeral was one of the most emotional ones Merrick had ever been to, and he had been to his fair share. Other than Chris, he had been the only one present to even speak with Andrea when she was alive. As he stood and looked down at the grave in his own backyard, at a fairly young healthy woman who had been shot and bled out, he realized that his tears were not only for Chris and his daughter Mia, but also for himself.

The world was a different place now. Life was fleeting. No matter if you were old, young, strong, or sick, it was entirely possible that you could die at any moment with little or no warning. Merrick could see the empathy of those present.

Bruce started the service by talking about Chris's obvious love for Andrea and how their time together had been robbed from them. Merrick almost fell over in shock when Bruce asked Andrea's spirit to guide them and her husband to those who had taken her life. He would have half expected Ryan to make a statement like that, but Bruce was the most passive one in the group. Only a couple of weeks had passed, but he could see how each person was adapting in his or her own way to the new conditions they found themselves in.

Merrick thought of Reese and Indiana and couldn't even remember the last time he had seen them fight since this thing started. Normally they were at each other's throats after being in the same room for more than thirty seconds. For the past few weeks, though, they had been together 24/7 and sleeping right beside each other with no issues. People were changing. He wondered if he had changed as well and how, but was drawn back into the funeral service by Amy.

While holding Mia in her arms, Amy spoke of the sacred bond between a mother and her child and how Mia would always feel the loss of her mother. She also said that Mia was not alone, that she had Chris and a whole family of people who would watch over her and help her grow. When she was done speaking, there were no dry eyes.

Merrick had intended to speak, but as he struggled to say something about Andrea, to say something on behalf of his friend, he could not get out two syllables without sobbing to the point that it took him a full minute to recover. He felt like he had failed his friend for not being able to say anything when Lydia stepped to his side and put her arms around him.

Lydia spoke about how much Andrea had endured by being married to a cop, to someone who had been in the military. Merrick look at her as she lightened the mood with humor, and he realized how resilient she was. He felt like he could breathe again knowing that Lydia had always been the backbone of their family, and she was there now to help him through the horrible nightmare they were facing.

Everyone returned back to the house, staying fairly silent during the sobering introspection that followed most funerals.

Chris walked up to Merrick holding an empty plate and said, "Do you put crack in that French toast? Because it's amazing." Merrick smiled back at his friend and saw that the rage was gone from his eyes.

"It's a special mix of crack and meth that coats the outside and gives it that special flavor. You want some more?" Merrick asked.

"Please," Chris said, but Merrick could tell he was going to say something else.

"If I am going to do any good scouting this thing out," Chris continued, "I will have to leave soon."

"You don't have to go," Merrick said.

"Who else you got?" Chris said, tilting his head slightly. Merrick didn't respond. "I know the area, and I have the skills and experience."

Merrick shook his head, trying to find a reason to keep his friend there and safe.

"Relax," Chris said. "You saved my life already."

"What do you mean?"

"Before the funeral I was in a bad place, but you pulled me back," Chris said, his voice breaking at the end. Merrick grabbed his friend in a big hug.

Merrick served Chris some more French toast and talked about some of the details of scouting out the armed group. Chris then said goodbye to Mia and asked Merrick to keep her safe. Merrick gave his word that he would protect her like his own.

He hated sending his friend out alone into an area full of hostile people. He hoped and prayed he would see his friend again, but the one thing he knew for sure was that the group of criminals who had taken Chris's wife would regret the day they had crossed this man.

CHAPTER 43

The group at the Albright house still had three hours till the neighborhood meeting, and Merrick was hoping to get Chris's first intel report so they could start figuring out their strategy. He lay down in front of the fireplace to relax while he could.

He could feel someone standing over him, so he opened his eyes and saw Mark and Ryan.

"What's up, guys?" asked Merrick.

"Don't you think we should start planning for this thing?" asked Ryan.

"We could try, but without hearing from Chris, it would be almost pointless. We don't know how many guys we are dealing with, what they are armed with, how protected they are, or most of all, if they are even still there. Let's not pour a bunch of energy into something until we know something." Merrick returned his focus to the warmth of the fire and its gentle crackling sound.

A few minutes later, Merrick's alarm went off, indicating it had been two hours since Chris had left. They had agreed that Chris would check in every two hours and give updates.

Merrick found a notepad and a pen, and walked outside to try to get the best reception possible. The metal roof was great 99 percent of the time, but when it came to radio transmissions or cell reception, it stunk.

"Chris, this is Merrick. Do you copy?" Merrick said over the ham radio.

"Wait one" came in over the radio in a hushed tone. Merrick waited but did not feel very patient hearing his friend in a hushed tone. He found himself pacing and looking down every few seconds at the radio, making sure it was still on. He wondered why Chris would be close enough for someone to possibly hear him. Was he trying to take out guards? He hoped not. Without Chris's information, the group would not be able to form any kind of plan.

"All clear. Go ahead for Chris" finally came in over the radio.

"I hope you're being careful out there; we need you. We're trying to put a plan together, and a little information would go a long way."

"Relax. Half of these guys are drunk or passed out. I could sneak up on them in a Mack truck. They're still in my neighborhood, just north of the Prairie View Apartments. I'm in the tree line just north and east of the main body. I'll have to move around a bit to get a better idea of their numbers, but I would guess that their numbers are more like 150 to 200 guys. They have some trucks and supply vehicles that they bring up once they clear a block, and then they load up what they want. They don't seem like they're in a huge hurry to go anywhere. They're just eating and drinking as they go. Most of them looked like they're armed with a rifle or shotgun."

"Have you seen them react to anyone resisting them?" Merrick asked.

"I've only seen one house put up any kind of resistance since I've been here. They surrounded the house and shot the place up pretty good, then breached it from multiple directions at roughly the same time. It's nothing fancy, but against one or two people it's effective."

"Thanks. That's good information. Any technicals or heavy weapons?" Merrick wanted to know how much firepower they had.

"No, just long guns," said Chris.

"It'd be nice to know if they have a base with more assets or if they simply move and bed down wherever they find themselves at night."

"I'm not sure, but I'm not going to get that information by just observing. I might have to ask one of them that directly."

"Just be careful. Our plan is sunk without you. Also, we should figure out how often we're going to communicate. You kind of took off before we hammered out some of the details."

"Yeah, thanks for not trying to stop me. I didn't want to have to hurt you." Merrick could hear the playfulness in Chris's voice again.

"I didn't want that either," Merrick joked back.

"How about I check in with you every even hour on the hour?"

"Sounds great. Eventually it'd be helpful, too, if you scout out some good infill locations," Merrick suggested.

"Got a couple places in mind already: 117th Street and 111th off 152nd Avenue are both good. You're covered by the wood line and have a direct path in. I'll get some on the other sides as I move around," Chris said.

"Okay, thanks. Talk to you in two hours."

"Over and out."

"What did he say?" asked Ryan, who had appeared next to Merrick along with several other group members.

"He hasn't been there that long, but the group is still in the same area, and he said it seems like they're in no hurry to leave. The bad news is they have closer to 150 to 200, including their support units."

"Support units?" Ryan asked.

"They have supply trucks that hold whatever they scavenge from an area."

"I think we should hit their trucks first," Ryan said. "That way it's harder for them to get away ,and they'll be less likely to just abandon all their supplies. Then all we have to do is just surround them and pick them off."

"Downing their vehicles will be one of our main objectives for sure, but I think we should do a couple shaping operations first."

"Shaping operation? What's a shaping operation? Is that a military term?"

"Yes, it's a military term. It's not easy to talk about military tactics and not use the lingo, but I'll try to explain. A shaping operation basically helps you set up the battlefield so you have the ideal conditions for your main objective." Merrick looked around and could tell most of the group still didn't understand. "Okay, you know in *Braveheart* when he insults the English, provoking them, and then sends away their horsemen, making them look weak?"

"Yeah," Ryan said. "Then they used the hidden spears to take out their entire cavalry."

"Bingo. Shaping operation," said Merrick.

"Ah, I see. So in a shaping operation, you're manipulating the enemy to fall into your trap."

"Yes, exactly. So we decide what ideal conditions we want and see if we can manipulate the enemy into it."

"Okay, you lost me again," Ryan admitted. "Don't we just want them dead? How else do we want them?"

"Do you want to engage when they're in the open or when they're in buildings?

"In the open."

"Do you want them mobile in their vehicles or locked down?"

"Locked down. Okay, I think I get it, but how do we get them in the open and away from their vehicles?" Ryan asked.

"Well, that's where the shaping operation comes in. If we have a couple of guys lightly engage them, they'll think it's just some local people and they'll swarm after them, thinking they can take them out with their sheer numbers. If we attacked hard, they'd either take off in their vehicles or hunker down. This way, we can draw a good number of them away into the open, then we can drop the hammer on them. If at the same time we can move a group in behind them, we can cut them off from retreat or reinforcement," Merrick explained.

"That's good, like divide and conquer, but what about their vehicles?" asked Ryan.

"What do you think they'd do if we started shooting up their vehicles from the direction of our secondary team?"

"They'd probably hightail it out of there," guessed Ryan.

"I think you're right. So we set up another team to ambush their vehicles when they're in the open. Hopefully, this way we have the element of surprise multiple times throughout the battle, and we get all their forces drawn out in the open."

"Ha! I knew we kept you around for a reason. General Merrick Patton!" laughed Mark as he slapping Merrick on the back.

"Don't go promoting me to general yet. There are still a million things that can go wrong with the plan that we have to consider. What if they don't pursue our guys? What if their trucks don't retreat or go a different direction than we anticipate?" Merrick pointed out.

"I'm a visual person," Ryan said. "Can we look this location up and draw in what we know about our plan on a whiteboard?"

"Reese?" Merrick said.

"On it," Reese answered, already moving to go get one.

"Are we all going out there in one big convoy?" asked Miranda.

"With limited communications, backup, and everything, I think it's our best option. Hopefully, if they do get warned that we're in the area, we'll be in position before they're able to get mobile."

"Maybe this is a bad idea with no fire department, but what if once we pin them down, we just burn down the houses they are using?" Ryan asked.

"It's not a bad idea, but fire can be hard to control. We wouldn't want to endanger our own forces, and it would be difficult to make sure homes in the area were clear of any civilians. I don't want the death of innocents on my conscience." Merrick shook his head.

"It's winter in damp Washington. I think we have to worry more about the fire not catching than we do about it getting out of control," Mark pointed out.

"What about making explosives? They're easier to control," Reese jumped into the conversation as he came in with the whiteboard.

"I like explosives better, too, but we're also limited on materials and time. When are we planning on kicking this thing off? Didn't I hear Chris give you a twenty-four-hour ultimatum?" asked Ryan, looking at Merrick.

"He did, but getting this done sooner rather than later is not just about him. The longer we wait, the more likely they are to move in an unknown direction where the setup could be far worse. The devil you know is always better than the devil you don't know. Let's draw this up on a map and continue to try to think of what we can do and what the enemy might do. For now, let's plan to make explosives and firebombs, but we'll hold the firebombs in reserve unless we really need them."

"It's better to have and not need than need and not have," quoted Ryan.

"That is the prepper mantra," Merrick said with a smile.

CHAPTER 44

"Frank, do you have a minute?" asked Merrick as everyone was getting ready to eat.

"Of course. What can I do for you?" asked Frank.

"We're going to the neighborhood meeting in just a bit, and I think it would be good if you were there."

"Sure. Debbie too?"

"She can come if she wants, but you're the one I need there. When I try to convince them to let you stay in one of the houses, the main selling point is going to be that you're a retired cop and know how to handle yourself," Merrick explained.

"I'm not a young buck anymore, but I don't expect a free ride."

"So you're okay with coming with us to fight this group?"

Frank nodded.

"Okay," Merrick said. "That'll make it easier to sell to the neighborhood, but we'll have to eventually break the news to your wife . . . and mine."

"I was thinking we just wouldn't," suggested Frank.

"Like you just jump in the truck at the last moment and not tell them?" Merrick questioned the wisdom of Frank's plan.

"No—I think they both know but haven't thought about it yet. So when the time comes, I'll load up with everyone else, and if they say something, then we'll explain it to them, but I think there's a decent chance that we'll just load and go without having to spell it out. Why upset them if we don't have to, right?"

"It's your call, but if that day comes, you have to be the one to break the news to them."

"Fair enough," agreed Frank.

The group drove toward Keith's house about twenty minutes early, but there was a problem. Cars lined the entire roadway as they neared Keith's. Merrick was shocked and suddenly feeling a little uneasy about presenting his plan to such a large group of people. They parked the car and started walking toward the house. They could see another dozen cars finding a place to park farther down the street.

"Wow, looks like we might not be fighting alone after all. You ready for this, General?" said Mark jokingly.

"If I were you, I'd wipe that grin off your face since you'll probably end up as one of the team captains," Merrick replied with a fake grin back.

"Okay, hold on there a second. I have no problem going and fighting, but there are going to be dozens of guys here that have actual military experience that could lead one of the teams."

Merrick understood exactly how Mark felt because he felt the same way. This whole situation had fallen into his lap, and he felt like if he did not step up, the whole thing would fall apart. He did not like the responsibility of leading this group, but he wasn't about to be responsible for what would happen if he shied away from his duty.

"You're probably right, but I don't know them or trust them. I want people I know and trust leading those teams, and I trust you." Merrick put one of his arms around Mark's shoulders.

"Well, thanks for ruining my night. Now that's all I'm going to be able to think about." Mark slouched slightly as if he were carrying a physical weight on his back.

Keith's house was fairly large, but not nearly big enough for the gathering tonight. There was a good number of people in the house, but most had already made their way into the backyard and were gathered around the paved firepit area. In the moment, Merrick thought it was odd to see so many people together. He guessed that there were about 200 people there so far. He finally spotted Keith talking to Paul Jacobs on the edge of the crowd.

"I'm going to talk to Keith really quick. Can you guys make your way to the firepit area and set up a spot for us? Reese, there are too many people here for the whiteboard to be of any real use. Can you just keep it covered? Sorry you had to tote it all the way here for nothing," Merrick said apologetically.

"It's fine," Reese said with a shrug.

"I don't think any of us should wander off alone tonight, especially you. There are a lot of armed people here that we don't know," said Ryan as he looked around at the large crowd.

"All right—let's pair up and stay together. Frank, you want to come with me? I'll introduce you," Merrick said, motioning for Frank to follow. They walked over to Keith, and Merrick introduced his father in-law.

"Keith, this is quite the turnout," said Frank.

"I'm shocked people could even find the place without Google Maps," Keith said. "Some of them started showing up an hour ago trying to grill me for information. They wanted to know about everything, like when is the power going to be back on, when will the hospitals be working, where is this large group, are they coming this way? I finally had to stop greeting people because it just made me a target for all their questions. I honestly think that's the main reason people are here. They're just starving for information."

"Well, they're going to leave here disappointed then, because I don't have the answers to most of those questions. Plus we really need to focus on the current issue." Merrick started to feel nerves set in. Public speaking didn't bother him too much, but he worried that these people expected too much of him, and he knew all too well how very human he was.

Keith looked down at his watch and said, "We still have about fifteen minutes before we're scheduled to start. Do you want to try to answer some of their questions now?"

"I think I'll wait. I don't want to have to repeat myself again for people that show up on time, and everyone will want to know about the threat first thing." Merrick paused a second before saying, "I did want to get just our neighborhood together for a second, if possible. Could you help me round them up?"

"Sure. I think most were hanging out just to the side of the firepit area." Keith pointed in that direction.

Merrick, Keith, and Frank made their way through the crowd toward the firepit. Merrick couldn't believe how packed the place was. If he had known that they would get this kind of response, he definitely would have tried to hold this at a school or church. He was impressed with how relaxed Keith seem to be, because he knew if it was his place, he would be freaking out with all these strangers running around.

Once the three men got to the side of the firepit, it took a few more minutes to get everyone from the neighborhood huddled together without drawing too much attention from the main crowd.

"Hey everyone, thanks for being here. I know you have a million questions about what's going on, and I'll give you all the details when I talk to the whole group, but the bottom line is this criminal group is moving through the area and taking over entire neighborhoods at a time. If we do nothing, we risk that eventually this group will show up here, and when they do, they might overrun us. Right now we know where they are, and we have a chance to take them out. We can't fight them alone, but we can't afford to do nothing either. Hopefully I can convince a good number of the people here to join together and set up an ambush for these thugs tomorrow. I know this all seems like it's happening fast, but if we're going to do something, we have to act now. I don't know half the people here, but I trust all of you. I hope a couple of you can be there tomorrow and help me out as team leaders." Merrick looked around the group and saw people nodding.

"Don't worry. We'll be there for you," Dale said.

"Yeah, and there's no way we're going to let you have all the fun," Paul said with a smile.

"Well, thanks. There's another issue I wanted to talk to all of you about. As most of you know, I have a house full of friends and family that have been there since the beginning of the collapse. Frank, my father-in-law, is an ex-cop and just made it out here. He would be a great asset, especially with this thing we're facing. With you guys' permission, we'd like to set him and his wife up in one of the empty houses in the neighborhood. We also thought it would be smart if we go into the other empty houses and collect the supplies for people in the neighborhood who might be running low. What do you guys think?"

"Personally, I think it's better to have someone in the houses than have them empty," Keith said.

"Sure, I'm okay with it," answered Dale.

Most of the other people in the neighborhood nodded in agreement. Merrick sensed that he could ask for just about anything right now and probably have them all nodding. As he looked at his neighbors, he realized they were looking at him a little differently tonight—not as Merrick the cop next door, but like Merrick the military leader. The only real change from the last meeting was the looming threat and the hundreds of people gathered around to listen to him. Perhaps that elevated his status in their eyes to the point that they were more willing to follow. Either way, he was glad and humbled at the same time.

"Okay, sounds like everyone's in agreement. The closest house to our place that's empty is Jill and Kim's place, so for right now that's where Frank and his wife will be. Dale, once this thing is over, can you and your boys check the other empty houses and gather up any supplies and store them at your place? If any of you are low right now, let Dale know so he can drop a few things off to tide you over, but let's wait till the next meeting and we can discuss anything more. If there's nothing else, let's start this thing so we can give Keith his house back and have our neighborhood quiet again."

CHAPTER 45

"Everyone, please gather in! We're going to get started!" Merrick yelled twice before lowering his voice. "Please try to minimize the side conversations so everyone can hear. My name is Merrick, and I'm a police officer with the sheriff's office. I was in the Army for more than twelve years. I know many of you came here with questions about when things are going to go back to normal, but I don't have any answers for you about that. What I do know is there's a large group in the east Orchards area that's going into entire neighborhoods and looting the place and killing anyone who puts up any kind of resistance." He looked out at the crowd.

"How do you know this?" someone yelled.

"I know this because another deputy friend of mine lived in the neighborhood they just hit, and his wife was shot and killed while they were trying to get out of there. This group that took over his neighborhood consists of 200 armed men with supply trucks."

The crowd murmured slightly.

"We have no idea where they'll be going next. It could be here or it could be one of your neighborhoods. This threat is not one we can turn a blind eye to, and we have to strike while we know where they are. I'm planning a well-coordinated, multifaceted assault that should be fairly low risk to the assault teams, but I cannot do this alone. The only way all of us can ensure our safety is by banding together. Separately they'll overpower each of our neighborhoods, but together with the element of surprise, I am confident that we can eliminate this threat for good. Tomorrow morning at 5 a.m. we're meeting at Hockinson High school to go over the plan in detail and then leave from there to carry it out. If any of you can handle a firearm, drive a vehicle, or has medical training, we need you there.

"This is one of those defining moments in all of our lives. Will we band together and protect each other, or will you cower at home and let others risk their lives so you can live?"

Someone started clapping, and it soon spread to the entire crowd. Merrick waved the crowd to hold their applause and let him finish. "Just a couple more things, then I'll open this up for questions. Tomorrow at five o'clock, bring whatever equipment you have or think you will need to fight with: weapons, water, jackets, etc. If you have a special skill, like you know how to make explosives or have special medical training, please come over and see my friend Ryan over there in the red shirt. Ryan, wave for me. Please see him before you leave so we can get your help. Okay. Questions?"

"Why can't you go over your plan now?" asked another person.

"Good question. In the military we called it 'operational security.' It can be potentially dangerous for people who are not going to be a part of the mission to know the specific details of our plan. I don't know all of you, so we're keeping those plans to the inner circle for now. Tomorrow, if any of you have a suggestion, we can adapt our plan if needed. Like I said, there is a fairly low risk for our people, but for it to work, I need your help."

"How do you know the group is even there still?"

"I have a friend who is an ex-Special Forces operator observing and giving us regular updates." Merrick could see heads turn and nod as he said this.

"What are you planning on doing with prisoners if they surrender?" It was a good question, one that Merrick hadn't taken time to really consider, so he made up his answer on the fly.

"These people have already displayed extreme violence toward unarmed civilians. We're not going to try and negotiate before we attack. We're going to hit them and hit them hard with the goal to totally eliminate this threat. Taking prisoners is not a priority. The hard reality is that we're not set up to house or care for any prisoners. If something happens and part of the group wants to surrender, then we'll hold a field trial that will decide what to do with them."

"How many people do you need tomorrow?"

"As many as we can get. The more resources we have, the less likely we are to lose any of our own people." Merrick waited for any other questions for a few seconds, but none came. "Before you go, we'd like to set up a kind of communication tree so even after this is over, we can share information with each other if needed. Keith, standing right over there with the Seahawks hat, will be standing by to collect contact information from at least one person from each neighborhood. Be safe getting back to your homes, and I hope to see all of you again tomorrow."

For two hours Merrick didn't move. He was surrounded by people wanting to talk with him privately. Most of the people wanted to thank him and tell him that they would be there tomorrow. Some were ex-military guys describing their military experience and saying they'd be willing to help plan and lead a group tomorrow. As the time went on, he loathed the fact that he felt like a politician with a fake smile, pretending to care even though he had lost interest after the first twenty people. To make matters worse, he hated being in crowds, and all he wanted to do was go home and spend some quality time with his family and make explosives. He now understood how hard the game of politics could be and he knew he wanted no part in it, then or ever.

"You done kissing babies?" asked Ryan.

"Just get me out of here, and please shoot anyone else that tries to talk to me, okay?" said Merrick, sounding exhausted.

"Hey Merrick! Hold on a sec!" yelled Keith. Merrick looked over at Ryan, who was grinning ear to ear and pointed toward his handgun, asking if he wanted him to shoot Keith. The entire group laughed at Merrick.

"Oh, shut up, all of ya!" Merrick said as he walked toward Keith, who was standing with another man.

"Keith, I need to get home. What's up?" Merrick said, hoping Keith would get the hint that he was ready to leave.

"This guy was saying he has a pretty nice drone that he could use tomorrow to help out, but he just needs a way to charge the battery and the tablet he uses to fly it."

"You didn't happen to bring it with you by chance?" Merrick asked the man.

"I did."

"I'm sure we can make that happen. How long does it need to charge?"

"About four hours or till the light turns green on the charger. I have four batteries. I'm not sure how many you want to charge up."

"All of them. What kind of range can you get on your drone, and how long can it stay in the air?" Merrick was considering just how valuable an asset this could be.

"It can stay up for almost thirty minutes and it can go out about four miles, but if it's raining, I can't fly it at all."

"That's impressive. What's your name, sir?" Merrick said as he extended his hand.

"Jacob Hall," he said as he shook Merrick's hand.

"Well, Jacob, if you could be there a little before five o'clock tomorrow, I'll have your stuff all charged up for you. I'll probably send you out early with a group to start getting us intel."

"Okay, but will I be safe? I'm not really a gun guy." Jacob looked and sounded a bit worried.

"Yes. You giving us a bird's-eye view of things will be extremely valuable, and we won't let anything happen to you," Merrick replied with a smile.

"Okay, thanks. I'll grab the stuff out of my car," Jacob said before he walked off.

"Thanks, Keith. It'll make a huge difference," Merrick said, grateful his neighbor had stopped him before he left.

"No problem. Do you think we'll get enough people?" Keith asked.

"If we get a third of the guys who showed up today, we'll have plenty."

"Is there such a thing as having too much help?" Keith said with a laugh.

"There might be, but I've never seen it. The biggest issue with this group won't be too many or too few people. It'll be command and control. We're an army that has never fought or even trained together. We don't have a chain of command structure, and most don't even know basic soldiering skills." Merrick had command experience, but that was with trained soldiers.

"I'm glad you didn't say that during your speech. I'm pretty optimistic, but now you're making me worry," Keith said.

"With a good briefing, and if things go as planned, we'll be okay." Merrick didn't say it, but he knew that the battlefield could be a very dynamic, constantly changing environment, and it was then that good leadership and basic soldiering skills became the difference between life and death. "Let's just pray things go as planned."

CHAPTER 46

"We have to watch the 300 Spartans standing up to a massive horde. It'd totally get us pumped for tomorrow!" Reese said excitedly.

"Yeah, except for the fact that they all die in the end. I wouldn't call that motivating," Mark said as he shook his head.

"Honestly, we shouldn't even watch a war movie. We should watch a comedy or something. Let's keep it light tonight and just enjoy being together," Lydia suggested.

It took almost ten minutes of debating to finally settle on a movie. Reese continued to try to persuade everyone to watch *300*, but with children present, it was a losing battle. They finally decided on *The Princess Bride*. Since the generator had to be fired up to charge the drone anyway, they had decided to celebrate a little bit with pizza and a movie.

The adults who were not involved in making pizza were creating homemade explosives. They made about forty firebomb explosives similar to a Molotov cocktail. The bottles were filled with the oldest gas they had combined with a little oil. To ignite each one, they duct-taped storm matches and jerry-rigged a pull string friction ignitor. Merrick also had a few mortar ball fireworks left over from the Fourth of July. They glued scrap nails and bolts to the balls, turning them into mini frag grenades.

Once the movie ended and the young kids were asleep, everyone gathered again in the family room to discuss the elephant in the room: who would be going tomorrow.

"I know a lot of you feel pressure to go tomorrow, but none of you have to. All of you can make the choice not to go. I would prefer that one person max from each couple go, and I think no one under fifteen years old should go," Merrick said.

"What? That's a bunch of crap, Dad!" Indiana objected.

"Shh! Kids are sleeping," Lydia said, scowling at Indiana.

"I bet I can shoot better than 99 percent of the people who are going tomorrow. I can move faster and know more military tactics than most of them too. What does my age have to do with anything?" Indiana continued at a lower volume.

"It's not because of you. I can barely handle the thought of letting Reese go. Worrying about both of you would be too much for me. I need a good shooter here to watch over things and keep everyone here safe. I think you'd do great, but please, for me, I need you to stay." While Merrick spoke, Lydia walked over to Indiana, put her arms around him, and whispered something in his ear that seemed to melt his resolve.

"I still don't like it, but I'll stay. Just know that next time I am going, and good luck trying to stop me," Indiana threatened.

"So do you think Will and Jake should go?" asked Mark, since they were both over fifteen.

"That's a decision for your family to make, but Mark, I was hoping you'd stay behind and take command of things here."

"Are you sure you don't need me out there?" Mark asked.

"Look, I'd love all of you to be there, but we don't have to risk everything. From the turnout at the meeting, I think we'll have a good amount of help, but I want to make sure we have something to come back to. Everyone that was at that meeting knows that a good number of people will be leaving their homes tomorrow, and someone could try and take advantage of that. I have to go, and I'd like Ryan and Bruce to come as well. Bruce, you would stay with the vehicles and be in charge of the field hospital and any medical staff. Ryan, it'd be nice to have you as one of the team leaders, but that's a choice you and Amy have to make. Like I said, none of you have to go, but let's talk it out now."

"I want to go," Miranda said.

"No, that's not necessary. You heard Merrick say they'll have plenty of people there," Mark argued.

"I am going," reaffirmed Miranda.

"No. Merrick, tell her. Tell her she doesn't have to go," Mark said, looking for an advocate.

"Mark, she knows and she wants to go. This is between the two of you. I can't tell her not to go." Merrick did not want to choose sides.

"But there'll be plenty of men there tomorrow to fight, so she doesn't—"

"Excuse me?" Miranda cut off Mark.

"Mark, a couple of weeks ago Miranda brought to my attention that I might have been unconsciously sheltering the women in our group," Merrick said. "I've been thinking about it more and more, and I think she was right. Tonight, on the eve of battle, is not the night to end up in the doghouse. If you were going, would you want her to be understanding and supportive of you?"

"Yeah, I would," Mark admitted.

"Then my advice is to do the same, even if it hurts," Merrick said.

"I'm going with you, Mom," Will said confidently. Mark looked at both of them, feeling defeated and knowing there was no point in arguing.

"I'm in too," said Ryan.

"Me too," said Bruce.

Merrick nodded and looked around at them. They were not battle-hardened soldiers, but they stood on the eve of a battle, sober and ready to face their enemy.

"Okay. Let's get some sleep, and tomorrow at 4 a.m., be ready to roll out."

CHAPTER 47

When Merrick and his group arrived at the high school, it was obvious that it had been vandalized at some point. There were broken windows and papers scattered across the floor of the gym. With no power, it was as dark as night inside. They were able to remove the center bar in one of the double doorways and fit a small vehicle inside the gym. With its lights bouncing off the wall, the gym grew fairly well lit.

Merrick had already sent an advance team to meet up with Chris and set up patrol bases for the field teams. Jacob Hall had also gone out with the advance team and met up with Chris. They were already feeding Merrick detailed information.

As people arrived, they were divided into different groups. There were three main categories of people: those with military or tactical training, those without, and those with specialty equipment or training. They were then subdivided into different teams with an aim of trying to spread those who had experience as equally as possible. Family and friends were allowed to stay together and just went with whoever the most experienced person was. Merrick was happy to see that among the group as a whole, there were four police officers he knew.

Once the teams were divided, the top leaders from each were called together. They were given a detailed briefing on the overall plan and their individual objectives. The team leaders were given the freedom to subdivide their own teams as they saw fit. Each team was given maps, radios, and explosives, and had a separate rally point where they would meet up with the advance team already on-site and scouting the area.

When all questions were answered, Merrick shook all the leaders' hands and wished them luck. He then climbed onto the top of the car they were using for light, stood up on the roof, and looked out over the crowd.

The gym was buzzing with activity and people getting to know each other. No directions were spoken, but slowly people stopped talking and turned to face Merrick. It spread slowly at first, but gradually picked up speed. Silence washed over the crowd like a wave and hung in the air for a moment as people waited for Merrick to speak.

"As I look out and see all of you here, it gives me hope. For years I've felt like America has been in a downward spiral. Then after the recent attacks, our nation completely fell apart into chaos. I've been wondering if we're ever going to recover. The answer can be found by looking to those who stand to your left and right. This country was founded by people who were willing to stand up and fight. It's going to take those same kind of people to save it now. Who here is willing to fight?"

The crowd roared in response.

"There—right there is our hope and the very spirit of America. Once the battle today is won, you cannot stop fighting if we want a future, if we want a better tomorrow. We are going to have to continue to fight for it. The good news is we will not be fighting alone. We will fight this fight together."

The crowd roared again.

"Your team leaders will explain the details of your mission, then when all the convoys are ready, we'll roll out together. All of you be safe, watch out for each other, and give 'em hell."

The sun had not yet risen, but the sky began to fill with the promise of dawn. During his military career, Merrick normally preferred assaulting the enemy in the dead of night. He had always been technologically superior to the enemy, and his soldiers could move like ghosts through the darkness with ease. Today they were on an even playing field with their foe. He wanted the daylight so his people would know full well what they were shooting at. It would lessen the chance of friendly fire and make it harder for the enemy to slip away.

Merrick walked along the rows of vehicles that were preparing to leave, trying to find his son. It pained him to know that he would not be fighting next to Reese and that if anything happened, he would not be able to get there in time. His only comfort came from knowing that Ryan was leading the team Reese was attached to and would do his best to watch over him. He found Reese sitting in the back of a pickup with a .50 caliber BMG rifle leaning up against him.

"You ready, Spartan?" Merrick asked as he approached Reese.

"Yes, sir," Reese answered with a smile. The BMG was a big rifle for any man, but Reese was just fifteen years old, and holding it made him look even more like a boy. Ryan had been the one to suggest that Reese operate the .50, and his logic was hard to argue with. Reese was a long-range rifle shooting champion. Combine that with the awesome power of a .50 caliber sniper rifle, and any enemy would be shaking in his boots.

Ryan was convinced that Reese could single-handedly stop the enemy trucks. But Merrick didn't like that once the .50 started barking out rounds, it would be hard to miss and make Reese a hell of a target.

Merrick reached over the bed of the truck and pulled Reese into a hug. The hug wasn't their best, for both of them were wearing body armor with magazines and gear attached. Even though the hug was awkward, Merrick didn't want to let Reese go. "I couldn't be more proud of you, and I love you. Be careful, and change positions if you start taking fire."

"I love you too. Don't worry. I'll be okay," Reese said.

"Promise?"

"I promise."

"I didn't raise you to be a liar, so I'm going to hold you to that." Merrick leaned in for one more hug and whispered, "This battle means nothing to me if I have to lose you. Nothing today is worth your life, okay?"

Merrick knew his son and how he glorified valor and self-sacrifice. He also knew he was mostly to blame. The stories, movies, and his example had been incredibly biased in that direction. He looked at Reese, pleading with his eyes to come back safe.

"I gave you my word, and I'm planning on keeping it, so don't worry."

"Okay. Just know if something happens to you, then you might as well kiss me goodbye. Your mom would kill me—no joke," Merrick said with a playful grimace.

"You're probably right." Both of them smiled at each other one last time.

Merrick walked back to the command convoy and jumped into one of the vehicles. Within a few minutes, all team commanders radioed that they were ready to roll out. They drove with no headlights on and kept the speed below forty-five miles per hour to keep a low profile. One by one, each group splintered off to its own patrol base and infill location. Merrick allowed himself one last thought of Reese and how much he wished he was fighting by Reese's side. He then pushed his concerns to the back of his mind so he could totally focus on commanding.

The convoy drove down to the end of 114th Street and circled around so it was ready to leave. Merrick looked up at the sky, trying to spot the drone flying overhead, but he couldn't see or hear a thing. Chris emerged from one of the houses on the dead-end street and walked over to Merrick. He was wearing military camo and decked out in tactical gear, including a pair of night-vision goggles affixed to his helmet. His face was painted with blended patterns of green, brown, and black. Everyone but Merrick took an unconscious step backward from this figure, who looked like he'd stepped right out of *Call of Duty*.

"Morning, Chris. You leave any guys for us?" Merrick asked.

"There are plenty to go around, but you better believe I haven't met my quota yet. This house was empty, and I thought it might make a good command headquarters. Jacob is in there now flying his drone around."

"Sounds good." Merrick turned to retired Sergeant Major John Kessel, who he'd asked to coordinate all of the HQ personnel. "John, can you get everyone set up in the house?"

"On it. What do you think about using the garage as a medical bay?" John asked.

"Great idea. If you'll see to things, I'm going to get the latest intel from the drone and push it out to the teams. Just make sure we have our security element set up as soon as you can." Merrick was glad he had John to depend on.

"Roger."

Chris led the way into the family room of the abandoned house. Jacob was sitting on a couch watching a little screen with a controller attached to it. On the far wall, there was a rough map of the area that looked like it had been drawn with a Sharpie. The map had markings that looked like enemy positions and even identified the area their teams would attack from.

"I like your artwork," Merrick told Chris, looking at the map.

"It could use some color, but I did what I could." There were multiple X's marked around the outside of the enemy position.

"What are the little X markings?" Jacob glanced up for a moment and looked at Chris, then back down at his drone screen.

"Sentries that wandered a bit too far out and didn't make it back," Chris said as he winked at Merrick. Merrick started counting up the X's around the map. "There are about a dozen, and don't worry; I didn't leave their bodies to be found. They probably think the guys just walked off and are AWOL."

"Great job. Seriously, both of you guys' work is what made this possible." Merrick put a hand on his friend's shoulder, trying to let him know he meant it. "Are there any new developments that we need to consider before we get the Bait Team moving?"

John Kessel walked in with a group in tow whose arms were full of gear. "John," Merrick said, "this is Jacob Hall, our eye in the sky."

John walked over and shook Jacob's hand. "Good to have you on the team."

"Nice to meet you too. To answer your other question, everything's pretty quiet out there right now," Jacob said.

"Once they engage, we'll want you to keep a close eye on things. We need to make sure that the Bait Team doesn't get into trouble and get pinned down. We also need to make sure that Team Two is able to move into position without raising any alarms too soon," Merrick explained.

"I'll do what I can, but honestly you should probably have someone with some military experience directing me."

Merrick's eyes naturally looked over at Chris.

"Fat chance," Chris objected. "Once we kick this thing off, I'm out of here. I'll probably go in with Team Two so I can be in the middle of the action."

"Whoa! I just looked at you; I wasn't volunteering you. It will probably be me or John helping direct you, Jacob. That way, we can instantly relay information and direct things on the radio," clarified Merrick.

"Good, because there was no way I was going to miss this fight," Chris affirmed.

CHAPTER 48

Everyone in the command room held their breath as they waited for the two-man Bait Team to fire on a small group of unexpecting combatants gathered in the street. They were given directions to fire on the group, but not to be too accurate. If they dropped all of them with deadly accuracy, odds were they'd be less likely to pursue, and that was the whole purpose of bait. They fired about ten rounds between the two of them and hit only two people. Both of them, wearing brightly colored jackets, then took off running. Merrick wondered if the bright jackets made it too obvious that it was a trap. They almost had a neon sign saying "Come and get us."

The response was immediate. Those in the group who were not injured fired back toward where the Bait Team had been just moments ago. There was no audio on the small tablet screen that was displaying the drone images, but Merrick could see rounds hitting and splintering the side of the house. He was blown away at just how clear the image was. Doors to nearby houses flung open and people poured out. They were running out of the houses and still putting on clothes, and some appeared to be staggering from a few too many the night before. A couple ran off after the Bait Team, but most of them waited in the area for more to join. When there were about thirty enemy combatants assembled, they moved out, fanning out only slightly.

"There are about thirty combatants moving out east in pursuit of the Bait Team. Remember, everyone, we want to draw them away into the ambush, so stay out of sight." Merrick watched as the Bait Team set up behind the next set of houses, waiting for the disorderly mass to draw closer so they didn't lose them.

"It's like watching a video game," Jacob said.

"Not for those guys down there. When you could die and there's no respawning, there's a very real feel to it." Merrick watched the screen closely and saw a lone male approach the Bait Team well in front of the main group.

"Bait Team, you have a male approaching your position on the northwest side. He's going around a charcoal-colored house with a red sedan parked in the driveway. Take him out if you can before he crosses the street."

Sure enough, the male came around the side of the car and got lit up once he tried crossing the street.

"Target is down; good job," Merrick radioed. "Main group is about 200 yards behind him, but they're moving toward you at a pretty good pace. Keep moving, but make sure you're easy to follow."

The Bait Team zigzagged from house to house at a slow jog. They stopped occasionally and fired a shot or two. They were not trying to pick off the enemy—just trying to leave bread crumbs for the large group to follow.

The Bait Team had to cover a slight larger open area to get to the next group of houses. The two guys had almost reached the safety of the house when one tripped and landed hard on the ground. The enemy group rounded the corner of the house and saw the man on the ground shaking off the fall. The first male stopped, and Merrick could tell he was trying to decide if he should help or just get to cover.

"God, no! Get up! Get up and *MOVE*!" Merrick screamed at the screen. He could see the gunfire erupt and follow them till they got to the safety of a house. The hostile group seemed to ignite and began running toward the Bait Team with new vigor. It was like seeing a pack of wild dogs close in on their prey as it hopelessly scurried before them. Merrick could literally see the change in energy in the hostile group's movements.

"Okay, that did it. They're running for you guys now. Get out of there and run east until you reach Team One's position. Team Two, you can start moving in slowly."

"Team Two copy, moving."

"Team One, the second the Bait Team is safe, open fire on these guys." Merrick watched the Bait Team continue to move east. "These guys deserve medals," he said, amazed at their bravery.

"And an Academy Award; their acting is really good. Look how that guy is dragging his leg a little like he's hurt," Jacob said.

Merrick leaned closer. "I don't think he's acting; I think he is really hurt," he said with a frown. He knew it was unrealistic to think his people would be able to go through this thing completely unscathed, but he suddenly felt a wave of guilt seeing this man run for his life on an injured leg. "Team One, Bait Team is nearing your location, but one of them might be injured. Have medics standing by," he said over the radio.

"Team One copies."

"Team Two, you probably have two minutes before Team One will start to engage."

"We copy. We're already in position to cut them off, just waiting until Team One engages."

There were still a million things that could go wrong, but the main body of the enemy was exposed and cut off from retreat. A small amount of hope fueled Merrick. Momentum was a powerful tool in battle. The enemy thought they had it, but it was about to be ripped away in an instant.

"Any movement of their trucks?" asked Ryan from Team Three. Merrick was so focused on what was happening that he had almost forgotten. Jacob zoomed in on the vehicles; they were still sitting in the same spot, but it looked like they'd beefed up their security around them.

"The trucks haven't moved, but they have . . ." Merrick leaned over the drone feed to estimate the number of people around the vehicles. "There are about thirty guys guarding them right now."

"Copy."

Merrick could see the enemy group closing in fast on the Bait Team; they now numbered at least sixty strong. The Bait Team still had fifty yards of open ground before they got to the safety of Team One's position. He quickly tried to calculate whether they'd make it before the enemy had a clean shot. It was going to be close, and he didn't feel like gambling with these brave men's lives.

"Bait Team, Bait Team, enemy forces are closing behind you. I need you to drop and stay down while Team One engages over the top of you. Do you copy?" No response was heard over the radio, but through the drone camera he saw the two Bait Team members drop flat in the grass. Moments later the hostile group ran into the field searching for the Bait Team. They started to spread out and comb through the tall grass looking for them. Then it happened: a barrage of gunfire erupted from fifty concealed positions. The firing lasted only a few seconds, but no one was standing when the firing ceased. It was hard to tell exactly how many were dead and how many had dived into the grass to avoid being mowed down. From his bird's-eye view, Merrick could see that at least fifteen to twenty appeared to be alive and were low-crawling back toward the houses.

"Team One, good shooting! About twenty of them are crawling low in the grass, making their way to the nearest house." Merrick was trying not to micromanage the teams too much, but it was difficult. His role was to coordinate and give intel, not to direct individual battle movements.

"Team One copies." Merrick watched the Team One commander give some type of order to his troops but couldn't tell exactly what he was telling them to do. He then saw a group of about fifteen moving along the right flank of their formation, closing in on where the enemy was crawling to safety. Most of them took up kneeling positions, but a couple reached into a bag and retrieved something Merrick recognized: the modified mortar fireworks. Their fuses were lit, and then they were thrown toward the enemy position. Merrick could see the enemies on the ground roll and scatter away from the explosives. Two were fairly stupid and jumped up trying to make a run for it. They were shot down almost instantly.

BOOM! A massive flash of green sparks and light exploded in all directions. Merrick was surprised by how much bigger the mortar explosions looked on the ground than when they were in the air, but as impressive as it looked, it didn't do very much damage. There was no crater left behind, and as far as he could tell, no one appeared to be affected by the shrapnel of the first explosion. A moment later, the second one flashed on the screen. This time Merrick saw that it detonated just in front of some unlucky guy. He was now holding his face and rolling away from where the explosion had occurred. The third explosion went off at almost the same time as the second had, but it had landed in an area that had no personnel nearby.

Merrick then saw about five of the remaining hostiles try to stand up with their weapons held up in the air. The first three who stood up were shot down before they were even able to stand up completely. The last two just stood there with their heads turned away, as if they were expecting to be shot.

"HQ, this is Team One. I have a few trying to surrender." Just as the radio broadcast Team One's message, two other males tried to make a run for the house using their own people as human shields. They had no such luck. All four were gunned down.

"HQ, disregard my last; they aren't trying to surrender anymore."

CHAPTER 49

"Did our people just shoot those guys that were trying to surrender?" asked Jacob.

"No, they were shooting the enemy and those guys got in the way," Merrick replied. People liked to think war was black and white, good guys versus bad guys. Merrick thought that was probably why World War II was one of the most popular wars ever depicted in movies. The Nazis were the perfect bad guys everyone could hate together. He knew the reality of most conflicts was a little more on the gray side of things.

Politicians and rebel leaders fed lies to their people in an effort to justify their wars, but their motives were often ambiguous and questionable at best. The frontline soldiers on both sides of a conflict usually had no great ambition or stake in the fight. Those looking in from the outside often asked the soldiers how they could fight and kill in a war they didn't completely understand. Those who had been downrange knew that soldiers, in the moments when bullets were flying, were not fighting for some political reason, but for each other and to make it home alive. That was why Merrick gave soldiers and cops the benefit of the doubt in most circumstances.

Merrick believed that for years, the general public had unrealistic expectations for police, soldiers, and the justice system in general. Juries now wanted DNA, fingerprints, or some other CSI super science for every crime. People expected police officers to be able to shoot the gun out of a suspect's hands and to be able to physically dominate anyone they were trying to arrest. People expected soldiers who were in the middle of a gunfight not to hit a civilian who ran right into the line of fire. All Merrick expected was that his troops acted in a reasonable manner in the specific situation they were in.

"HQ, this is Team Two. We just hit the security team guarding the trucks pretty hard, and a couple of their trucks are hightailing it out of there, but the majority of them are still sitting here."

"I see them. Team Three, it looks like one of them is going south toward your position and the other is going east toward a dead end near Team One. Both Team One and Team Three, be ready to receive those trucks. They're coming at you at a pretty good pace," Merrick announced over the radio.

"Just so you know, I only have a minute or two before I have to fly this thing back and change out the battery," Jacob said.

Merrick's gaze pierced into Jacob. Jacob leaned away from Merrick like he was suddenly afraid of him. "Get it back here right now and change it out as fast as possible," Merrick responded briskly.

"Okay. Sorry," Jacob said apologetically.

"It's not your fault, but from now on, try and give me a countdown of how much time we have left: fifteen minutes, then five minutes, and so on. We're about to reach the most pivotal point in this battle, and I would prefer not to be blind during it," Merrick said more calmly.

"I'll have it switched out and back out there in five to ten minutes," Jacob promised.

During a conflict, ten minutes was an eternity. "Understood, but try to make it less."

Merrick got back on the radio. "All teams, be advised that our bird in the sky is refueling for the next few. Please send up sit-reps at least every three to five minutes." With no view of what was happening on the ground, Merrick found himself pacing in the room and looking up at the map every few seconds.

"HQ, we have a truck coming your way with some wounded."

"Copy," Merrick said over the radio, then turned to John. "Can you make sure our security detail and medical team are ready to receive them?"

"On it, sir," John said, moving away at a half run.

Merrick heard the drone touch down on the back porch. Jacob sprinted over to the sliding glass door and almost threw it off its track as he opened it. With the door open, Merrick could hear the sounds of the distant battle being waged. Then he heard the deep rhythmic booming of a larger weapon system being fired every few seconds. He knew what it was: Reese on the .50 BMG. He said a silent prayer that Reese would be all right.

Jacob slammed the sliding door shut as he rushed back to the couch to grab his remote. The drone shot straight up with what seemed like impossible speed.

"HQ, this is Team Three; both vehicles have been stopped. Team Two, any more vehicles leaving?" Ryan ask over the radio.

"Four trucks just took off heading southwest, and I think they're going to be the last of them. There are only a handful of fighters still left here, and most of them are pinned down."

"Okay, I'll be back in view in just a minute," said Jacob. Merrick noticed beads of sweat on his forehead.

"Perfect. Let's try and focus on what's happening with those four vehicles that just left." Merrick thought that maybe he'd put too much pressure on Jacob and added, "That was very fast, Jacob. Good job."

Back on the radio, Merrick said, "Team Three, let me know if you can see those vehicles. We'll have our bird in the sky back in just a minute."

"HQ, I can barely see them moving west. They're using the neighborhood as cover as they move west. We won't have a shot till they make it to the field on the west side," Ryan replied.

"Copy. Team Two, do you have anyone over there covering the west side?" Merrick asked.

"Sure, but not with anything heavy enough to stop a bunch of vehicles."

"If you can, engage them as they enter the field. It might slow them down enough for Team Three to engage."

"Copy, will do."

Merrick looked over at Jacob's screen; the drone was just reaching the neighborhood. Then he heard the deep bark of the .50 engaging again. Finally the fleeing vehicles came into view as they were driving recklessly fast across the grassy field. The trucks were loaded with supplies, and as they hit natural bumps in the field, supplies tumbled out. Merrick could also see men in the back of the trucks bouncing around. Some of the men were spraying rounds toward his people while holding on with one hand. None of their shots could have been very accurate; they were just spraying and praying. Suddenly the first truck exploded.

"What was that?" Merrick asked.

"Maybe they hit the gas tank?" Merrick didn't even answer Jacob's guess. This wasn't the movies, and cars didn't suddenly burst into flames by regular bullets hitting it, no matter where they hit.

Then another vehicle exploded. Merrick felt his gut twist with a horrible feeling.

"Zoom out, zoom out, and look to the west," Merrick said quickly. As the view widened, what he saw was so shocking that he just stared at the screen.

"Is that—" Jacob started to speak but was cut off by Merrick getting on the radio.

"All units: cease fire, cease fire!" Merrick then suddenly went pale as he saw a home to the south demolished by multiple exploding ordnances hitting it. Reese was in that area with Team Three, and the house had just been hit by a MK19, a fully automatic grenade launcher.

"All units: cease fire, cease fire! The US military are in the area and are engaging anyone that is hostile. *DO NOT FIRE!*" Merrick urged.

"HQ, say again. Did you say the military is here?"

CHAPTER 50

"John, can you hold down the fort? I'm going out there," said Merrick.

"Sir, I don't think that's wise," John objected. "You're still needed here."

"The battle is over, and I need to talk to whoever is in command of that convoy and make sure they don't shoot any of our people," Merrick pressed.

"Sir, the battle is never over till you get all your people home. There are capable people out there; let them do their job out there and you do your job in here."

"You know you're a pain in the butt, right?" Merrick said.

"Yep, been a pain in the butt for many officers during my career, because the one thing all officers have in common is they need a good kick in the butt by an enlisted guy from time to time."

Merrick laughed. "Whatever." He thought of how best to approach a military convoy that had already opened fire. "Chris, are you up to go and try to talk these guys down?"

"Sure, send a suicidal guy on a suicide mission. I like your style," Chris responded.

"Hey, do me a favor and don't get yourself killed, and if you could, also try not to piss these guys off. All our butts are on the line."

"What do you want me to tell them?" Chris asked.

"The truth. Tell them you're a cop, ex-military, and that there was a hostile group in the area looting and killing and we had to take them out," Merrick said matter-of-factly.

"Okay. Here goes nothing," Chris said in a relaxed tone.

It took a minute, but Chris emerged and started walking west toward the convoy with his hands held high. It felt like forever watching him walk across the field. Merrick hoped Chris was the right person to send as an ambassador. With what he was wearing, Chris looked like he could be in the military, and Merrick hoped that would be enough so they wouldn't shoot him as he walked up.

Chris had served long enough in the Army to know how to talk to them, but the only gamble was his current state of mind. He was on edge and still filled with rage from his wife's death. If these guys were dicks, this might go bad—really bad—but Merrick hoped that even though Chris might be careless with his own life right now, he would restrain himself for the sake of the rest of them.

Merrick saw Jacob push the joystick forward slightly, following Chris toward the convoy.

"Stop. Don't get too close. They'll probably try to shoot you down if they see the drone. That and their vehicles will probably have a jammer that'll kill your signal if you get too close," Merrick warned him.

"Okay then. I'll just hang out right here," Jacob said, his eyes widening.

They all watched as Chris got down on his knees with his back facing the convoy. A couple of soldiers moved forward and detained him using what looked like zip ties. They walked him back to the convoy. For ten minutes they watched but saw no movement or sign of Chris. Then Chris walked away from the convoy just holding his radio. When he was about 200 feet out, the radio keyed up.

"HQ, do you copy?" Chris asked.

"Go ahead for HQ," Merrick said, eager to hear from Chris.

"They'd like to talk to whoever is in command. You want me to direct them over to you?"

"Yes, that's fine."

"Just a heads-up: their commander doesn't seem too happy."

CHAPTER 51

"Good morning, Colonel. I'm Deputy Merrick. We're very glad to see you," Merrick said with his hand outstretched to shake the lieutenant colonel's hand. He had walked outside to meet the convoy and left John inside to monitor and command things.

"Are you in charge of this renegade group?" the lieutenant colonel asked without shaking Merrick's hand. The military had all types of people, just like every other organization. There was a chance that Lieutenant Colonel Hafer was just having a bad day, but Merrick guessed that wasn't the case. He was just a dick. Chris, who had guided the military convoy to HQ's location, was now standing at the lieutenant colonel's side with a dumb smile on his face as if to say, "I told you so."

"Yes, sir. I'm in charge here, and as a local police officer, I organized this group to deal with a large hostile group in the—"

"Yeah, yeah. Your other guy gave me the same song and dance. I've been assigned to the Clark County area to restore order, and I will not tolerate people running around killing each other for supplies. I'm relieving you of command, and all of your men will surrender their weapons and return to their homes," Lieutenant Colonel Hafer said, waving his hand dismissively.

"Sir, I'm glad that you won't tolerate people going around and killing each other because that's exactly what we are here trying to stop as well," Merrick tried to explain diplomatically. "My men are just good Americans defending their lives and homes against a murderous mob. For weeks these people have been abandoned by both the local and federal governments. They've been barely holding on and trying to simply survive long enough for law and order to return. If you have been assigned to this area, I'm sure you're going to have your hands full. You're going to want the cooperation of these good citizens, and you're probably going to need their help getting things back to normal. You have an opportunity to gain an ally and not make an enemy today."

"Are you refusing to obey a direct order to surrender your weapons while under martial law?" the lieutenant colonel asked, putting his hands on his hips.

"It's not a lawful order if you're asking me to do something illegal. Have you ever heard of the Disaster Recovery Personal Protection Act?" Merrick asked back.

"No, but I'm sure it doesn't apply."

"Actually, it applies precisely to this situation. During Hurricane Katrina, a few military officers thought it was a good idea to start disarming people. Afterward, those officers got in trouble, and Congress passed the Disaster Recovery Act specifically stating that lawful citizens cannot be deprived of their Second Amendment right to protect themselves, even in a state of emergency or under martial law." Merrick was fairly proud of the puzzled look on Lieutenant Colonel Hafer's face.

"Are you some kind of activist or something?" the lieutenant colonel said, narrowing his eyes and showing slight disgust with Merrick.

"No, I'm just a cop who used to be a military police officer, and now I'm trying to do what I can to help everyone around me pull through this. Put yourself in these people's shoes. If your family was in danger, would you give up your weapon?" asked Merrick.

"I'll let you go home with your weapons today." The lieutenant colonel leaned in closer to Merrick and said, "But you better believe I'm going do some research, and if I find out that this Disaster Recovery Act thing is bogus, your door is the first one I kick in. Do you get me?" He pointed his finger in Merrick's face.

Merrick leaned in even closer and said, "Do your research, and do yourself a favor and check your ego, because for someone who's here to bring order, all you've done since you've gotten here is to try and start a fight."

The lieutenant colonel, with an unhappy look on his face, turned around and walked away without so much as a goodbye or handshake. He signaled his men to prepare to roll out. Chris stepped beside Merrick and looked oddly pleased with himself.

"So he's a real piece of work," Chris said with a smile.

"I think I'd rather have our roving looters back than this guy." Merrick crossed his arms and shook his head at Lieutenant Colonel Hafer.

"And you were worried about me ruffling his feathers."

"The guy's on a power trip and he shot at . . ." Merrick keyed up his radio. "All teams, the military is going to be leaving the area. Start getting things ready to move out, but wait to move out until I give the all clear that they're gone. Then meet back at the school for a debrief." Merrick paused and then asked, "Team Three, are your people okay?"

"A few of us have some scrapes from having to get out of there fast, but we're *all* okay," Ryan said, emphasizing the word *all*. Merrick understood. Ryan was telling him that Reese was okay without saying his name over the radio. "We have another problem over here we need to deal with, though. When the military started blowing up all their vehicles, it must have scared the crap out of the bad guys here because those who were left surrendered. What do you want me to do with them?"

"How many are we talking about?" Merrick asked.

"Seven—well, seven and a half. One is pretty wounded and probably won't make it anyway."

"Stand by." Merrick turned to Chris. "Stop that dick colonel—"

"On it," Chris said as he ran after the convoy. The front few vehicles had just started to move as Chris finally got to the rear vehicle, which radioed the rest to stop. Merrick jogged up to the convoy and saw his new friend, the lieutenant colonel, step out.

"Sir, we have eight people from that hostile group I told you about that want to surrender to you," Merrick said, breathing hard from the jog.

"No," the lieutenant colonel said matter-of-factly.

"No? What do you mean? Aren't you the law in the area now?" Merrick said, puzzled at the response.

"First of all, I'm not set up yet. Secondly, five minutes ago you were trying to convince me you were a police officer leading a lawful group. Where I'm from, we have a rule: you catch 'em, you clean 'em. This is your mess, so you get to clean it up."

Merrick hated this guy, but it was hard to argue with his logic. The lieutenant colonel saw the understanding in Merrick's face, and with a grin of satisfaction, he ordered his convoy to move out.

CHAPTER 52

Merrick looked at John and asked, "Any advice?"

"I don't have much advice to give on this one, other than to say it's like everything else in life. You're damned if you do and you're damned if you don't. You can't let them go in good conscience, knowing they'll probably hurt more people. On the other hand, you don't want to become an executioner either. So you're damned if you do and damned if you don't. Might as well pony up and choose what you'd rather be damned for," John said.

"Are those my only two options? Is there some other way? Couldn't we punish them without killing them?"

"Sure, you could cut off a hand, remove an eye, break their legs . . ." John said, listing off the horrible things they could do like he was reading a shopping list.

"Okay, okay. I get it. That sounds more brutal than just shooting them. I'm not going to delegate this one; I'm going out there. Can you wrap things up here and meet us back at the school?"

"Yes, sir, and just so you know, you're doing the right thing." John nodded in approval.

"How do you know what I decided?"

"A sergeant major wouldn't be worth half his salt if he couldn't read his commander," John answered with a half smile.

"Well, John, I really appreciated your experience and wisdom today. I couldn't have done this without you. Thanks." Merrick extended his hand, but John snapped to the position of attention and saluted.

"Sir, it has been my pleasure to help you today, and I enjoyed being a pain in the butt to a good officer again. You're a good man, and you did well today. You let me know if the need should ever rise again, because I'll be there."

Merrick saluted John back. John gave one more nod to Merrick, then walked back toward HQ.

Chris and Merrick then found a vehicle and headed to where Team Three was guarding the prisoners. As they pulled up, they were directed down a few streets until they found them. They were all sitting against a cedar fence along one of the homes in the neighborhood. Ryan walked over to meet Merrick as they pulled up.

"Merrick, thank you for coming out here. I thought I might have to be the one to do this," Ryan said, looking relieved.

"No, this one's on me, but I do need you to do something for me. Find me ten crusty soldiers that can handle being on a firing squad. The rest of the guys can head back to the school for the debriefing. I don't want to make this a spectacle," Merrick said, not looking forward to what had to be done.

"Okay, give me a few," Ryan said.

"Hey Ryan, I'll be one of your ten," Chris said to Ryan as he walked away. Ryan nodded and continued to gather his people together.

"You haven't spilled enough blood yet?" asked Merrick.

"I'm past my need for vengeance, but I'm still dealing with it. If you're looking for hardened soldiers who won't be kept up at night for shooting these guys, I definitely fit that bill. By the way, I never thanked you for organizing this little war for me; it was very kind of you." Chris elbowed Merrick gently.

"Of course, what are friends for if they won't organize a little war for a friend now and again, right?" Merrick elbowed Chris back.

"Right." They both laughed, unconscious trying to use humor to distract themselves from what was literally staring right at them.

The prisoners were sitting along a fence line just to the right. Their eyes were on Merrick and Chris as they watched them laugh and joke. When nine men walked up about thirty feet in front of them and lined up parallel to them, most of them caught on to what was about to happen. A nasty, overweight man who was all tattooed up started yelling obscenities at them. A few others started to shift around, feeling uneasy where they were sitting.

"Okay, listen up, all of you. You have been accused of being part of a group that participated in the murder of men, women, and children, looting people of their property, homes, and food, raping and enslaving countless people. Each of you will be given a chance to say whatever you want on your behalf, starting with you on the left," Merrick said loudly as he scanned the group.

Most of them didn't have much to say. A few cursed at Merrick. The second to last guy stood up and whined about how he was just trying to survive and had been caught up in the whole thing. Merrick yelled at him to sit back down. After refusing to sit, he took a couple of steps forward and was shot in the head instantly by Chris. Two others on the edge of the group tried to run, but the only thing running achieved was an early firing squad for them.

There were only four guys left alive. They were not blindfolded or standing shoulder to shoulder bravely like in the movies. They were sitting down to avoid the temptation to run, and they were either spewing pure hatred at their accusers or so scared that they were cowering and pissing themselves. The command was given, and the ten shooters opened fire.

CHAPTER 53

Once everyone got back to the high school, Merrick got the final casualty count. There were twelve wounded and two dead from their own ranks. No one was buried on the battlefield on both sides of the fight. The enemies were left where they lay, and the two of their own who had fallen were loaded onto a truck to be taken home to their families. John and a few others who knew the two dead men volunteered to deliver condolences to the families.

Merrick's group was also able to salvage a considerable amount of supplies. Most of the supplies were being given to the two families who had lost someone. The remaining supplies were divided among those who were wounded.

Ryan had said that Reese was fine, but Merrick still felt uneasy until he saw Reese with his own eyes. He could see other members of Team Three coming up to Reese, shaking his hand and saying goodbye before they went their separate ways. Merrick walked up to him and grabbed him in a giant hug.

"Easy, Dad." Reese sounded like he could barely breathe.

"Why, are you hurt?" Merrick said, pulling away from him and looking him up and down.

"No, but if you squeeze me any harder, I might be," Reese said with a smile.

"Whatever. I'm just glad you're okay. When I saw that house blow up, I almost lost it."

"I made you a promise, didn't I?" Reese asked.

"Yes, and thanks for keeping it. Now your mom won't have to kill me."

Miranda and Ryan walked over and joined Reese and Merrick.

"Is Chris coming back with us?" Ryan asked.

"I have no idea. I thought he might live down the street in the house with my in-laws, but I haven't talked to him about it yet."

"How is he doing with everything?" Miranda asked.

"He still has some things to work out, but I think he will be okay. Let's go home; I'm done. I just want to go home and not have to make any more decisions today."

"All right. We'll figure it all out later," said Ryan sympathetically.

"Merrick, what do you want for dinner? Or is there a special dessert we can make for you?" Miranda asked mockingly, and they all laughed as they loaded up their truck.

"I hate you all, and I just might shoot you guys to get some peace and quiet tonight."

Merrick climbed into the bed of the truck, lay down, and closed his eyes. The truth was he didn't hate them at all. They'd been friends for years, but living together and working through some tough times had brought them even closer. They had all become like family.

THE END OF BOOK ONE